PRIMAL
VENGEANCE

JACK SILKSTONE

BOOKS

By Jack Silkstone

The Primal Series

PRIMAL Origin
PRIMAL Unleashed
PRIMAL Vengeance
PRIMAL Fury
PRIMAL Reckoning
PRIMAL Nemesis
PRIMAL Redemption
PRIMAL Renegade
PRIMAL Deception
PRIMAL Exodus

PRIMAL Vengeance is dedicated to the Intelligence Analysts, 2s, Deltas, 18Foxes, Three Letter Agency LOs, Bears, Spies, and others who work endless hours to ensure that operators are at the right place at the right time. You are appreciated.

Vinci Books

vinci-books.com

Published by Vinci Books Ltd in 2025

1

Copyright © Jack Silkstone 2015

The author has asserted their moral right to be identified as the author of this work in accordance with the Copyright, Designs and Patents Act 1988. This work is a work of fiction. Names, characters, places and incidents are the product of the author's imagination or are used fictitiously. Any resemblance to actual persons, living or dead, places and incidents is entirely coincidental.

All rights reserved. No part of this publication may be copied, reproduced, distributed, stored in any retrieval system, or transmitted in any form or by any means, including photocopying, recording, or other electronic or mechanical methods, nor used as a source for any form of machine learning including AI datasets, without the prior written permission of the publisher.

The publisher and the author have made every effort to obtain permissions for any third party material used in this book and to comply with copyright law. Any queries in this respect should be brought to the attention of the publisher and any omissions will be corrected in future editions.

A CIP catalogue record for this book is available from the British Library.

Paperback ISBN: 9781036701918

Printed and bound in Great Britain by Clays Ltd, Elcograf S.p.A.

Prologue

Extract From News Article: South Sudan's Independence—A False Hope

Published: 13 June 2012

South Sudan's decades-long conflict was supposed to have ended when the region won independence in 2011. Freed from the oppression of Khartoum's reign and with a peace agreement ratified by the UN, the future looked promising. With over half the Sudanese oil fields situated south of the border, dreams of prosperity and development were rekindled. Some of the world's poorest people could finally look toward the future with hope.

Now, a year later, harsh reality has set in. Conflict in the border region continues and refugee camps are overflowing. Khartoum still controls the vital oil infrastructure, pumping liquid gold into the Chinese market. The hope that any of the billions of dollars of oil revenue would be shared with the south is fading rapidly, and the old fighters from the civil war are preparing for a new struggle.

"Again we must take up arms against Khartoum," said Garang Abango, a freedom fighter who had been educated in the United States. "We are not an army, we have no tanks, no fighter jets, no money. But we have our freedom and we will fight for what is rightfully ours."

Chapter One

KHARTOUM, SUDAN, 2012

GARANG'S HANDS WERE SWEATING, despite the cool air that flowed from the air-conditioning vent behind his head. He was more at home in the African bush than here in the boardroom of a major petroleum corporation. Not to mention that the PETROCON building was situated in downtown Khartoum—the heart of enemy territory and a thousand miles from his adopted home in South Sudan. It had been years since the civil war between Sudan and South Sudan had officially ended, but deep wounds heal slowly.

Garang's job now was to keep his tribal chief safe, and surrounded by hostile Sudanese forces, it was no wonder his palms were sweating. He wiped them against his olive drab combat fatigues and returned his attention to the two men at the negotiating table.

"This is a good deal; we both know it. You would be a fool not to agree," the Sudanese oil minister addressed the chief sitting opposite him. Garang had noticed that every time the man finished a sentence he licked his lips, almost as if he could taste the crude oil he coveted so desperately.

The chief leaned forward and pushed a pile of legal documents back toward the fat politician. "You want my people to sign their lands across to your Chinese masters for only four percent? We are not simpletons who can be swayed with a handful of beads, Omar. We are a proud people. The Dinka lands belong to the Dinka and that is final."

Omar slapped his thick hands against the table, upsetting a glass of water and spilling its contents across the table's surface. "You either take this deal or we take the lands from you!"

"Your threats are idle," the chief replied calmly. "You couldn't take our lands in two decades of civil war and—"

The politician slammed his hands against the table again. "Look around you, old man." He gestured toward the floor-to-ceiling glass windows that overlooked the bustling city. From thirty-six floors up people looked like ants. "You're a long way from your grass huts. Times have changed and your shitty little tribe has been left behind. Now I have the power. I have the money. This is a new era and your people will not survive unless they submit. Sign the papers and I promise, you will spend your final years a wealthy man."

He paused, squinting across at Garang. "What about you, boy? Do you want your people to live in squalor or do you want to be a part of this?"

Garang swallowed, wiping his hands against his pants as he rallied the courage to speak. Before he opened his mouth his chief spoke for him. "There is no Dinka who will sign your worthless papers, Omar." The elder was dressed like

Garang, olive fatigues tucked into battered combat boots. He was lean, dark skin drawn and leathery, a veteran African warrior. "We will fight to the last man to keep our lands."

Omar remained seated. "Yes, you'll get your fight soon enough. Before too long I will have more tanks and artillery to pound your pathetic tribe into the dust." He pushed his own chair back and pried himself from its clutches. "Your women will spend their final days being stuffed with Janjaweed cocks."

At the mention of the fearsome Arab militias the doors at the end of the conference room opened and a fourth man entered. He crossed the room to stand behind the Sudanese politician.

"You probably already know of Sagrib," Omar said.

At the mention of his name the man's lips peeled back to reveal a mouth almost devoid of teeth. Then he laughed, a revolting cackling sound not unlike the bark of a hyena.

The Dinkas knew the man only by reputation. The leader of Omar's private Janjaweed army was renowned for his brutal acts of violence. He was dressed in desert combat fatigues and had cloth wrapped around his head, the tan material draped over his shoulder. A gold Rolex adorned his wrist, hacked from the arm of one of his countless victims.

The Dinka chief ignored Sagrib and looked the oil minister squarely in the eye. "Your Chinese masters can give you all the weapons they want, Omar. Your forces will never defeat the Dinka while you continue to send pigs to fight us."

Sagrib turned his head slightly, angling his mirrored Ray-Bans toward the chief. Garang kept his mouth shut. He was starting to regret volunteering to protect the old man.

It was Omar who broke the silence. "You and your

people are all alone. No UN, no Americans, no helicopters, and no tanks. I will ask one last time, sign the papers and your people will have a chance to live." He waddled across to a side table, retrieved a manila envelope, and threw it on the table.

"What about you, boy? I hear you were born in America. I'm sure you understand the value of this contract." He leaned across the table. "Get the old man to sign it and I will make you rich."

Garang paused for a second, his eyes drawn to the envelope.

The elder Dinka pulled him back. "This meeting is over." The chief's voice had a slight tremor. "Garang, we are leaving."

"You're making a very big mistake, gentlemen," Omar said as the pair retreated to the boardroom doors and into the path of a heavily armed security detail.

Garang spun on his heel. "What is this?" he yelled, pointing his finger at Omar. "You promised us safe passage!"

Omar shook his head. "You are too trusting, but you will learn. This will be an important lesson for you." He turned to Sagrib. "Kill the old man and make an example out of the boy."

The Janjaweed mercenary nodded, snapping an order at the guards, "Take them to the basement!"

It took only minutes for the guards to cuff the two men and move them into the elevator to the lower levels of the building. There, among the PETROCON vans, they forced the Dinka tribal leader to his knees.

Garang struggled against the guards who held him. One of them drove a baton into his stomach, doubling him over.

His legs turned to jelly as he gasped for air but he was held up, forced to watch.

Sagrib stood over the Dinka chief, a rusty saw in one hand. With the other he grabbed a fistful of hair, wrenching the man's head back.

The old man looked up at the mercenary with hate in his eyes. "You can kill me, but you cannot kill all of us. Mark my words. Dinka warriors will bury you in the carcass of a pig."

"No, they will die like you. Like fucking lambs to slaughter." Sagrib brought the saw up against the man's throat and hacked it back and forth. The rusty blade chewed deep into the flesh and the chief gasped involuntarily as the jagged teeth tore through his jugular and windpipe. Crimson blood spewed out of the horrific wound as Sagrib sawed through the spine, laughing like a mad man as the tribal elder gurgled.

Garang screamed and thrashed against the men holding him. The baton returned, smashing his legs out from under him. The guards beat him savagely while Sagrib continued to hack at the once-proud elder's head.

The old man died without so much as a whimper. The last thing Garang saw before he succumbed to unconsciousness was Sagrib holding the severed head aloft, his uniform drenched in blood, toothless mouth grinning.

THEY FOUND Garang on the outskirts of Khartoum, badly beaten and dumped in a pile of trash. Next to him was the chief's head, the body missing. Garang screamed in pain as they loaded him into the truck. None of them wanted to touch the severed head of their chief. Eventually it was a young warrior named Jonjo who rallied the courage to take the head and wrap it in a sheet. Tears rolled down his cheeks as he placed it in the passenger seat of the truck.

They drove south, trying to avoid the potholes in the old highway, as every jolt caused Garang to moan in pain. Jonjo was not sure the American would survive the long journey. He was not sure if any of them would make it home. If Omar had rescinded their safe passage and the Sudanese army found them, they would all be dead.

Chapter Two

PIRATE ALLEY, GULF OF ADEN

THE *TIAN HAI* churned its way through the lukewarm waters of the Gulf of Aden, heading north, bound for Sudan. Sitting low in the water the heavily laden cargo ship made a steady fourteen knots, slowly working its way through the region known as Pirate Alley.

High above the water on the ship's bridge a cigarette glowed faintly in the darkness. A shower of ash disappeared in the wind as the butt was stubbed out on the handrail and tossed into the inky black water. The Chinese security contractor pulled night vision goggles down over his eyes, a copy of the US-designed PVS-7, and scanned the horizon.

He was on the lookout for pirates, Somali criminals intent on seizing the ship and her cargo. Already the *Tian Hai* security detail had fought off two attempts to board the freighter. The pirates hadn't fared well, but the sharks had.

The guard almost wished for pirates as he mechanically scanned his zone of responsibility. The ambient light from the new moon struggled to penetrate the low cloud base, and through his goggles he could barely see past the end of the ship, over two hundred meters to his front. He lifted the goggles and reached for the packet of cigarettes tucked into a pouch on his assault rig.

"The cigarette will give away your position. Do not smoke again!" a voice spoke in Mandarin.

The contractor snapped his head around to see Yang step out of the shadows and into the faint glow cast by the ship's navigation lights. He was a slim figure dressed in black combat fatigues and a baseball cap. His only weapon was a sidearm on his hip.

"Yes, sir." The guard's hands flashed back to the QBZ-97 assault rifle slung across his chest.

"Have you checked your sectors?"

"Yes, they are all clear."

"Are they?" Yang nodded into the darkness.

The guard flipped his goggles down and scanned the horizon. At the very edge of the sensor's range he could just make out the faint glow of a fishing boat. The vessel was heading away from them. He flipped the goggles up and turned back to Yang.

"Sir, how ...?"

The man had disappeared back into the shadows.

TEN NAUTICAL MILES ahead of the *Tian Hai* an unusual-looking aircraft hovered above the ocean. In the darkness it resembled a giant dragonfly, loitering on the surface of a pond as it searched for prey.

The AW609 was a civilian evolution of the US armed forces V-22 Osprey. Like its military cousin, it relied on a pair of giant propellers for conventional flight that when swiveled skyward allowed it to hover like a helicopter. The tilt-rotor had the speed and range of a fixed-wing aircraft, yet unlike a seaplane it could support water operations in the heaviest of seas.

The gray tilt-rotor hovered a few meters above the swell, the downward wash of the twin blades whipping the surface into a frenzy of spray and froth. It rotated slowly until its nose faced into the wind. The door on the left side slid open revealing a faint green glow from the cabin.

A black-clad figure appeared, quickly scanned the surface, and pushed a large bundle out into the ocean below. A number of smaller bundles followed before the man dropped from the aircraft and disappeared into the water. He was followed by a second man, who splashed into the ocean beside him.

With a roar the tilt-rotor climbed away into the dark sky, leaving the two men alone in the Arabian Sea, nearly a hundred nautical miles from shore.

"Beautiful night for a swim, mate," the first man said cheerfully as he treaded water, holding on to the side of the large bundle he had pushed from the aircraft.

"It is nice, Bish, but I think I'd prefer a boat ride," Mirza replied from the other side of the bundle.

"Probably need a boat then. Get clear, I'll inflate."

"Roger." The former Indian Special Forces soldier pushed off the bundle and bobbed in the black water.

Bishop tore open a Velcro panel on the side of the package. With one hand bracing against the rubber he pulled hard on a plastic handle. There was a pop and a hiss as it split open and unfolded slowly. The hissing continued until it took the form of a small inflatable boat.

Both men climbed into the compact rubber craft, dragging in the various dry bags behind them. They worked quickly, preparing their personal equipment. The pair pulled on body armor over their wet suits and donned lightweight helmets. Everything was black, from their gloves and ropes to the suppressed MP7 submachine guns that hung from slings attached to their armor. Mission success was dependant on stealth.

"Rubber Ducky, this is Dragonfly," the pilot of the tilt-rotor checked in, his English accent broadcasting through the men's earpieces.

"Ducky here, go ahead."

"How's the water, chaps?"

"Surprisingly cool for this time of year."

"Told you to go the five mil over the three mil. Rookie error, boys."

Bishop laughed. Their pilot was also the PRIMAL team's equipment specialist and resident technician. He had helped them set up for the mission and had recommended thicker wetsuits.

"This is Africa, Mitch, not some shitty beach off Scotland. We'll be fine."

Mirza interjected, "I hate to interrupt, gentlemen, but we have a ship to catch."

Bishop laughed again. "Yeah, Mitch, now where the hell is she?"

"OK, I have the *Tian Hai* on scope. She's eight nautical miles from your location to the southeast and closing."

"Cheers, Mitch, we're ready to roll."

"Roger, chaps, I'll be in a loiter here, keeping an eye on things. Drop me a bell when you need exfil."

"Too easy. Bishop out."

Bishop activated the data link on his iPRIMAL, the combat interface on his forearm that communicated wirelessly through the satellite radio attached to his back. Through the touch-screen he could access information being beamed from Dragonfly, or from PRIMAL headquarters over eleven thousand kilometers away. Scrolling through the available feeds he found the one he was looking for and activated it with a tap. On the screen he could now see the radar image from the tilt-rotor. It showed their own location and that of their target, the cargo ship *Tian Hai*.

Mirza activated the electric drive motor and the two men lay low in the boat while it skimmed through the water at ten knots. The small vessel sat a mere two feet above the water and there was no chance the navigational radar suite on the *Tian Hai* could detect its approach.

The combat interface on Bishop's forearm vibrated, letting him know they were eight kilometers out from the target. He retrieved a long cylinder from one of the dry bags and propped it against the inflated wall of the boat. Flicking off a safety bail in the middle of the tube he pressed a rubber switch. There was a loud thud, followed by a snap as the modified Switchblade drone shot out of the tube, flying into the darkness with a whirr.

The visual feed from the Switchblade appeared on Bishop's iPRIMAL. His fingers danced over the flex-screen to plot the UAV a route to the target. The sensors on the miniature aircraft easily detected the thermal signature emitting from the merchant ship's exhaust. An automated flight program would keep the UAV in a holding pattern above it giving the PRIMAL operatives an all-seeing eye in the sky. Now all they needed to do was get on board.

The *Tian Hai* appeared in Mirza's night vision goggles as a grainy shape. At one mile he could not make out any of the ship's detail. He aimed the inflatable slightly to one side of the mass and glanced at his partner. Bishop had his night vision goggles flicked up and was inspecting his combat interface.

"Looks like at least three hostiles topside." He whispered despite the throb of the freighter's engines as it bore down on them. "One on each of the bridge wings and one roving on deck among the containers. The port side looks like the best approach."

Mirza gave a nod and corrected their course. When the ship was only a few hundred meters in front of them he throttled back.

"She's sitting low in the water, Aden, must be fully laden," Mirza said.

"Just thinking the same thing. Looks like Chua's intel is solid."

Both men gripped the sides of the boat as they hit the wall of water being pushed forward by the bow of the cargo ship. The little craft launched into the air as Mirza powered over the wash. Thumping back onto the water he whipped the little craft around in a tight circle, accelerated, and edged forward until they were bouncing in the white water just behind the bow.

Their boat came in against the metal skin of the ship and Bishop leaned out and slapped a pair of rubber-coated electromagnets against the hull. They thudded in place and he pulled the tether ropes tight, locking them to the hulking freighter that towered above them.

Even with the *Tian Hai* sitting low in the water the distance between the rubber boat and the deck was over twenty feet. Bishop checked the UAV feed. One of the guards was now walking directly above them. Bishop looked up and spotted a gloved hand resting on the rail.

"Tango above," he whispered over the radio, flicking down the night vision goggles and raising his MP7. Seconds ticked by and Bishop's shoulders started to ache from holding the submachine gun at a high angle.

A glowing object dropped from the sentry and arced toward the men in the boat. Through night vision goggles it looked like a blazing meteorite trailing a shower of sparks. Bishop ducked as the cigarette bounced off the side of the boat and was extinguished by the waves.

"Filthy fucking habit," he whispered and checked his iPRIMAL again. The guard was moving away.

"Aden, did you see the glow?" Mirza asked.

"Yeah, NVGs. Chua's intel is definitely spot on." The PRIMAL intelligence officer had briefed them that the Chinese army had arranged the guards for this vessel. "Guys like this aren't going to be protecting containers of pirated DVDs and Armani knock-offs. Let's roll."

Bishop let his weapon hang from its sling and secured it to his side with a strap. He opened one of the dry bags and pulled out a coiled rope complete with a black rubber-coated grappling hook and an auto-ascender. He lobbed the hook high; it sailed over the rail and landed on the deck of the ship with a thud. With a sharp tug it caught on the handrail.

Bishop hefted another dry bag onto his back and hooked into the auto-ascender. He thumbed the activator and the tubular device bit into the rope hauling him up the side of the ship. In a couple of seconds he reached the handrail and pulled himself over. With a deft hand he unsnapped the device and let it slide back down the rope.

"All clear." He raised the MP7 to his shoulder and slipped into the shadows between the containers.

"Coming up." Mirza picked up his own dry bag before being hauled up the rope. He pulled himself over the rail, unhooked the grappling iron, and let it drop into the boat below. Moments later he was crouched next to Bishop on board the *Tian Hai*.

They hid in the darkness cast by the containers stacked on the immense deck. Bishop checked the UAV feed again. It was all clear. They crept forward, weapons held at the ready. Dressed in black, they blended into the shadows cast by the ship's dim lighting.

Mirza led them toward the rear of the ship, their sophisticated night vision goggles fusing ambient light with thermal signatures, turning the darkness into a hazy green world.

"Target door ahead."

They stopped at the entrance that led from the ship's external walkway to the internal cargo holds. Mirza spun the wheel and the steel door swung open. Inside was pitch black and he could feel the hot, thick air. Only the superstructure and crew quarters were air-conditioned.

Mirza stepped into the darkness, activated the infrared light on his helmet, and paused.

"Reed switch," he stated, inspecting the entrance. Invisible to the naked eye, his infrared light filled the stairwell with a green glow when viewed through their NVGs. The illumination clearly showed a magnetic switch attached to the door.

Bishop swore, pushed in after Mirza, and closed the hatch behind him. Switching on his own light, he inspected the device, adjusting the focus on his night vision. Someone had attached a magnetic alarm to the door.

Bishop ran his hand slowly along the cable that connected the switch to a radio transmitter. He was sweating in his wet suit, beads streaming down his face. The eighty-pound dry bag on his back weighed him down. He checked the UAV feed; the guards on deck seemed to still be in their normal routine. Go or no go? he asked himself.

"Aden." Mirza spoke with urgency. "We need to make a decision now!"

"OK, let's do this as quick as possible. Consider the mission compromised: shoot to kill."

"Roger. We need to take the stairs down three more levels to the cargo hold."

"Lead the way."

They moved cautiously, keenly aware that someone could be responding to the triggered alarm. At the bottom of the stairs they reached another door. Mirza opened it and Bishop moved through holding his MP7 low, using its infrared flashlight for extra illumination.

Within the cargo hold the air was even thicker and the throb of the ship's diesel engines incessant. They closed the door and pushed deep into the hold, squeezing past stacked crates.

Bishop froze and held up his hand. "Holy shit!"

"What is it?" Mirza asked, creeping forward.

"Look!"

Through his NVGs Mirza could make out the hulking shape of an armored vehicle. Turning his head he could see a whole row of tanks.

Bishop climbed onto the front of a tank. "There's got to be over a battalion's worth of armor in here." He let out a low whistle. "The ChiComs have gone all out on this one. Chua's source was right on the money."

Mirza jumped up beside him. They had a clear view of the cavernous hold. "Main battle tanks, APCs, BM-21s," he observed. In front of them was an army of military vehicles. More of the squat main battle tanks packed in with boxy armored personnel carriers. Beyond that was a row of trucks sporting multiple rocket launchers. Vehicles filled the entire hold as far as they could see. "Aden, the rebels wouldn't stand a chance against this."

"Yep, Khartoum would eat them for breakfast. We need to deep-six this lot ASAP."

The pair split, moving quickly to each side of the cargo hold. They identified the vital points that Chua had briefed them in the pre-mission package. From heavy dry bags they drew out lengths of cutting charge. The prepackaged explosives had been specifically designed to slice through the ship's thick steel hull. It took them fifteen minutes to lay the charges.

"Charges set?" asked Bishop once they met back at the first tank.

"Yes, just as we practiced."

"Excellent." Bishop keyed his iPRIMAL and activated the two radio detonators, synching their initiation sequence. Numbers appeared on the screen, a countdown from ten minutes.

They ran back toward the door that separated the cargo hold from the stairwell, lighter on their feet, no longer burdened with explosives. As the exit came into view, the hold's lighting activated, dim globes appearing bright white through their NVGs. They froze, eyes drawn to the steel door. The locking wheel in the middle of the hatch started turning.

The two PRIMAL operatives dashed for cover, flipping up their NVGs as they slid under the closest tank. Seconds later the door opened and harsh Chinese accents echoed over the throb of the ship's engines.

Mirza counted the guards as they entered, assault rifles held at the ready. "Four tangos," he whispered. The men split into two pairs, starting to systematically search the shadows with flashlights attached to their rifles.

"Only four," Bishop replied into his mike. "If they find the charges, we're screwed." He paused to think. "We'll take them down in pairs. Closest two first. Silent kills, yeah."

Mirza had crawled out from under the tank and was focused on the armored personnel carrier alongside, his brow furrowed in thought. "We may not have to fight. I have an idea."

"Now's not the time, mate. Eight minutes left." Bishop flicked off the safety catch on his MP7.

Mirza pointed at the stubby smoke grenade launchers mounted on the APC and explained, "I'll set them off, we get out. They're not going to find the charges in the smoke."

Bishop gave a wry smile. He couldn't argue with the logic. "Well, hurry up then, MacGyver."

Mirza's knife was already stripping the wires and he pulled out a spare radio battery. "NVGs ready?"

Bishop flipped down his goggles. Mirza touched the battery to the bare wires. The smoke canister assembly spat four grenades into the air. With a clang they slammed into the roof and ricocheted onto the deck. Gray smoke billowed from the grenades and filled the hold.

Shouts in Chinese were soon replaced by coughing. The smoke pod had been designed to create a thick smokescreen to hide tanks in the open. In the confines of the cargo hold it rapidly filled the space. The PRIMAL operatives took a deep breath and made their way toward the exit door. The thermal sensors on their goggles saw through the smoke, detecting the body heat of the guards. Treading softly, they avoided the heavily armed contractors and headed straight through the exit.

They secured the metal hatch behind them and hurried up the stairwell. "Five minutes," said Bishop between breaths. As they hit the deck level an alarm commenced wailing and red lights flashed. Mirza approached the exterior door cautiously, hoping the other guards were slow to react. It was already open. He covered the hatch with his MP7 as Bishop checked the feed from the Switchblade drone.

"Bird's on the wrong side of the ship," Bishop whispered. "I'll bring it round but we can't wait for the feed. Four minutes left!"

Mirza hesitated. "It would be wiser to wait."

"No time, mate, gotta go." Bishop moved past Mirza and bobbed his head out of the open hatch. He snapped it back as a burst of automatic fire blasted inches from his face, ricocheting off the open metal door. "Fuck me!" he exclaimed.

A metallic clang resonated up the stairwell from below. The cargo hold door had been opened.

"Looks like company from below." Mirza pulled a stun grenade from his vest and flicked it down the stairs. The electronic hearing protection in their headsets canceled out the explosion as it detonated.

"Switchblade's coming round." Bishop checked his combat interface again. "I've got three tangos on the walkway with weapons."

"I don't think you'll get a second chance if you stick anything out that door."

The footsteps coming up the stairs were getting closer. Bishop was starting to wish he hadn't let Mirza convince him to let the guards live. He ripped off a fragmentation grenade, pulled the pin, and lobbed it down the stairs. Fuck them, he thought as the grenade detonated. The stairwell lighting went dark and the noises stopped.

"Here's the plan," he said. "I'll use the Switchblade to hit the ChiComs. You make a beeline for the boat."

"And you?" asked Mirza.

"I'll be right behind you. Now stand by."

Mirza braced himself next to the doorway, pulling a carabiner from one of his pouches.

At a thousand feet above the *Tian Hai* the Switchblade drone pitched forward, the nose camera feeding a picture to Bishop's iPRIMAL.

"Ten seconds, Mirza."

The little craft gathered speed as it dove.

"Five seconds."

The picture showed the three Chinese guards covering the walkway.

"Four, three, two, one, impact!"

The Switchblade detonated a meter above the guards, half a kilogram of high explosive shredding the men with tungsten pellets.

Mirza sidestepped through the doorway and fired a long burst into the bodies that littered the gangway. He needn't have bothered; the kamikaze UAV had done its job. He sprinted past the bodies, Bishop's footsteps close behind him. When he reached where their boat was moored, he snapped the carabiner onto the rail and leaped over the side of the ship. The lightweight line fed through a descender attached to his chest from a pouch on his thigh. He pulled the line tight as he raced downwards, slowing to a complete halt when his boots hit the rubber boat.

Bishop was checking over his shoulder when Mirza jumped the rail. The walkway was littered with debris from the airstrike. The alarm was still wailing, the ship bathed in red emergency lighting. He glanced at his wrist; only two minutes until the charges detonated. He grasped the rail with one hand and made ready to snap onto Mirza's line.

That was as far as he got. A shadow leaped from one of the containers above, slamming him into the safety barrier.

Bishop's body armor bore the brunt of the impact and he bounced off the rail, raising his MP7 at the attacker. A savage kick tore it from his hands, breaking the sling's clip and sending it over the side of the ship.

His assailant was Chinese, small and lightly built, dressed in a black uniform, with only a holster on his hip. The man seemed deathly calm despite the fact he was facing a well-equipped operative.

Bishop snatched his pistol from its holster as the steely-eyed fighter unleashed a savage volley of kicks, forcing him back along the walkway. Even in the tight confines the Chinese fighter was able to unleash a maelstrom of blows against the larger PRIMAL operative. Bishop's pistol was knocked from his hand, NVGs were smashed off his helmet, and the comms cables were ripped out. Desperate, he covered up, using his arms to protect his face.

His combat interface vibrated on his wrist, a reminder that the timer had hit the sixty seconds mark. Bishop dropped his shoulder and charged forward. He was counting on his mass and the weight of his equipment to overwhelm his lighter opponent. He was wrong.

Yang sidestepped at the last moment, landing a blow against Bishop's jaw as he careened past. Stunned, Bishop tripped and slammed into the deck, his helmet saving him from being knocked unconscious. Instinctively he rolled onto his back, ready to fend off any further attacks.

Yang laughed. "You Westerners are all the same. You fight like a bull: all brute force, no finesse." The man hissed the final letters of the word like a snake.

Bishop rose to his feet, taking a fighting stance. He wiped the blood and mucus from his face with a glove. His other hand drew a combat knife from his armor.

An evil smile appeared on Yang's face. "Oh, so you want to try again?"

Bishop shuffled forward, the knife held blade down in his leading hand. Yang lashed out with a kick. The blow landed on Bishop's fist, knocking the knife to the ground. The lean Asian darted forward, stepping inside Bishop's guard, throwing a strike at his throat.

Bishop managed to deflect it and Yang grunted in pain as his fist struck an ammunition pouch. The PRIMAL operative seized the smaller opponent and pulled him closer, head-butting him with his helmet. The broken NVG mount dug into Yang's face, the solid plastic shell shattering his nose.

Yang sprang backward, shocked by the blow. Bishop grabbed his knife off the ground and pressed home his advantage, slashing upwards. Again the Chinese operative sidestepped and drove a powerful kick into Bishop's thigh.

His leg spasmed in agony but he hobbled forward, slashing wildly. Yang moved in under the blade and unleashed a volley of punches. Bishop covered up, absorbing the blows, hoping for an opportunity to retaliate.

Sensing the PRIMAL operative was nearly finished Yang positioned his leg to deliver a finishing kick. As he swung his boot forward Bishop lifted the combat knife and drove it into the man's thigh.

Yang grunted in pain but continued to press forward with another hail of punches to the face, knocking his opponent against the bulkhead. The blows stopped and it took Bishop a few seconds to regain his feet. When he did so he was staring down the barrel of a pistol.

Yang did not look happy. He was standing a few meters away with the knife sticking out of his inner thigh. Blood streamed from his nose where it had been smashed in by the head butt. The pistol in his hand was aimed directly at Bishop's face and did not waver.

"Tell me why you are on my ship!"

Bishop nodded at the knife sticking out of the man's leg. "Should get that looked at, champ."

"Answer me now or you will die."

"That nose doesn't look so good either."

Yang smiled. He looked comical with his bloodied, smashed nose. "As you wish."

The Chinese operative squeezed the trigger. At the same instant there was a muffled explosion and the deck lurched beneath them. Yang staggered and the bullet went wide, ricocheting off the bulkhead. Bishop lost his footing and fell back against the safety railing. Yang fired again as Bishop rolled over the railing and disappeared overboard.

Mirza was climbing back up his rope when Bishop flashed past him. He slashed the line and hit the surface a split second behind his partner.

Weighed down by armor, equipment, and ammunition, Bishop sank like a stone. He yanked the tabs attached to his floatation pouches. One of them inflated, slowing his descent, but the other pouch failed, the punctured bladder spewing forth a torrent of bubbles.

Mirza was also sinking, searching for Bishop. There was zero visibility through the black water and the throb of the freighter's propellers filled his ears. He started running out of air when his fingers brushed Bishop's arm. The bigger man was paddling frantically, trying to swim upward. Mirza gripped the arm firmly and yanked his own floatation tabs. For a split second they hovered underwater before the buoyancy of Mirza's pouches overcame their weight and dragged them to the surface.

Both men fought for air, floating in the wake trailing the *Tian Hai*. Despite her mortal wounds, the ship was still plowing stubbornly forward.

"Fuck me, I thought I was cactus," Bishop said between breaths, still holding on to Mirza.

"You and me both, Aden. What happened?"

"Some prick jumped me at the rail. He got off a shot that must have punched through my gear. One of the bags didn't inflate." Bishop threw away his helmet and started to dump ammunition, stripping off unnecessary weight. "You're starting to make a habit of hauling my arse out of the fire, Mirza."

"Isn't that why you keep me around?"

"Yeah, something about strength in numbers. Now, what's the go with the ship?"

The two men were over a kilometer from the *Tian Hai*. They could barely see her lights in the distance.

"The charges definitely fired," said Mirza.

"Yeah, I can confirm that. It's the only reason I'm still alive. Can you raise Dragonfly? My comms are buggered."

Mirza checked his combat interface and keyed the communications tab. "Mitch, this is Mirza."

There was a short pause. "Mirza, my good man, how's the water?" The tilt-rotor was tracking their GPS transponders.

"Damp. Can you pick us up?"

"Roger, I'm inbound now, mate. Knock-up job on the *Tian Hai*. She's breaking up and the crew are abandoning ship."

Mirza relayed the information to Bishop, who gave a thumbs-up.

As the two **PRIMAL** operatives bobbed in the water, they could faintly hear the death throes from the sinking ship. The charges had cut through her central support structures and now the weight of her deadly cargo was tearing her in two.

"We've bought South Sudan at least six more months of freedom," Bishop said as they floated side by side. "Job well done!" The satisfaction of mission success was stronger than the numerous aching wounds inflicted by the Chinese assailant. "Now all we need to do is get the UN to approve an increase in peacekeepers. Too easy, really."

They listened as the moans and shrieks of tortured metal cut through the cool night air until the turboprops of the approaching aircraft blocked out the eerie sounds.

Chapter Three

KHARTOUM, SUDAN

"THOSE MOTHERLESS WHORES!" Omar threw his phone across the room. It smashed into the wall and broke into pieces. "The entire shipment is gone! All of it! The tanks, the rocket launchers, all of it!"

The Sudanese oil minister paced in front of his desk. His cheap shirt was stained with sweat, the buttons struggling to contain his girth.

A voice emitted from the video conferencing system. "Do you know who is responsible?"

"Those infidel Dinka dogs." Omar slumped into his chair, reaching for the bowl of candy on his desk. "Who else would it be?"

"While it is wise not to underestimate your enemies, it is also foolish to assume that poorly trained rebels could conduct such a sophisticated attack."

The man who lectured Omar spoke excellent English with only the slightest of Chinese accents. His name was

Han Zhu and he was the chief executive officer of the Chinese Petroleum and Energy Conglomerate, PETRO-CON. With the backing of the Chinese government, Zhu had almost limitless resources to secure resources for his nation's energy-guzzling economy.

"What about the Americans then. Perhaps they had help?" Omar stuffed another fistful of candy into his mouth.

"This is unlikely." On the video feed, Zhu stroked his short beard as he weighed up the situation. The sinking of the cargo ship was a significant loss, but unlike Omar he viewed it dispassionately, a business setback, a problem to be solved. "American interests in Africa are orientated mainly toward Islamists. They have their hands full with their own wars in the Middle East."

"What about the British then, or the French? They had men in Libya. Maybe they have sent them south? Or the South Africans? They're always meddling in our affairs."

"You chase shadows, Omar. Leave the investigation to my people. We will find those responsible."

"Bah! Your people. It was your people who failed us in the—"

Zhu cut him short. "Do not snap at the hand that feeds you, Omar. Without me you would still be squabbling in the mud with the rest of your pitiful nation. Look out the windows of your palace and remind yourself who makes it so."

He gritted his teeth as Zhu continued, "The shipment is no longer your concern. I will find who is responsible and they will be dealt with. Now, you must find new ways to push back the rebels and claim the oil fields."

"Without tanks it will be difficult."

"Difficult but not impossible."

"No, not impossible. We will need more equipment and

better weapons to exterminate the vermin." He looked up eagerly at the camera. "If you could supply gas shells for our mortars my men would soon kill them all."

Zhu's eyes narrowed. "No, we cannot afford to bring the world's attention to their plight. Gassing them would condemn us."

"No one would know."

"Don't be a fool, Omar. If the UN thinks that you are using chemical weapons their observers will descend upon you like locusts. The Western world will occupy your country with their armies and China will lose her influence. No, we must use conventional means to crush our enemies."

"Without the additional equipment the president will never approve the use of the army. That was the deal!"

"What about your own fighters, the horsemen?" asked Zhu.

"The Janjaweed already raid the border tribes to the west. They spread fear but do not have the weapons or the vehicles to push the southern militias from the area."

"China will provide all you need. Our Abyei refinery will be the logistics base and we will support your horsemen against the southerners. I have an agent I will send. He will organize your rabble into an army and they will defeat our enemies."

Omar shook his head. "The Janjaweed will not accept an outsider. Send guns and ammunition but do not send men."

Zhu stared into the camera at Omar. "Believe me when I say, they will accept this man."

OVER TEN THOUSAND MILES AWAY, in the skies above Mongolia, Zhu terminated the video call with Khartoum.

Omar irritated him; a small-time thug in a position of great influence and responsibility. A man whose stupidity he was forced to entertain, for now. He nodded toward the pretty flight attendant who responded with a warm hand towel and a glass of Maotai. Relaxing into his chair, he sipped the traditional Chinese liquor and stared out the business jet's window at the bleak landscape below.

Zhu's thoughts were interrupted by the stewardess. She handed him the aircraft's satellite phone. "It's him, sir."

Zhu handed her his glass and took the phone.

"Yang, what have you learned?"

"Not as much as I would like. No one on the coastline saw the aircraft. It must have stayed out to sea."

"Perhaps another vessel? One of the counter-piracy task force?"

"No. I have already checked with my contacts there. None of their helicopters were in the area."

"This man you described to me, could he have been South African?"

"A mercenary? It is possible. I cannot place his accent. His equipment was modern, he was definitely well trained. Perhaps one of our competitors has hired outside help."

"It would seem so. I want you to hand your investigation over to MSS," Zhu said referring to the Chinese civilian intelligence and security agency. "Your skills are needed in Sudan."

Yang did not respond immediately. The humiliation of the *Tian Hai* being sunk was still sharp and handing over the investigation would be a further embarrassment.

Zhu continued, "I promise you, Yang, if the investigation reveals anything, you'll be the first to know. I need you in Sudan."

"I can be at the refinery within twelve hours."

"Contact me when you arrive."

"Yes, sir."

Zhu ended the call and handed the phone to the waiting stewardess, who replaced it with a fresh glass. He sipped the liquor and studied the Mongolian steppes through the window. Why is it that oil is always found in the most miserable of places, he thought.

Juba, South Sudan

The teaching hospital in Juba was a single-story brick building nestled in the heart of the South Sudanese capital. The streets that surrounded it were hard-packed earth, the dwellings ramshackle huts of corrugated iron and salvaged materials. Juba was a city of poverty despite the wealth of natural resources betrothed to the fledgling nation.

Dr. Jess Hutton had been working at the hospital for over a year. Idealistic, free of spirit, and fresh out of medical school she had tried to sign on with Médecins Sans Frontières. The Doctors Without Borders had turned her down with a rejection letter that had advised her to gain more experience. Unperturbed, she dipped into her own savings and bought a ticket to Juba. On arrival she had offered her services to a not-for-profit organization providing support to the teaching hospital. Twelve months later Jess was running the modest establishment. She managed a cadre of local nurses and took care of the endless stream of victims from the ongoing conflict.

It was four days since the Dinka warriors had brought Garang to the hospital. He had slipped in and out of consciousness during the long drive from Khartoum and by the time they reached Juba he had degenerated into a partial coma. Jess had met them at the gates with a stretcher and orderlies. She did not recognize the battered body when they unloaded the stretcher from the vehicle, the face mangled beyond any form of recognition.

It was Jonjo who had broken the news that the badly beaten soldier was in fact her lover, Garang. With tears streaming down her cheeks she had rushed him into the tiled room that served as their emergency department. Without the technology of a modern hospital there was little she could do other than insert an IV drip into his bruised body and monitor his vitals. It had taken four long days before Garang began to stir.

"Doctor Hutton, Doctor Hutton!" the Sudanese orderly ran yelling down the hospital's single corridor.

Jess appeared from one of the doorways, a finger raised to her lips. "Quiet, Samir, we have patients recovering." Dressed in her whites and with her long, brown ponytail the American doctor resembled a star from a TV hospital drama.

"I'm sorry, Doctor Hutton," the orderly whispered excitedly as he skidded to a halt. "But it's Garang; he's awake."

The smile that split Jess's oval face filled the gloomy hospital with energy as she hurried to his private room. The two had met not long after Jess's arrival in the country. With their shared American backgrounds, they quickly became friends. It had not taken long for the impressionable young doctor and handsome freedom fighter to become lovers.

Garang was sitting up in bed, his once handsome face still swollen beyond recognition. He turned to Jess, dull eyes staring as she entered the room. She sat next to him and took his hand.

"They killed him," he croaked.

"I know."

"They cut off his head, Jess, and I couldn't do anything." Tears ran down his bruised face as he gripped her hand tightly. "They have it all: the oil, the money, the weapons. What do we have?"

"Brave men like you; men willing to fight."

"Is it enough? When our leaders are fools? They sent us to Khartoum to beg for scraps. Men of courage don't send their bravest warriors into the heart of enemy territory to have their heads hacked off with a rusty saw. They're cowards, not leaders." Garang met her eyes, a pained look on his battered face. "They're dragging us kicking and screaming down a path of submission, Jess. Khartoum will rape us of our wealth and our leaders will argue over a few drops of oil."

"But we can fight!" A young man of around seventeen stood in the doorway dressed in olive fatigues, a battered AK-47 slung over his shoulder. Jonjo was one of the few Dinka warriors who spoke good English, a result of his upbringing in a Christian orphanage. "The army can fight and we can beat them."

"The SPLA is finished, Jonjo," Garang said referring to South Sudan's fragmented military. "They fight among themselves for Khartoum's money. The independence movement is drowning in greed."

"Then start again," said Jess.

"What? Build another army?"

"You were in the US Army, Garang, you have more training than anyone else. Who better to do it?"

"That's true," he agreed, glancing at the young soldier

standing in the doorway. "I mean, I taught Jonjo how to shoot."

Despite only receiving basic training in the US military and having worked in supply, Garang had impressed the soldiers of the SPLA. Many of them had never even been taught how to use the sights of their weapons.

"The men will follow you. The chief trusted you." Although Jonjo was only seventeen, his youthful features had seen a lifetime of violence. Like Garang, he had hoped the Referendum of 2011 would be the end of the civil war. With peace would come the oil companies and prosperity, but the beheading of their chief and savage beating of Garang crushed that dream. The only chance now was to continue resisting and hope the international community would pay attention.

"Jonjo, how many men do we have?"

"Thirty or so. More if we can get guns."

"The Arabs won't stop until they have raped all they can from our land," Garang spoke with conviction. The dull throbbing of his wounds was forgotten as his thoughts went to revenge and glory. "If you and the men will follow me, Jonjo, I will lead. We will fight Khartoum and if we hold out long enough the Western world might support us."

Jonjo's eyes lit up in hope.

Garang continued, "We will fight and when the oil companies come to us, then we will inherit what we deserve." He slowly sat upright and swung his legs off the bed. Grimacing in pain, he reached for his boots. "Get the men together. Today will be the first meeting of the Southern Freedom Fighters."

"Yes, Garang." Jonjo left the room at a trot.

He struggled to get on one of his boots, his arm still too

bruised to function properly. Jess gently pried it from his hand and placed it back on the floor.

"You need to rest a little more, Garang. Your body is yet to heal."

"Stop it with your mothering, woman." He reached for the boot again. "There is work to be done. If I cannot build an army then who will protect the villages? I need to get back to the Dinka."

"Fine. Go!" She kissed him on the cheek. "But make sure you rest. Let Jonjo do the running around."

Garang managed to pull the boot over his sock. "I will rest once we have what is rightfully ours and Khartoum is no longer stealing our oil!"

Chapter Four

PETROCON OIL REFINERY, KURDUFAN DISTRICT, SUDAN

THE PETROCON REFINERY was located in Sudan within fifty miles of the still disputed Abyei border region. Constructed, manned, and owned by PETROCON it towered over the surrounding bushland, a monument to Chinese engineering. Twenty-four hours a day, seven days a week, it belched flames and smoke into the clear blue skies and spilled oil on the red soil. A tall chain fence shrouded in plastic adorned a wall of earth, barricading the expensive infrastructure from threats. The only parts visible were the tall smokestacks, huge oil tanks, and the pipes that led to the oil fields. Animals and locals alike avoided the area, terrified of the flames and smoke that spewed from the burn-off towers.

Jonjo lay in a patch of thick bush watching the Chinese security detail patrol the strip of earth that surrounded the facility. The four-man team were dressed in black fatigues and walked casually, their assault rifles slung. Although the morning sun had risen the guards did not see him lying in the undergrowth, his AK-47 cradled in his arms.

Jonjo shook his head slowly. These men had no place in the African bush. They walked straight over the tracks he had attempted to hide the night before; a good bushman would have seen the subtle disturbance and known something was amiss. Not these men. Jonjo had seen better bush skills from ten-year-olds.

Despite his youth the Dinka warrior was a veteran of the civil war and an experienced scout. Five long years ago, at the age of twelve, a raiding party had snatched him from an orphanage and he had been destined for a short life of rape and abuse. It had been the Dinka who had ambushed the raiders and freed him. It was the chief who had taken an AK-47 from a dead body and placed it in his hands.

As the guards disappeared around the corner of the facility Jonjo relaxed and reached for his backpack. Inside were his supplies: food, water, radio, and spare magazines for the AK. He rummaged through it and pulled out a battered exercise book and a pencil. Flicking it open he turned the pages past where the doctor, Jess, was teaching him to read and write. At the back of the book he had drawn a map of the refinery. Despite a lack of education Jonjo was a talented artist, one of the reasons that Garang had given him this mission.

The sketch map that Jonjo had drawn was detailed. It showed the perimeter fence with its guard towers and heavily defended front gate. He had measured the size of the facility; it was four hundred paces on each side.

The previous night he had crept across the oil-stained clearing, sliding alongside one of the pipes that brought the crude oil from drill rigs in the south. Scrambling up the bank of earth topped with the wire fence, he had peered through a tear in the thick black material to see what was inside. The bright lights had revealed a miniature city: machinery, towers covered in lights, rows of box-like buildings. Back in the safety of the bush he had marked the positions of the tanks and pipes, as well as the parking lot filled with trucks.

Jonjo checked his sketch map again and identified a number of suitable locations to stage fighters, marking them on with an X. The plan would be to ambush a petrol tanker as it came through the entrance; with any luck it would set fire to the whole base. Garang's instructions were clear; to destroy the refinery, not the pipelines or drilling sites. He wanted a spectacular attack to draw more fighters and support to the newly formed Southern Freedom Fighters.

Satisfied with his map he shuffled back from his hiding spot and worked around the facility to the side overlooking the front gate. The dirt road snaked in between a set of heavy concrete blast walls overlooked by two guard towers. Heavily armed security personnel searched every vehicle that entered.

Jonjo left his backpack and slid forward on his stomach into the hide he had constructed the day before. He pushed cut branches forward for concealment as he watched the comings and goings of the refinery. He wanted to wait for an oil tanker in order to observe how the security guards reacted to the vehicle leaving the facility. Then he would head south, back into radio range with Garang and the rest of the SFF.

The growl of vehicles alerted him to the approach of a convoy, not yet visible from his position. As the sound grew louder Jonjo could see that the guards at the checkpoint had retreated to their firing positions. The convoy drove into sight and he could see why. They were technicals, battered Toyota Hiluxes and Land Cruisers with heavy machine guns bolted to their trays. The five trucks were filled with dark-skinned warriors wearing headscarves. Jonjo reached for his AK; they were Janjaweed raiders.

He watched the standoff at the gate. One of the Chinese guards had come forward to confront the men. Jonjo waited for the shooting to start. The weapons on the technicals were pointed at the towers, and the facility security forces were ready with their own guns. What were the Janjaweed thinking, he wondered. Were they raiding the refinery? Demanding protection money? Surely they weren't working together.

With a wave the security guard confirmed Jonjo's worst fears. One by one the trucks snaked through the security checkpoint and into the facility. He watched the last of the convoy disappear and crawled back to where he had left his pack. He threw it over his shoulder and trotted off away from the refinery, back toward the border. If the Janjaweed were working with the Chinese, he needed to get into radio range and let Garang know as soon as possible.

INSIDE THE CONFINES of the refinery, in front of the accommodation buildings, Yang had started his morning fitness regime. Dressed in black combat pants, boots, and singlet, he worked through a series of warm-up exercises, testing his injured leg. A Somalian doctor had stitched the wound and he was lucky the blade hadn't cut anything vital. Confident that he could carry the weakness, he began hitting a standing bag with punch and elbow combinations. His face was still swollen, another painful reminder of his failure on the *Tian Hai*. As his body warmed he sped up the combinations, unleashing his rage on the spring-loaded heavy bag. Unable to bear the weight of a roundhouse kick on his bad leg, he focused on low front kicks.

"Sir." One of the refinery guards interrupted his routine.

"What?"

"The Arabs are here."

Yang paused mid-combination and turned his head. "Really? I do not see them."

The guard spoke into his radio. "Let them in."

He returned to his routine as the Janjaweed trucks pulled into the parking lot behind the gates. He completed another series of punches as the Arab raiders gathered in front of the trucks. There were more than forty men, all dark-skinned, clad in mismatched camouflage, with weapons slung over their shoulders.

Yang finished his punches and stepped away from the bag wiping the sweat from his face and arms with a towel. He threw it onto a chair and walked across to the waiting men.

"Who is in charge?" he asked in English.

The Janjaweed stared at him with open animosity. Omar had told them to report to the Chinese man, a notion that did not sit well with the fiercely independent warriors.

There was silence as Yang met their gazes. Then one of the men stepped forward.

"You think you are a fighter, Chinaman?" The Janjaweed warlord glanced at the standing bag. "Do you fuck pretend women as well?"

Some of the men laughed, translating the joke into their dialect. In a few seconds the entire group was cackling.

Yang stood in silence, turned his head from side to side,

scanning the ragtag group of raiders. He fixed his stare on the largest of the group. The Arab stood at least six foot nine, a full foot taller than the Chinese operative. Like Yang, he was lean and well muscled.

The Janjaweed leader smiled, revealing a mouth devoid of teeth. "Ah, I think our friend prefers the boys, yes!" Once again his men translated the comment and they started laughing.

Yang raised his arm and pointed at the fighter that towered over the others. The Janjaweed boss nodded at the hulking Arab. The man grinned, shrugged off his ammunition belts, and placed his machine gun on the ground. He swaggered across the sand toward Yang while the others gathered around.

With a roar he leaped forward, his arms wide to catch Yang in a death grip.

The Chinese operative sidestepped and ducked. There was a loud slap and the bigger man roared like a wounded bull. He spun to face Yang. His right cheek glowed red and his eyes watered. Yang waited with his arms relaxed by his side, feet slightly apart.

The Janjaweed fighter was cautious now. He approached slowly, his fists in a defensive guard. Yang, raised his hands, palms open, and let him close. The Arab swung a punch and Yang caught it under his left arm, pivoted with the motion, and slammed his boot into the side of the man's knee.

The Arab screamed and dropped his guard. Yang continued to pivot, driving an elbow into the side of the bigger man's head. The scream stopped as he collapsed onto the sand, unconscious.

Yang dusted his hands and once again adopted a passive

stance. He watched the Janjaweed leader who was staring at the inert body.

"I like this man!" the Arab announced to his men as he stepped forward offering a hand.

There was an awkward pause as Yang left him hanging. Then he grasped the Arab's hand.

"My name is Yang and I am here to help you defeat our enemies."

"I am Sagrib." The Janjaweed Warlord's mouth opened into a broken smile. "And I like you even more." He laughed and slapped the Chinese man on the shoulder.

Yang led the men across to where guards were working on eight tan four-wheel drives. The team was slotting Chinese-built QJZ89 heavy machine guns into the turret mounts and lighter PKM machine guns to the front pintle mounts. Other men were loading weapons and boxes of ammunition into the back of the trucks.

"The vehicles are yours. My men will provide ammunition, fuel, and repairs as you need them," said Yang.

Sagrib translated for his men. They looked at each other in disbelief then rushed forward to inspect the modern equipment.

"And what do you want from me?" Sagrib asked, eyeing the Chinese agent suspiciously. "I work for Omar, not Chinamen."

Yang placed a satellite phone in the Janjaweed warlord's hand. "I am here to help you destroy Sudan's enemies and reclaim her wealth." He took a map from his thigh pocket and unfolded it. He had circled the villages that he wanted the Janjaweed to raid. "These villages are where we need to attack first. If we push the Dinka off the land, then Sudan can claim it and drill for more oil."

Sagrib inspected the map. With his new vehicles and

heavy weapons he could hit them hard and withdraw before any of the South Sudanese army units or the UN could respond. He smiled at the thought of how many of the *kafirs* his men would kill.

"I will give you regular intelligence updates," said Yang.

"You have people in the south?" asked Sagrib.

"We have people everywhere."

Chapter Five

KALJAK VILLAGE, ABYEI DISTRICT

TECHNICALLY THE VILLAGE of Kaljak was located in South Sudan. In reality it resided in the contested Abyei District, an area claimed by both Sudan and the newly formed South Sudan. During a UN referendum in 2011 the population had voted overwhelmingly in favor of splitting from Sudan. However, democracy meant little to the powerful men in Khartoum. They simply wanted the oil.

The village, if it could be called that, was a cluster of single-story, mud-and-thatch-roofed dwellings around an open marketplace. Normally filled with traders and their goods, the market was now abandoned.

To one side of the dusty square stood a medical clinic constructed with humanitarian aid money. It was the only medical post for forty miles. Manned by a team of Western volunteers, it was a basic, single-story building with a large water tank. Its modern wood-and-plastic-sheet construction contrasted with the mud-brick huts.

"You don't understand. They will come and they will kill everyone!" Garang was arguing with the missionaries who ran the clinic. The evangelists refused to abandon the village despite the dire warning that Garang and his men had brought.

The leader of the group was a stern American woman. She reminded Garang of his junior-high librarian. "God did not abandon us in our time of need. We will not abandon these people."

"God has nothing to do with this and the villagers are already leaving. The Janjaweed will not care what god you pray to. You will die here."

She jutted out her chin. "I would not expect you to understand. You are not a believer."

"For God's sake, die here if you want. But don't force these women to die with you." The other members of the missionary team were a pair of idealistic American college students.

"God will not forsake us, young man. We will negotiate."

Garang threw his arms in the air and stormed away. "These people are brainwashed. Jess, you talk to them." The doctor was overseeing Garang's men loading the village's elderly into a battered military truck.

"I'll try." She walked over to the missionaries.

Garang had brought six armed men, the military Unimog truck, and a four-wheel drive to the village. It was all he could scrounge on short notice. Jonjo's radio transmission revealing the Janjaweed at the oil refinery had reached them the day before. By the time they had picked up the teenage soldier the Janjaweed were already on their way to Kaljak.

The news had been shocking; the nomadic Arab tribes

had never worked with the Chinese before. Their raids were usually focused out west around Darfur.

The SFF had moved fast but still they were running out of time. As they reached Kaljak, Janjaweed warriors had already raided a number of the nearby settlements. The streams of refugees brought stories of horror: entire families massacred, women gang-raped, markets pillaged, cattle butchered, homes burned. Their masters in Khartoum wanted the villagers forced off the lands so they could claim the territory. The Janjaweed were simply happy to be slaughtering infidels.

Garang watched the villagers fleeing. Women, children, and the elderly, hampered by the few things they could carry, walked as fast as they could. A couple of rusted vehicles also departed, crammed full of people and the last of the livestock. Most of the cattle had already been driven south by the able-bodied men. Everyone was heading deep into South Sudan, away from the violence and toward the refugee camps.

Garang slammed his fist down on the bonnet of his Hilux pickup. If only he had more men and more weapons. He could make a stand against the Janjaweed, drive them from the oil fields, and bring riches to the country. He shook his head in disbelief as a white UN Land Cruiser overtook the stragglers, leaving them in its dust. No doubt the observers would report the incident, then in a week or so a patrol of poorly equipped Nigerians would come out to survey what was left of the village. He spat in the dust as he watched the four-wheel drive disappear down the dirt track.

"Garang, Garang!" The radio attached to his belt transmitted with a burst of static. It was Jonjo reporting. The young warrior was watching the approaches to the village.

"Jonjo, report."

"The Janjaweed are coming. We have ten minutes at the most."

Garang looked back to where he had left Jess negotiating with the missionaries. She had given up and was now taking photos; more evidence of the atrocities, as she called it. His men had finished loading the weak and wounded into the Unimog truck and were now focused on stopping desperate refugees from climbing onto the vehicle.

"OK, pull back, Jonjo." He dropped the radio back onto his belt, unslung his AK, and yelled at the top of his lungs. "Mount up. We're leaving!"

Two of his men climbed into the back of the Unimog and lifted the tailgate. The driver turned the truck engine over as Jess climbed up into the cab. The other three men were in the Hilux.

Garang strode over to the missionaries who were watching from in front of the medical clinic. "Last chance, ladies. We are leaving."

The old lady stood firm. "We're staying."

"May God be with you then." Garang strode back to the truck. The driver was struggling to get it started.

In the distance a heavy machine gun thudded, followed by the crackle of small arms. The gunfire panicked the remaining villagers and they started running into the bush. The elderly missionary bundled the younger women into the clinic and shut the door.

"Get that damn truck started!" ordered Garang as he jumped into the Hilux.

More gunfire sounded in the distance, villagers trying to protect their homes. They would die in vain, ruthlessly gunned down.

"The truck is broken," Jess yelled from the front seat. "It won't start."

Another volley of heavy machine gun fire echoed through the marketplace.

Garang leaped from the Hilux, yelling at his driver, "Get in front of the truck and tow-start it!"

The SFF man skidded the pickup in front of the Unimog and jumped out, then hooked chains to the bull bar of the truck.

"Hurry the hell up!" screamed the SFF commander.

"Garang!" Jonjo yelled from the other side of the square. He was running, his AK-47 held close to his chest. "Why is the truck still here?"

"Because it's broken," snapped Garang.

Jonjo grabbed a worn PKM machine gun from the SFF pickup. Looping a belt of ammunition over his shoulder, he ran to the medical clinic. It was the tallest building in the village and a ladder led up the adjacent water tank. He scrambled to the roof to get a better view.

The gunfire from the edge of the village had stopped but the rumbling of approaching vehicles could be heard. Jonjo lay at the roof's edge, adjusting the PKM, sighting the weapon on the Janjaweed convoy in the distance.

"We've got inbound, four vehicles," Jonjo yelled.

"Slow them down!" Garang screamed from the Hilux.

Jonjo opened fire with a short burst from the PKM. The vehicles were still well out of effective range for the weapon and the rounds smacked into the dust, short of his intended target. The young soldier adjusted his point of aim, as Garang had taught him, and pumped out another volley.

Twelve hundred yards away the rounds slammed into the lead vehicle in the convoy. The driver reacted quickly, bouncing the truck off the road and into the bush. The other vehicles followed, bashing through the trees. The gunners in the weapon turrets unleashed their machine guns, blasting away at the village.

Jonjo ducked instinctively as bullets snapped through the air. The rooftop offered good fields of view but no protection. He let off another burst into the trees where the vehicles had driven. Inaccurate return fire peppered the village and the marketplace.

"Garang, we need to go now!"

"Goddamn it, I know!"

The Hilux struggled to pull the Unimog, its worn engine screaming. Slowly the truck inched forward, gaining momentum. As it gathered speed the truck driver dropped the clutch, there was a lurch and cough of smoke, and the old diesel spluttered to life. Both vehicles halted, their engines running, and a SFF fighter detached the Hilux from the truck.

Back on the building Jonjo watched the location of the Janjaweed vehicles, partially concealed among the trees. His sharp eyes registered a flash and he caught a glimpse of a black dot heading skyward.

"MORTARS!" the young soldier screamed as he leaped from the rooftop.

The bombs slammed into the square, screams filling the air as flying shrapnel inflicted horrendous wounds on a family of refugees. A woman thrashed in the dirt, both of her legs blown off. Another round detonated on top of her, finishing her misery, spraying her body across the ground.

The Unimog truck roared as it surged forward, black smoke pouring from its exhaust. The driver didn't need prompting. He swerved around the Hilux and took off down the track that ran south.

"GO, GO, GO!" screamed Garang as more rounds slammed into the village. The roof of the medical clinic exploded in a cloud of splinters, the water tank collapsing, sending a wave out over the packed earth.

The SFF driver paused, watching his side mirror. Jonjo burst through the dust and smoke. Waiting hands hauled him over the tailgate and the driver gunned the engine following the cloud of dust trailing the Unimog.

The two heavily laden SFF vehicles sped clear of the village, refugees running with outstretched arms as they tried to catch them.

Jonjo's knuckles were white as he clutched the tailgate of the Hilux. Tears of rage streamed down his face. In the front Garang pounded his fists against the dashboard. Jeeps, heavy machine guns, and now mortars. The Janjaweed had it all! He slammed his fist again. What did he have to fight back with? AKs, old men, and boy soldiers!

SAGRIB RAISED his pistol and shot the old man through the face. The body remained upright on its knees for a moment before it toppled into the dust. The infidel had served his purpose. Now Sagrib knew why the village was almost empty. He knew why there were no cattle and he knew who had fired at them, killing one of his men.

The Dinka men had warned the villagers. A group led by the American from the meeting, no less. The battered body his men had dumped outside Khartoum hardly seemed like a threat at the time. According to the old man, Sagrib had only just missed the foreigner and his band of would-be warriors.

The Janjaweed warlord surveyed the prisoners his men had captured. Half a dozen old men and a few women were hardly the bounty he had promised them. Still, the three

American women would go a long way to easing their disappointment. The two young ones and the old lady were squatting in the dirt with the rest of the prisoners. Their capture had been the only highlight of an attack that had cost him the life of one of his men.

A single burst of fire from a machine gun had hit his lead vehicle, shattered the windshield killing the driver. It was the first casualty they had taken since commencing the raids. The first real resistance. Still, the new Chinese weapons had quickly turned the battle in his favor.

"Bring her!" Sagrib pointed to the old American missionary. She had already attempted to sully his ears with all manner of infidel words.

He strode toward one of the village huts. The mud walls were scarred with bullet holes but otherwise intact. Two of his men dragged the woman behind him.

The protests of the two younger women stopped Sagrib in his tracks. He turned back to his men guarding the prisoners. "Those two are yours; share them with the others."

His men eagerly dragged the white women from the group. An elderly Dinka rose to protect them and was clubbed to the ground with the buttstock of a rifle. Sagrib grinned. The bitches had no idea what was in store for them, he thought.

As his men dragged the old woman Sagrib stopped to take a bag from the back of his open-topped jeep. In front of a hut he unclipped the bag and emptied the contents on the ground. He ordered his men to pin the woman against the mud-brick wall.

"Nothing you can do will scare me!" There was a look of defiance in her eyes. "The Lord is with me."

Sagrib picked up a hammer and a metal spike from the ground, one of three used to peg a long-range radio mast to the ground. "Oh, he will be soon." He held up the spike. "They crucified your prophet, didn't they?"

The old woman gasped, her eyes wide. She struggled against the guards but they held her firm, pinning her arms to the wall.

Sagrib brought his face close to hers, his lips peeled back in a hideous leer. "You should have stayed in your own country, witch!"

"No, no, you wouldn't!" She shook her head in disbelief as he placed the spike on the back of her hand. He paused, savoring her fear, then smashed the spike with the hammer. The shaft of metal punctured her flesh, bones, and tendons with a sickening crunch. She screamed in agony as he bashed the peg home, driving it into the mud wall. She continued to scream as he repeated the process on her other hand.

Sagrib stepped back to survey his handiwork. The old woman was now suspended by the spikes in her hands, crucified. She whimpered and gasped for air as her feet scrabbled against the dry mud wall.

"Look how close you are to your God now, infidel." He spat on the woman's face.

She looked at him with sad eyes. "I forgive you, my son," she whispered before the pain overwhelmed her, her head bowed, and she passed out.

He stared and shook his head. He was no stranger to killing but the women's deathly calm disturbed him. Usually they begged for their lives, right up until their last breath.

"Get the vehicles ready. We're leaving," Sagrib ordered one of his men as he turned his back on the woman. She would take hours to die. Suitable punishment for bringing her lies to his country, he thought.

He checked his Rolex. They had been in the village for

a little over an hour. It was time to move. There was a slight chance that the SPLA or the UN would send a patrol. So far they had seen neither the South Sudanese army nor the peacekeepers but Omar had warned him that he was to avoid conflict with any official security forces.

The shrill scream of one of the American girls pierced the air. Sagrib smiled. His men were enjoying themselves. No need to interrupt them just yet. He reached into his four-wheel drive and grabbed the satellite phone Yang had given him. The Chinese operative would want to know about the American and his men. Perhaps he would have some intelligence on their home base.

Chapter Six

LASCAR ISLAND, SOUTHWEST PACIFIC

SANEH'S HEART was pounding in her ears as she crested the ridgeline. She paused for a second to savor the cool ocean breeze that penetrated the thick jungle. In the valleys the humidity and heat were oppressive. Her clothing and equipment were drenched in sweat.

The former Iranian intelligence officer wore a lightweight belt rig. It contained four magazines for her Micro-Tavor carbine, a water bottle, and a pair of fragmentation grenades. She rarely wore the armored chest rigs that the men wore. Not only was she unlikely to be directly assaulting enemy objectives, but also the ballistic plates weren't designed to fit an ample chest. She preferred the comfort of a lightweight shirt. Her camouflage cargo pants were covered in mud, boots drenched from the dozen creeks she'd traversed.

She had started out at the crack of dawn, following what the rest of the team called the Punisher: a ten mile obstacle course, shooting range, and endurance test. PRIMAL operators ran it regularly to keep in shape. It was one of many training activities that had been set up on the island, each one designed to challenge a different set of skills.

Saneh was a recent addition to the PRIMAL team. Formerly an agent of the Iranian Ministry of Intelligence and Security, the alluring spy had been recruited into the vigilante organization more by chance than plan. She had been sold out by her old organization following a mission to secure a chemical weapon. Homeless, nationless, and without a friend in the world, PRIMAL offered her a second chance. She was a perfect fit for the clandestine organization: striking, audacious, ruthless, and a bit of an altruist. PRIMAL had appealed to her from day one; a renegade team of former intelligence and Special Forces operators dealing out justice to the world's untouchables.

Having caught her breath Saneh stepped off again. She scrambled down the narrow jungle track, her boots cutting into the slick mud. When she hit the bottom she searched for the red arrow that marked the route. It was nailed to a tree, indicating she needed to follow the creek. The cool water was refreshing as she waded downstream. It rose up to her chest and she held her Tavor high.

The next arrow directed her out of the creek and she clambered up into a clearing with a track running downhill. A buzzer sounded and she racked the action on her carbine. The shooting range had detected her GPS transponder and activated the targets. She brought the weapon to her shoulder and stalked along the footpad.

Man-size targets popped up randomly, Saneh firing at them as they appeared. She progressed steadily, double-tapping and changing magazines on the move. Within minutes she had cleared the course, unloaded her weapon, and was jogging down the track toward the ocean.

Two miles later she burst out of the jungle onto a pristine white beach. The PRIMAL operatives used this part of the island as a recreational retreat. A cluster of huts was hidden underneath a canopy of palm trees.

Saneh downed the last of her water, dumped her equipment on the deck in front of one of the huts, and tore off her boots. Peeling off her sweat-drenched T-shirt, she dropped it onto a sun bed and stepped out of her cargo pants. She strode down the beach in her underwear, shaking out her long, dark hair.

As she entered the water, Bishop appeared in the doorway of the hut dressed in blue swim trunks and a pair of aviator sunglasses. Sipping from a glass of iced tea, he walked out onto the deck and watched her dive into the ocean. He deposited the glass on a side table, lay on one of the loungers and closed his eyes, savoring the sun on his bruised body.

"Good morning, lover." Saneh stood on the deck in her sports underwear having finished her swim. Water dripped from her dark hair, running down her body to pool on the deck.

Bishop looked over the top of his sunglasses, drinking in every curve of her athletic frame.

She parted her lips, revealing a near-perfect smile. "You're looking a little less battered."

He sat up and threw her a towel. "Nothing a little rest couldn't fix."

She caught it deftly and began drying her hair.

"Hey, babe."

"Yes?"

He took a deep breath. "Look, it's just..."

"Spit it out, Aden."

"OK. Well, it's just there's something I wanted to talk to you about. Something important."

She smiled at him coyly. "What?"

"I, uh, want to talk about us. Wanted to talk about where this is going."

"I've been waiting for this."

"Huh, what do you mean?"

"I've been waiting for you to bring it up." She sat down on the other sun bed and faced him. "I'm not a giddy schoolgirl, Aden. I'm an experienced operative."

"I know that. I just thought..."

"You thought? Please, we both know that thinking's not your strong suit, Mr. Shoot-from-the-hip." She flashed him another smile. "Now, what did you think? That I was in love with you?"

He looked up at her sheepishly. "Well, yes. I didn't want to be the only one.'"

She laughed. "Of course I love you, Aden. But I'm also a realist. I know your loyalty is with the team and the mission."

"That doesn't mean—"

"Yes it does. You're an idealist with a stupidly big heart. You won't rest until you've saved every last kicked-and-beaten underdog on the planet."

"I guess we're similar like that."

She smiled again. "I guess you're right. Although you do seem to get all the good missions."

It was Bishop's turn to laugh. "That's a lie and you know it. You're the one that bounces straight out of recruitment in Istanbul into an operation in the UAE."

Both had been redeployed to the Emirates to help deal

with a threat to PRIMAL's wealthy benefactor, Tariq Ahmed.

"So did you."

"I had to. I wasn't about to let Tariq down, was I?"

"Nobody would let that man down; he's handsome, educated, and oh so charming."

The founder of PRIMAL was renowned for being a lady's man. The sheik had been rather taken with Saneh and had lavished her with attention.

Bishop raised an eyebrow and she continued, "You're such a little boy, Aden Bishop. A little boy that doesn't want to share his toys with anyone else."

He pretended to sulk and Saneh straddled him on the sun bed. She leaned forward and kissed him gently. "It's OK, little boy. I only have eyes for you... for now."

His hands slid up the side of her body and around her back until they reached the latch of her bra. With a flick he unsnapped it and the bra dropped from her chest. He took a second to fully appreciate her ample breasts before pulling her even closer to him, kissing her passionately.

The embrace was interrupted by the buzzing of a phone.

"Are you shitting me?" he said as she reached across and grabbed the device from the side table.

"You've been recalled to the Bunker."

"Now? That'd be right."

She jumped off him, scooped up her bra, and slipped it back on. She cringed as she slid the filthy cargo pants over her legs and gathered up the rest of her gear. Bishop was already inside the hut grabbing his own kit. He reappeared dressed in a T-shirt carrying a shoulder bag.

"Here, wear this. Yours stinks." He threw her a spare T-shirt.

"What do you think is going on?" Saneh asked as she pulled on the shirt and laced her boots.

Bishop strapped her Tavor carbine to the side of his bag. "Not sure, but if I had to guess I'd say it's got to do with Sudan."

The pair grabbed their bags and followed a track that led from the huts to an open-sided vehicle shed.

"Mirza's been keeping an eye on the situation. Both he and Chua think it's getting worse."

Bishop's partner had already moved to Abu Dhabi where he could be closer to the action should intervention be required.

At the shed they threw their gear into the back of an ATV. Saneh swung into the driver's seat and started the engine.

Bishop stood next to the powerful buggy with his hands on his hips. "Is that so...?"

"It certainly is, lover boy. Now get in and I'll show you how it's done."

Saneh raced the ATV down a short track before they hit the beach. Once the tires hit the sand she unleashed the 1000cc engine. Sand rooster tails arced off the back tires as they rocketed down the beach, heading back toward the airfield.

She slowed the buggy as they left the beach and bounced onto the apron of Lascar Island's single runway. Checking for aircraft, she accelerated across the tarmac and into a hangar butted-up alongside the extinct volcano that towered over the airfield.

An abandoned Japanese World War Two base, the island now masqueraded as a maintenance and refueling depot for Lascar Logistics, the air freight company owned by Tariq Ahmed. It was here, thousands of miles from any prying eyes, that PRIMAL staged its operations.

The irony of a covert organization basing itself on an abandoned island with its headquarters deep within the bowels of an extinct volcano was lost on Saneh. Growing up in Iran she had missed out on Bond villains and the *Thunderbirds* TV series. To her the concept made sense. Where else in the world could PRIMAL hide without being exposed?

They entered the hangar and drove under the wing of a Lascar cargo aircraft, stopping for a moment at the back wall. There was a whir of electric motors and two portions of the wall separated, wide enough for the buggy to enter.

On the other side of the doors was a vast cavern the size of a football field. Carved from volcanic rock it once housed Japanese bombers. Now it was the home of PRIMAL's own fleet of aircraft. Present in the hangar was a heavily modified Il-76 transport aircraft that the team called the Pain Train. The four-engine airframe was a surveillance platform, transporter, signals intelligence collector, and when required, a gunship. Parked with its nose under the wing of the hulking jet was a Gulfstream business jet.

She stopped the ATV at the back of the hangar, in front of a large service elevator. The pair swiped their access cards and rode the elevator down one level.

"Make sure you come see me once you're done." Saneh gave Bishop a kiss before exiting into the accommodation level.

"You still going to be wearing those pants?" Bishop said, clamping his fingers over his nose.

"Just for you, soldier boy." She laughed as the doors closed.

Bishop stepped out of the elevator on the third level,

swiped through a secure access point and entered the Bunker.

The PRIMAL operations center was quiet with only a few of the staff sitting in front of their terminals.

"Chua is in Vance's office," the watchkeeper said without looking up from a book he was reading. Clearly not much was happening.

"Cheers, Frank." Bishop walked across the operations floor to the staff offices. He knocked on the one that boldly declared 'THE BOSS'.

"Come in!" Vance, the director of operations, bellowed.

Bishop pushed the door open and stepped into the spartan office. Vance was not one for covering his walls in memorabilia and all that "crap," as he eloquently described it.

"Bish, how you doing, buddy?" Vance jumped up from behind his desk and pumped Bishop's arm vigorously. The former CIA operative was an ox of a man, built like Mike Tyson complete with shaved head and biceps like coconuts.

"Yeah, I'm OK. Healed up pretty good." Bishop's run-in with the Chinese on the *Tian Hai* had left him battered. He had spent a day in a hospital undergoing a thorough exam.

"Hey, Chua," Bishop acknowledged PRIMAL's chief of intelligence sitting across the room.

"Aden," responded Chen Chua.

"So, what's the go, guys? Things kicking off in Africa?"

"You picked it," said Vance. "Chua, fill Bish in on the details."

Chua took a sip from a can of energy drink then activated the screen on the wall of the office. Animated fish swimming through tropical waters was replaced with a map of Eastern Africa.

Bishop nodded as the map exploded with graphics. Animated icons highlighted important locations, recent activity appearing with call-outs denoting the key stakeholders.

"Considering your last mission, sinking the freighter, I'm going to jump straight into the new stuff. OK?" the intel officer asked.

"Yes."

"In the past week we've been getting a lot of reports from the disputed Abyei district between South Sudan and Sudan."

"Disputed? I thought South Sudan won control of the area through UN-run elections? What is there to dispute?"

"Khartoum is ignoring the result of the referendum. They're calling the election a sham and as a result they've been increasing their clandestine militia capability in the oil-rich region. I did a bit of a deep dive into the situation and reporting indicates that violence in the area has increased significantly with at least five villages raided. The UN estimates that close to thirty thousand refugees have fled south from the disputed border area. Media interviews with refugees lead me to believe that the raiding parties are Janjaweed militias."

"Damn, so the raid on the *Tian Hai* was a waste of time."

"No, not at all. Khartoum was intending to raise an armored brigade to bully South Sudan into giving up the oil fields. By sinking the *Tian Hai* we denied them that capability."

"Yeah, but instead they're sending Janjaweed scum out to murder and rape."

Vance jumped in, "Bish, look at it this way. We can work

against AK-waving horsemen. I ain't about to throw you and Mirza up against heavy armor."

"Is Mirza already in country?"

"He hit the ground in Juba this morning. Some of this info has come from his observations," said Vance. "He's laying the groundwork. We need you to punch in and hook up with one of the more effective southern resistance groups."

"There are a number in the area," added Chua. "I've been getting whispers of a new group that's led by a former American soldier. Haven't got a name yet but Mirza is tracking him down."

"Former US Army, in South Sudan?"

"Yes, quite a few families fled the region in the mid-eighties and were given refugee status in the US. It's probable that he served in the military then returned to help protect his people from extermination."

"Pretty worthy cause. Khartoum doesn't seem to be hiding the fact that it wants all of the tribes pushed out of the area or exterminated so they can grab the oil. This guy could be the perfect means to stop the Janjaweed."

"Exactly," agreed Chua.

"What about the Chinese. Are they involved in this or was the *Tian Hai* a one-off?"

"They're in neck deep," said Chua. "The CIA head of station in Juba submitted a report last night. His sources are telling him the ChiComs are bankrolling the entire operation."

Bishop shook his head. How the hell Chua managed to get CIA reports, probably before Langley had read them, was a mystery. The little guy might be teetotalling and risk adverse, he thought, but he was damn good at his job.

"So that fat bastard Omar is probably dancing on the end of a Chinese leash," said Bishop.

"Correct. Chinese big business backed by government resources. They're experts in influence and manipulation, and they'll be controlling all the key players. These people have zero scruples. They're not afraid to use bribery or violence."

"So, no doubt they will be up-gunning the Janjiwankers?"

"Yes, I assess they'll be flying in light equipment. Vehicles, small arms, and support weapons like mortars and machine guns."

"More than enough firepower to wipe out lightly armed freedom fighters." Bishop turned to Vance. "So what's the plan?"

"It's nice and simple. We punch you in to RV with Mirza. You ID and recruit a suitable militia, kit them up, train them, and neutralize the Janjaweed."

"It does sound like something the Company should be all over..."

"Negative. They've got their hands full chasing Al Qaeda around in Somalia and every other Timbuktu shithole. China got in first on this one and the CIA is taking a backseat. Got to remember who's lending them their cash." As a former CIA officer Vance still had his finger on the pulse of the US spy agency.

"Roger, sounds like a decent job. Happy to run with it."

"Yeah I thought it might be your sort of gig. Mitch and the Dragonfly will be in support. He's already stockpiled weapons in Abu Dhabi, courtesy of our Ukrainian friend."

Following a successful mission in Ukraine PRIMAL now had an arms dealer under their control. The man had access to bulk supplies of almost any weapon system they needed.

"Excellent. What about other stakeholders?" asked Bishop. "Does the UN have much of a presence in the area?"

"They have observers and some humanitarian aid types, but they're hopelessly undermanned and have their hands full trying to control the refugees," explained Chua. "China has vetoed any move to increase their numbers, and as long as it's in their interest to keep the UN hamstrung, that's not going to change."

"Good old blue caps, about as useful as tits on a bull."

"I disagree. It's not the UN at all," Chua said. "With a few thousand more troops they could probably keep the peace. The problem is with China vetoing every attempt to bring in more soldiers and equipment."

Bishop glanced at Vance in surprise. The PRIMAL commander nodded. Maybe he had a point, Bishop thought, although it irked him to think the UN could achieve anything useful.

"So what are we going to do about that? I mean apart from taking down the Janjaweed?"

"Chua and I are working on that. Our biggest priority is to get you on the ground to start training the locals. There's a Lascar flight due in for a refuel in two hours. That should get you to Abu Dhabi by tonight. Mitch will meet you there and he'll infil you using Dragonfly."

Chua pointed at the screen detailing the mission information. "I'll forward you the latest intel pack. You can check it out on the flight."

"No dramas." Bishop shook hands with both men and exited the office. He did a rough time breakdown in his head. Two hours was not a lot of time to pack his gear and squeeze in a visit to Saneh. He hit the elevator button for the first floor, smiling to himself. Maybe he would just grab his drag bag. It had most of the things he needed and Mitch could sort out anything he missed. Yep, that would work, he thought, as he made a beeline for Saneh's suite.

Chapter Seven

PETROCON OIL REFINERY, KURDUFAN DISTRICT, SUDAN

THE JANJAWEED RAID at Kaljak had shattered the morale of the newly formed SFF. The warriors felt shamed, forced to flee in the face of the enemy and abandon the villagers to a fate worse than death. They wanted blood and Garang knew exactly where to extract it. He would raid the Chinese oil refinery across the border. Not only would it bolster morale, it would also draw more fighters to their ranks.

The SFF leader had waited until runners brought reports of Janjaweed attacks further to the east. Now that the raiders were more than a day's drive from the refinery, they were unable to interfere with his plans. Garang was not deluded enough to think his ragtag band could defeat the well-equipped and battle-hardened Janjaweed. Contracted Chinese guards, on the other hand, were another matter.

They waited in their firing positions for dawn to come.

Garang and his thirty fighters were tense in anticipation, ready to unleash hell. Overnight Jonjo had led them from the vehicle hide to the refinery where the young warrior had guided each group to their firing positions. Garang had given them strict instructions: "Hold your fire until I shoot. Total radio silence." He would initiate the attack with his RPG.

The newly formed militia had only managed to scrounge a small number of RPGs and PKM machine guns. The majority of the Dinka tribe's heavy weapons had been cached in the mountains. The more experienced tribesmen were apprehensive of the young American and this attack would prove his mettle as a commander. Success would bring with it the respect and support of the entire tribe.

Dawn finally broke, the first fingers of light creeping over the horizon to cast a faint glow across the bush. Despite the lighting inside the refinery it had been difficult to make out any of the base's defenses. As the front gate became visible in the gray hues of dawn Garang could see how accurate Jonjo's sketch map was. The militia had placed a lot of faith in the young soldier and it had paid dividends; all three of their firing positions were sighted perfectly. They covered the gate as well as the machine gun towers at the entrance and each corner of the refinery. Together they could suppress all of the refinery's defenses on its western flank.

Garang pulled his RPG closer. According to Jonjo a tanker departed the facility most mornings just after dawn. It would be escorted by two jeeps armed with machine guns, more than enough security to deal with potential thieves. This morning they would get a lot more than they bargained for.

From inside the refinery Garang heard the rumbling of a large diesel engine. A cloud of soot rose up above the fence as the truck idled.

"This is it," Garang whispered to the man next to him. He shouldered the RPG, tucking it in against his cheek. Firers on each side of him did the same.

They watched as the guards slid back the gate and waved the first of the convoy through. A Chinese jeep drove out, weaved between the barriers, and stopped a dozen yards along road.

The tanker revved hard as it came through the gate, struggling with a full load of oil. The driver was experienced; he deftly threaded the truck through the concrete barriers.

Garang flicked the safety lever on his RPG and sighted the truck through the iron sights. The words of his weapons instructor from basic training raced through his mind: squeeze the trigger, let the weapon surprise you.

The explosion that launched the rocket was deafening, the back blast throwing up a plume of dust. The projectile screamed across the four hundred yard gap and slammed into the tanker with a thump.

The tanker detonated in an instant, a jet of flame leaping from the rupture as thousands of gallons of freshly refined oil ignited. Moments later a second and third rocket streaked from the position. Put off by the blast of Garang's initial rocket, they missed the tanker, slamming into the concrete blast walls.

Immediately following the rockets came the small arms, PKM and AK fire lashing the guard towers and blasting the sandbagged defenses. There was no chance for return fire. The guards hunkered down in an attempt to escape the overwhelming firepower.

The single jeep that had ventured out of the refinery was destroyed by 7.62mm rounds. Its occupants died instantly, their bodies riddled with bullets.

As the dust cleared, Garang surveyed the damage. The burning tanker blocked the entry point, black smoke billowing from the wreck. One jeep was destroyed and at least half a dozen guards had been trapped outside the fence by the blaze. They either burned or were shot down by the SFF fighters eager to exact vengeance for the recent Janjaweed atrocities. Garang grinned. The attack was a success.

"Garang, my team is ineffective. We cannot see the enemy," Jonjo transmitted over the radio.

Thick clouds of smoke from the destroyed tanker had completely obscured half the refinery.

"Wait, I am coming to you," Garang transmitted before turning to the man next to him. "Hand me all the grenades."

The Dinka warrior gave Garang a cloth satchel. The men in the group passed along their grenades and Garang gathered them up, placing them in the bag. His fighters provided cover, taking turns firing at the towers as he slid back into the creek line that ran parallel to the refinery fence.

Black smoke stung his eyes and lungs as he called out to the team. Jonjo's voice penetrated the haze and within seconds the young soldier appeared. Garang handed him the satchel of grenades. "Use the smoke for cover. Take two men forward and throw grenades into the compound."

"A good plan, Garang."

Jonjo threw the satchel over his shoulder and disappeared into the smoke. He ran blindly, using his memory of the ground to find his team of ten men. They were crouched behind a rocky outcrop, searching for targets in the thick smoke. Leaving seven of them to provide security, he took two forward.

They moved around the outcrop, Jonjo leading through the smoke. He slung his AK and pulled the pin from his first grenade, ensuring he held the lever tightly. Sprinting forward, he ran over a berm and barreled out of the smoke.

One of the guards in the tower spotted him and attempted to bring his weapon to bear. Jonjo let the handle fly off the grenade, cooking it off before he pitched it. It sailed through the air and detonated as it hit the wire mesh that screened the tower.

The other two SFF fired shots at the towers with their AKs, suppressing the guard posts. Jonjo emptied his satchel onto the ground and stood over the heap of grenades, yanking out the pins before lobbing them over the fence into the refinery.

Back in his position Garang directed the fire of his PKM machine guns. They were eating through ammunition quickly but he needed to buy enough time for Jonjo to finish his attack and withdraw. He couldn't help but grin as the grenade explosions added to the roar of the inferno at the front gate and snap of small arms fire.

WHEN THE TANKER EXPLODED, Yang was walking out of his accommodation. Grabbing his pistol belt, he sprinted across the vehicle park toward the front gate. Smoke and gunfire confirmed his fears. The refinery was under attack.

All the guard towers were being shot up and the front

gate was a raging inferno. Alarms sounded and guards rushed forward, attempting to reinforce the towers.

"Stop, you fools!" Yang screamed at them in Mandarin. If they attempted to climb the towers they would be killed. Held in reserve they could react to their attacker's next move. He rallied the guards and held them behind the concrete barriers that separated the vehicle park from the rest of the plant. Finding the senior-ranking mercenary, he issued him a quick set of orders.

"Hold your men here. If anyone tries to penetrate the wire, kill them. Do not attempt to reinforce the towers until I give word on the radio. Is this clear?"

The guard captain nodded.

A fire truck rushed forward to attempt to extinguish the flames. Yang waved it back. He would let the tanker burn. The fire would not spread and it stopped any assault from entering the compound. The enemy would eventually run low on ammunition and be forced to withdraw.

The thump of a grenade drew his attention to one corner of the compound. The tower was under attack, the guards killed or injured. As he watched, another grenade sailed over the wall and detonated, fragging a number of the Chinese jeeps. Then another sailed over the fence, and another, a stream of grenades arcing over the wall exploding among vehicles and accommodation buildings. One of them rolled into an ammunition pit dug for the Janjaweed stocks of mortar bombs. Yang hit the sand as it detonated. A huge explosion flipped one of the jeeps into the air and the blast wave washed over him.

He clenched his fists, watching the burning debris land on an accommodation building, setting it alight. His radio crackled, "Cobra, this is Slayer. We are ready for takeoff."

Yang got up and ran toward the helipad in the center of the compound.

GARANG WAITED until Jonjo was back in position before giving the order to withdraw. The PKM gunner next to him was down to his last fifty rounds, enough to pepper the towers while the SFF leapfrogged back. Jonjo's team would bring up the rear.

The northern team gave off a few more bursts before beginning their move. They scrambled into the creek line, the team leader accounting for all of his men. Spirits were high as they ran down the creek back toward the rally point.

Garang heard the thud of helicopter blades over the gunfire as the Chinese-built Z-9 screamed around the edge of the refinery. He watched in horror as the gun pods and rockets caught the withdrawing team cold, 12.7mm rounds ripping into the men. Rockets exploded in the creek, turning it into a burning hell of scorched flesh and blood. In one pass the aircraft decimated the team, all but three of the men killed instantly. None of them were left standing.

Garang hugged the earth in shock as the helicopter gunship roared overhead. A few of his men tracked it with their AKs, firing off the last of their ammunition. He fumbled with his radio attempting to raise the team leader. There was no reply.

"Garang, we need to go." The man next to him shook his arm, eyes wide with fear.

The rest of the team looked to him for direction, terrified.

"Everyone split up and run back to the trucks," Garang ordered, keying his radio so Jonjo could hear the order.

The men didn't need prompting. They burst into the bush as the helicopter circled around for another pass.

Garang fled as fast as his legs could carry him. He heard the helicopter's guns firing and rockets exploding near Jonjo's position. He crouched under a thick cluster of trees as the chopper roared overhead, searching for targets. One of his men raised an AK and blasted away. It was a pointless gesture; the gunship banked and unleashed another volley of rockets.

For the next half hour Garang crept through the thickest bushes he could find. Sharp thorns tore at him, drenching his shirt in blood.

The sound of the helicopter disappeared in the distance and Garang began to run again. He followed foot trails and animal tracks, putting as much distance between him and the refinery as he could. At a track junction he met with two of his men. They joined him as they jogged to the vehicles.

Two hours later, exhausted, they reached the trucks, the first to return.

"What happened?" Jess asked as she laid her basic medical kit out on the bonnet of their pickup. She started checking over the two fighters for wounds. "I heard the explosions."

"Chinese had a helicopter." Garang dropped into the sand breathing heavily.

Jess finished her inspection of the two men and made her way to Garang.

"And the rest of the men?" She made to inspect Garang.

"I don't know." He waved her away. "They are only scratches."

She ignored him, swabbing one of the bleeding slashes with an antiseptic wipe.

Garang pushed her hand away. "Damn it, stop mothering me." He walked stiffly over to where the two-man vehicle security detail was sitting under camouflage nets. Jess checked over her medical kit in silence.

Over the next few hours a few men trickled in. None of the first team that bore the brunt of the helicopter made it. Of Garang's own group, three had been lost, killed as they fled. There was no sign of Jonjo and his team. Garang could not contact them as he had lost his radio, forgotten during his frantic attempt to escape.

There was little work for Jess, a few scratches and a shrapnel wound. Everyone with graver injuries had died under the savage onslaught of the helicopter or bled-out in the dust.

Two hours later Garang had accepted total defeat. From a group of thirty fighters he now only had nine. He had lost all but one of his RPG launchers and all of his PKM machine guns. The mission had gone from total success to disaster in a matter of seconds.

The disheartened remnants of the militia pulled the camouflage nets down from the trucks and climbed in, ready for the long drive back to their village.

As Garang started the engine of the Hilux he heard a piercing whistle. He killed the engine and leaped out of the cab.

It was Jonjo, leading his men into the RV. Glistening with sweat they dropped onto the sand, exhausted.

Garang counted them. They were all there and still had their weapons. His losses, although brutal, were not as bad as he had thought. He squatted in the sand next to the exhausted Jonjo as Jess made her rounds among the men.

"How did you escape?"

Jonjo shrugged, matter-of-fact. "We hid in the smoke.

The helicopter has only so much fuel. So when it landed, we ran, and when it flew, we hid."

Garang allowed them to rest a moment before ordering them into the trucks. He had a long drive back to their base to dwell on the defeat. Convincing the other Dinka warriors to join the SFF, when he had left thirteen men behind, dead, was going to be next to impossible.

Chapter Eight

JUBA ARMS BAZAAR, SOUTH SUDAN

GARANG'S MEN returned directly to their base, an isolated Dinka village nestled in a valley. He had let them rest, confident the location was unknown to the Janjaweed.

While the fighters spent time with their wives and children, Garang had returned to Juba with Jonjo and Jess. After a long argument he'd persuaded Jess to lend him cash from the hospital's meager funds. Garang's supporters in the US had not sent any more funding.

Once Jess had returned to the hospital and handed over the money, Garang, together with Jonjo, headed into town to purchase weapons and ammunition.

The term 'arms dealer' usually evokes images of warehouses stacked with guns and rocket launchers, and dealers of death selling tanks and fighter jets to wealthy dictators. Juba's death merchants conformed to none of these stereotypes.

Garang and Jonjo wandered the narrow alleyway at the

back of Juba's traditional markets. They had paid the small fee to gain entry, stepping through the rusty corrugated iron wall as a guard peeled back a loose sheet.

The bazaar was merely a bunch of stalls selling the usual battered hardware. RPGs, PKMs, AKs, and other Soviet-designed weapons leaned on racks. Stacks of ammunition were piled high on makeshift tables. It was the same all over Africa; wherever there was conflict, opportunists made money hawking the weapons of war.

Garang stopped at a stall well stocked with RPG rockets. He hefted one from the seller's bench and inspected it.

The owner offered another of the missiles to Jonjo. "Only the best rockets from Nubu's stall, yes?" said the shopkeeper.

Jess had only given him five thousand Sudanese pounds and Garang wanted to ensure they got the best value for money. The rocket he inspected looked in good condition: the end cap was in place, the body free of dents and scratches. Even the booster charges looked new.

"How much?" asked Garang.

"Five hundred each."

Garang gave Jonjo a sideways glance. The young man shook his head and placed the rocket back on the table.

Garang handed his rocket to the seller. "Too expensive." He turned to walk away.

"Four hundred!" The man reached out and grasped his arm.

"Two hundred," responded Garang, peeling the man's grimy hand from his shirt.

"No, no, no. Too cheap! These are quality. Russian made."

Garang looked the man in the eye. "We tend to use a lot of them."

Jonjo had already moved on to the next stall. The young soldier had picked up a Dragunov sniper rifle and was handling it like it was a precious artifact. Even in poor condition it was worth more than the entire SFF budget. Garang made a move to join him.

"OK. OK. Two fifty."

"Two twenty-five and I will buy ten," said Garang.

The man wavered as Garang walked away. "OK! OK!"

"Jonjo, pay the man. We will load the ammunition once we are done."

The young soldier nodded, laying the sniper rifle back in its rack.

Garang crunched the numbers in his head. The rockets were the most expensive component of the purchase. It had used up half his funds. He still needed to purchase a dozen boxes of AK-47 ammunition. This would give the remaining SFF warriors enough to defend their camp and conduct some training. If he was going to launch any sort of offensive, he was going to need to find more money and more men. This was the part that had him worried. Perhaps Jess would be able to get funds from the NGOs. There was no way he was going to dip into his own savings without a guarantee from the oil companies.

Jonjo joined him at the next stall after paying the RPG salesman.

As they were inspecting ammunition, neither of the men noticed the eyes that watched them from across the market. A short, scruffy-looking African dressed in jeans and a T-shirt had been following them since they'd entered the bazaar. He had purchased an AK-47 and box of ammunition, then followed the SFF soldiers, appearing to be inspecting ordnance as he trailed them. At one stage he had held up a rocket, taking a picture of it with his phone.

Garang and Jonjo thought nothing of it; another purchasing agent buying weapons on behalf of one of many militias, private armies, or security contractors.

The man left the bazaar with his purchases, making his way back to his car. Within the vehicle he scrolled through the photos on his phone, selected one that showed the faces of the two men and sent it to the number he had been given. With any luck the bonus he would receive would be worth close to ten times what the AK and ammunition had cost.

PETROCON OIL REFINERY, KURDUFAN DISTRICT, SUDAN

Yang's guards had cleared the burnt wreckage of the tanker from the refinery gates by the time the Janjaweed warriors had returned from their pillaging. The shot-up sandbags had been replaced and contractors were busy mounting heavy machine guns in the corner guard towers. A pair of bulldozers pushed back the bushes in front of the fence, extending the clearing around the perimeter. The creek line that Garang's men had used to infiltrate into their firing positions had been leveled.

Sagrib inspected the three bodies that Yang's guards had laid out in the parking lot. "They are Dinka," he confirmed, inspecting the talismans that hung from a dead man's chest. "How many were there?"

"At least thirty." Yang was standing a few feet away, hands folded across his chest.

"And you killed how many?"

"Thirteen, possibly more. A number of bodies are still out there."

Sagrib turned to Yang with a confused look on his face. "You chased them?"

"We turned the battle with superior firepower. My helicopter arrived the day before the attack."

A sick grin spread across Sagrib's face. "Show me the helicopter."

Yang led him through the refinery infrastructure to where the gunship was based. High banks of earth surrounded the aircraft, protecting it from attack. Bunkers dug into the dry sand had been reinforced with sandbags to hold the helicopter's rockets and ammunition.

Sagrib grinned like a child as he ran his hands over the rocket pods attached to the sleek machine. The Z-9 was a Chinese-built helicopter originally designed for executive transport. This particular model had been heavily modified by PETROCON; a brace of 12.7mm fixed machine guns and rocket pods were slung beneath the stubby wings that protruded from its sides.

"If I call will you bring this to the fight?" Sagrib asked.

"Yes. When we have found the men responsible for the attack I will help you destroy them."

Yang's pocket buzzed twice as a message reached his phone. He moved away to check the device. The message contained a number of photos. He selected one that showed a man's face and walked back to the helicopter.

"Do you know this man?" he asked.

Sagrib studied the photo. "Yes, his name is Garang. He is an American, born of a bastard Dinka who ran from his duties like a scared dog."

"How do you know him?"

"He came to Khartoum with the Dinka chief. I wanted to kill him as well, but Omar would not allow it. He said he is not the same as the others. He is American so he is greedy."

"Greed can be a powerful motivator. How many men do you think he has?"

"Don't know. Twenty, maybe thirty. Not as many thanks to the helicopter." He laughed, displaying his toothless gums.

"Was he the one who warned the villagers in Kaljak and killed one of your men?"

"Could be. One of the infidel dogs said an American Dinka was there."

"He is certainly audacious, I will give him that. It takes determination to strike deep into enemy territory."

"Do you really think the Dinka are capable of this?" Sagrib pointed toward the blackened entrance.

"I think we both know the answer to that."

The warlord gestured to the phone. "From your spies, yes?"

Yang nodded.

Sagrib smashed his fist into his palm. "I should have killed the American when I had a chance. I will find him, his men, their families, and I will kill them all."

"If you get word of his base pass it to me immediately," said Yang as the pair walked back to the waiting Janjaweed.

"Yes, yes. And I have more men coming. Will you have more vehicles?"

"Five fast attack vehicles are arriving tomorrow with another shipment of heavy weapons and ammunition. My men will fit the machine guns to your trucks."

Sagrib nodded. "When we find their camp you will bring the helicopter, yes?"

"Of course. You find them and we will destroy them together."

Chapter Nine

NORTH OF JUBA, SOUTH SUDAN

SOUTH of the border another team was preparing to join the war. Mirza had driven across the border from Ethiopia two days earlier. He'd leased a small house in Juba, paying a full month's rent in cash before scoping the situation in town. Mirza was not one for tourism but he visited the bars, restaurants, and markets to get a feel for what was happening. In cargo pants, a khaki shirt, and combat boots, and with his heavy beard, he looked like any of the mining, oil, security, or NGO contractors floating around Africa. His dark Asiatic features could have come from a dozen different regions though his passport claimed he was a British national.

Within forty-eight hours of arriving in Juba, Mirza was ready to meet the next member of the PRIMAL team. He drove his four-wheel drive to the RV location just after sunrise. Ten miles out from Juba he followed an overgrown track off the main road. Parking in a dry riverbed among dense vegetation, he waited patiently to make contact with the incoming aircraft.

Mirza grabbed his iPRIMAL from the dashboard and checked it. Dragonfly's icon showed it was ten minutes away. He tapped the screen and opened a line of communication.

"Dragonfly, this is Wildcat. LZ is secure. Awaiting delivery of the package."

Mitch, the pilot, responded immediately. "Wildcat, I read you loud and clear. Got you on scope. We're seven mikes out."

"Roger."

"You better have a martini ready when I get there," said another voice.

"A bottle of cold H2O if you're lucky, Bish."

"Wow, sounds great. Good thing I'm bringing my own. See you on the ground in five," replied Bishop from inside the aircraft.

Mirza got out of his vehicle and used the last few minutes of the aircraft's approach to give the area around the wadi a quick scan. Apart from a family of warthogs hunting for grubs, it was all clear.

He slid the iPRIMAL from the pocket of his cargo pants and held it up in front of his face. On the screen he could see the flat ground to his front digitally overlaid with the landing zone he had marked. The same image would appear in Mitch's heads-up display, showing him the exact location and dimensions.

In the distance he could hear the faint drone of Dragonfly. It got louder as the speck on the horizon rapidly grew. The warthogs bolted into a thicket of swamp grass as the aircraft cycled through its landing process, the two giant propellers pitching skyward as it moved into a hover. It dropped toward the LZ, slowing as the powerful blades sent a wall of dust into the wadi.

The gray tilt-rotor touched down gently in the middle of the LZ. The side door was already open and a number of bundles were dropped to the ground. A figure jumped out and knelt as Dragonfly powered away, driving even more sand into the air.

In a pair of faded blue jeans and a lightweight khaki shirt, the PRIMAL operative held an old New York Yankees cap on his head as the downwash dissipated.

Mirza waited for the dust to settle before he walked over to help with the gear.

"Welcome to Africa, Bish."

"Good to be back, mate." Bishop took a deep breath of the crisp morning air. "It's been far too long," he said as he hugged his long-time friend. Sporting a five o'clock shadow and scruffy hair under his cap, together with his dark eyes and crooked nose, he looked like a troublemaker.

He grabbed the bags and followed Mirza into the wadi where the four-wheel drive was parked.

"A Bowler!" Bishop exclaimed. "Where the hell did you get a Bowler Wildcat?"

Mirza grinned. The tan-colored four-wheel drive looked like a Land Rover soft top but closer observation revealed a few key giveaways to the true nature of the truck. On either side of the bonnet were a pair of air intakes that allowed the supercharged 4.0 liter V8 to suck in all the oxygen it needed. The roll cage had also been modified; a canvas sunshade hid a machine gun ring mount. The Wildcat was a rally car with teeth.

Mirza patted the bonnet. "In Ethiopia I asked Mitch for a fast truck and this is what he got me."

Bishop laughed as he unzipped one of his bags, pulling

out his AK-104 assault rifle and a chest rig. He dumped the bags in the back of the Wildcat, and with his weapon and ammunition climbed into the passenger seat.

"Didn't you see one of these on *Top Gear?*" asked Bishop. It was well known that Mirza was a fan of the show. "You must have mentioned it to Mitch." PRIMAL's resident technician, pilot, and all round Mr. Fix-It was renowned for his ability to get the team anything they wanted.

Mirza turned over the engine and the Wildcat started with a throaty rumble.

"Now that's what I'm talking about," said Bishop. "How far is it back to Juba?"

"About twenty minutes."

Bishop checked the digital map on his iPRIMAL. "Terrain's pretty tough but I reckon you can get this beast to the safe house in under fifteen."

He caught a glimpse of a smile through Mirza's beard and the Indian pushed the accelerator to the floor. Bishop was thrown back in his seat. The Wildcat roared like an enraged rhino and accelerated out of the riverbed in a cloud of dust.

"I read your report," yelled Bishop while Mirza rallied the vehicle down the dirt track, the engine howling through the quiet morning air. "The girl, Jess, she's a long way from home. Pretty little thing out here in the sticks. Have you had a chance to meet her?"

Mirza shook his head. "No, I thought that would be better left to you. You always have better luck with the ladies."

Bishop laughed. "That's very charitable of you, Mirza. From what it sounds like, she's already taken."

"Yes, one of the NGOs said she was seeing the American freedom fighter."

"This Garang guy?"

"That's the one. According to our sources in Juba, he's trying to raise an army to fight the Janjaweed. There are rumors he launched a raid into Sudan to hit the Chinese refinery."

"Well, credit where credit's due. At least he's doing something. I wish the same could be said for the rest of the SPLA," Bishop said referring to South Sudan's official defense force. "So, when are we meeting her?"

"Tomorrow. That gives us a bit of time to check things out around Juba and follow up on a few leads."

"Sounds good, but first things first; let's sort some breakfast."

Chapter Ten

JUBA, SOUTH SUDAN

"DOCTOR HUTTON, there is a man here to see you." The orderly stuck his head into the room as Jess was finishing up with a patient.

"One minute, Michael." She tied off the final suture in the young boy's arm. "So brave!" She pulled the rubber gloves from her hands and gave the three-year-old a lollipop. The toddler had fallen on a sharp piece of tin and sliced open his forearm. Without proper treatment he probably would have lost his arm. "Bring him back in one week, OK," she told the child's mother.

"Thank you, Doctor Hutton." The mother thrust a bag of fruit into her arms.

"Oh, thank you!" Jess had tried to refuse her patients' gifts in the past. She had learned that this offended them.

She gave the boy a pat on the head, tucked the fruit under her arm, and left the treatment room. Michael was waiting for her. "He is in your office."

Jess walked down the dimly lit corridor to her office. She opened the door and was greeted by a stranger wearing a baseball cap and sporting a light beard.

"Doctor Hutton, my name is Aden." He removed his cap, uncovering a shock of dark hair, and offered her a hand.

"Please call me Jess. Everyone does." She placed the fruit on her desk and grasped the man's hand, noticing how rough it was. She studied his face: to her he had kind eyes, dark brown with wrinkles around them, suggesting he laughed a lot. His jawline was strong; his nose crooked, and his smile roguish. She put his age at around thirty-five. His slight accent threw her: a tinge of American, but something else, something crisper. Maybe he was from New York or maybe he'd spent time in England.

"Thank you for taking the time to see me, Jess. No doubt you are a very busy woman."

"It's never quiet, that's for sure."

"I think what you're doing here is pretty damn special," said Bishop honestly. "It takes a certain kind of person to give up life in the developed world and throw themselves into this environment. Not everyone can do it."

She blushed and looked down at her desk.

Bishop had already seen her photo attached to her intel file. He knew Jess was pretty, but in person she was even more so. Dressed in jeans, a T-shirt, and a white medical jacket, her long brown hair in a ponytail, she looked utterly desirable. Gray eyes, wide full lips, a round face, and a button nose; not the sort of woman he usually pursued, but definitely attractive.

"I wanted to talk to you about your dealings with South Sudanese fighters."

"What about them?" The coy embarrassment disappeared from her face and her soft features hardened.

"I take it that a number of the groups bring their wounded here."

"This is Africa, Aden. I see a lot of war wounded. Not all of them are fighters." She folded her arms across her chest.

"Of course. I apologize if I've thrown you a little." He pulled a card from his shirt and handed it across. "I'm from an independent US organization. We want to inject aid into South Sudan."

Jess examined the card suspiciously. Christians In Africa: CIA.

Aden certainly fit the mold of a government agent: broad, unshaven, the obligatory khaki shirt and baseball cap. No doubt he was also carrying a pistol.

"So what do you want from me?" Jess asked as she pocketed the card. "I'm guessing you're not looking to spend money on my hospital."

He shrugged. "Don't be so quick to write off the possibility. I'm sure there are a lot of things you need here." He took a pen and pad out of his jeans and pushed it across the table. "You should write me a list."

Jess raised her eyebrows. She paused a second before writing some of the hospital's key deficiencies on the pad. "And what would you want in return?"

"Not much, merely an introduction."

She stopped writing. "To who?"

"I've heard rumors of a newly formed group, the Southern Freedom Fighters. I've also heard they're led by a former American soldier. I'd like you to arrange a meeting with this man."

She finished the list and pushed the pad across the table.

"I haven't heard of any Americans but I can make some inquiries."

"I would be most obliged, Jess."

"How will I contact you if arrange the meeting?"

"I'll be around tomorrow to drop off some of these things. Perhaps after that we could go and meet him together." He pocketed the notepad. "If you need me before then, my number is on the card."

Bishop rose from the table and made his way to the door. As he opened it, he thanked her again.

Jess sat at her desk for a moment, her mind racing. The CIA in Juba! She had heard rumors but nothing concrete. This could be the support Garang was looking for, but what if it was a trap? What if the CIA wanted to arrest him and take him back to the US? She took her phone from her jeans and typed a text message. Garang would know what to do.

TEN MILES NORTH OF JUBA, SOUTH SUDAN

Bishop guided the Wildcat slowly up a dirt track. At low revs the engine was barely discernible over the hissing sound of grass rubbing against the side of the four-wheel drive. Fresh tire tracks indicated that vehicles had passed through recently.

Mirza sat in the back, his AK on his lap, ready to deal with any potential threats. Jess sat in the passenger seat. They had dropped off supplies at the clinic and picked her up. She had directed them out of town and now they were headed north.

"If you're cold there's a jacket in the back." Bishop kept

his eye on the track. "Mirza, can you pass Jess my puff jacket?"

It was early morning and the air was still cool. The wind flowing into the Wildcat through the open sides had a bite to it. Mirza handed the jacket forward and Jess draped it over her legs.

"Thank you." She smiled gratefully.

"So what brought you to Sudan, Jess?" asked Bishop. "And an airplane is not an acceptable answer."

She laughed. "I guess I wanted to make a difference. The idea of working in California didn't appeal to me. I wanted to do more than treat bunions and cankers so I hooked up with an NGO and here I am."

"Wow, big leap from California to here. Lots of sand but no beaches."

"I do miss that, but like I said I wanted to make a difference. What about you, Aden? Have you always worked for the Agency?"

"Spent a bit of time in the Army. I've always been in this line of work. The opposite to what you do, I guess."

"But equally as important."

Bishop shot her a questioning glance. "Not many doctors would have that view, especially ones that work for NGOs."

Jess brushed her hair from her face. "I'm not naive, Aden. My dad was a soldier. He had a favorite quote, George Orwell, if I remember correctly. Something about resting safe in our beds because rough men stand ready in the night to inflict violence on those who would do us harm."

"One of my favorites."

She laughed. "Of course it is, because you're one of them. The rough men that keep us safe."

They drove in silence for a few minutes before the Wildcat's GPS buzzed.

"We should be pretty close, yeah?" asked Bishop. "We're almost on top of the coords you gave us."

"Nearly there."

They dipped down into a dry creek bed and Bishop revved the engine slightly to propel them up the other side. As they crested, the track hooked to the right and revealed a barricade of wood held together with barbed wire.

The cobbled together barrier was manned by two men armed with AK-47s. They waved for the vehicle to stop and waited as the Wildcat pulled over to the side of the road.

One of them covered the vehicle with his weapon while the other walked up to the passenger side, his AK held casually in one hand. As he got closer he recognized Jess. "Ah, Doctor Hutton, how are you?"

"I'm good, David. How are you? We are here to see Garang. These men are friends."

"You are the CIA, yes?"

Mirza glanced at Bishop, who shrugged. "Yeah, that's us."

"That is good. We have been told to let you through. But the truck stays here."

Bishop nodded, opened the door, and alighted from the vehicle. The guard said nothing as the PRIMAL operative snapped on his chest rig and slung an AK over his shoulder. Weapons were an everyday part of life in this part of the world.

Jess walked to the other guard at the checkpoint. He smiled and slung his rifle across his back before hugging her.

"Which one has the medical supplies?" asked Mirza as he reached into the back of the truck.

"This one." Bishop slung the backpack over his shoulder

while Mirza grabbed his shoulder satchel and rifle. The backpack contained a full trauma kit, a gift to show Jess and the SFF they were serious.

"Don't touch the truck or it will explode," Mirza told the two men as he aimed a remote at the Wildcat. It emitted a beep and flashed its lights. The guards stepped away from it.

As they continued up the track Bishop turned to his partner. "Did Mitch rig the vehicle?"

"Not really," said Mirza. "I lied."

Jess led them a short distance to a cluster of huts. Smoke drifted and they could smell something cooking. A guard waved them forward. Grass-roofed mud huts surrounded an open patch of bare earth. Tall trees offered shade from the sun. A battered Unimog truck was parked behind the huts next to an old Hilux pickup. Two men sat around a low campfire.

Bishop and Mirza lay their weapons against a log at the edge of the clearing as Jess greeted the men at the fire. They were dressed as Bishop would expect of resistance fighters; battered boots, torn camouflage pants, and T-shirts. Both carried basic AKs, the weapons worn but well maintained.

Jess spoke first. "Mirza, Aden, this is Garang and Jonjo. They are representatives of the Southern Freedom Fighters."

Bishop sized up Garang as he grasped his hand. He was tall, muscular, and handsome, with a firm handshake. His face was bruised and battered but he stood tall. Whoever had given him a beating had not broken his spirit.

Bishop moved on to the younger man as Mirza shook Garang's hand. Jonjo was still really only a boy, tall but lean. He moved with the awkwardness of someone not yet confident in their own abilities. Bishop locked eyes with him. The kid already had the stare of someone who had faced and dealt death.

"Come. Sit." Garang invited them to the fire. They sat on logs as Jonjo stirred a pot of tea.

Bishop handed the backpack to Garang as he took a seat. "Just a small token of appreciation for this meeting. It's a combat medical kit. I thought the doctor might find it useful to help your men."

"I was under the impression you wanted to help us with our fight. Weapons and ammunition would be more useful."

"I don't bring guns to a first meeting. Sorry."

Garang nodded. "That's fair. Thank you." He handed the medical kit to Jess, saying, "This is men's business. Perhaps you could wait for us at the vehicles." Garang missed the angry look his girlfriend gave him as she picked up the heavy medical kit and struggled with it toward the Hilux. One of the guards came across and helped her.

Once she was out of earshot the SFF commander continued, "Doctor Hutton tells me you are looking to support us in our battle against the oppression of Khartoum."

"Yes, we represent an organization that wishes to bring peace to South Sudan."

Garang laughed. "The US doesn't want peace. You want to reduce Chinese power and gain control of the oil fields."

Bishop nodded. "And you want to bring peace and prosperity to your people by denying Khartoum control of your lands. I see these two goals as being aligned."

Garang considered the statement. "So why has the US ignored us until now?"

"The situation is complex. Needless to say, any support provided to South Sudan needs to be completely deniable and strictly controlled. You and your group provide us with a unique opportunity."

"You assume that we want your help."

"We offer weapons, ammunition, and training."

"What type of weapons?" interrupted Jonjo.

"What do you need?" asked Mirza.

"RPGs, AKs, PKMs, explosives, grenades, and... one Dragunov sniper rifle."

"Only one?" Mirza feigned surprise. He stood and walked over to where they had left their assault rifles. Methodically he removed the magazine from the modified AK and cleared the action. He walked back to the fire and handed it to Jonjo, taking a seat on the log beside him. "I find that with the correct attachments the AK-104 is a superior weapon to both the forty-seven and the Dragunov."

Jonjo took the weapon in his hands. The AK-104 was a modern version of the AK but it felt nothing like his own battered weapon. The woodwork had been replaced with tough black plastic. Rails had been attached on either side of the barrel and a short stubby suppressor was screwed on where the flash suppressor used to be. He grasped the front grip and lifted the weapon to his shoulder. The sight on top was nothing like the iron sights he was used to; it had a glowing red chevron with little markings to allow for different ranges. The magnification was minimal but the sight picture was crystal clear. The weapon was a masterpiece: reliable, tough, deadly. He made to pass it back.

"No, you can keep it," said Mirza. "I can get another one."

Jonjo's jaw dropped and he turned to Garang eagerly.

The SFF leader considered the two men for a moment then nodded. "The only question I have is can I trust you?"

Mirza rose from the log. "I think I will leave you two to

talk details. Jonjo, if it's OK with your boss I would like to show you how to use the sighting system on that rifle."

Garang gave the young soldier a nod and Jonjo jumped up with the weapon in his hands. He and Mirza walked across the clearing into the scrub behind the huts. The SFF leader waved one of the guards after them. The other stayed near the vehicle with Jess.

"So, what exactly is it that you want from us, Mr....?"

"Aden, it's just Aden."

"OK, what exactly do you want from us, Aden?"

"Being completely honest, I want you to destroy the Janjaweed raiders and protect the South Sudanese people and land from being eaten up by Khartoum. I want South Sudanese wealth in the hands of the rightful landowners and if China happens to lose a little influence in the mix, so be it."

Garang looked thoughtful. "As a show of faith, I would like you to deliver a number of things for us."

Bishop pulled a notepad from his pocket.

"We need all of the things Jonjo mentioned, mostly RPG rockets, PKMs, and ammunition, but also something special. We also need Stingers."

Bishop jotted a few notes on the pad. "I can provide all of the weapons and do better than Stingers! In addition Mirza and I would also like to provide training and other assistance where we can."

"If you deliver what we need, you will be more than welcome to train and fight with us. How long will it take for the weapons to be ready? Weeks or months?"

"We can make delivery tomorrow afternoon."

"That soon?"

"The quicker I get you weapons, the quicker we can

stop those murdering bastards killing innocent women and children. Will delivery at your base be acceptable?"

"I can give you a location."

Bishop handed across the notepad. Garang pulled a GPS from his pocket and copied a set of coordinates from the screen.

"My men and I will be heading north tonight. We will meet you at these coordinates and you can deliver the weapons. I expect to see only the two of you."

"There will be a third person in my team. The man responsible for bringing the weapons."

"That's fine, just make sure there are no surprises."

"I expect the same from your end." Bishop took a satellite phone from his pocket. "This is a secure phone and it will be the only means I use to contact you."

"Yes, I used a similar device in the Army."

Both men looked up as Jonjo and Mirza walked back into the clearing. The PRIMAL operative and the young soldier were engaged in an animated conversation, the AK tucked under the latter's arm. Mirza was telling a story and the guard trailing them was also grinning as he listened in.

"I was just telling Jonjo about the time in Sierra Leone when you nearly got me killed."

Bishop rolled his eyes and Jonjo laughed. "You two have been working together for a long time, yes?"

"Far, far too long," said Bishop. "But don't believe everything he says, Jonjo. I've saved his bacon more times than he'll admit."

With the mood of the meeting lightened, Garang waved Jess back to sit with them.

Garang moved across to Jonjo and Mirza to inspect the new AK. Jess was left sitting by the fire with Bishop.

"I hope it's all to your satisfaction." Bishop gestured toward the backpack.

"Yes. Thank you so much. I don't think I've ever seen a medical kit that comprehensive. I could operate with what's in that bag."

"Yeah, I've amputated a leg using that kit."

Jess raised an eyebrow. "You're a doctor."

"Not really. I dabble. More by necessity than choice."

"I guess in your business you see a lot of suffering."

"More than any man's fair share."

There was a pause and Jess stared into the fire. Then she looked up at Bishop. "Do you have a family back home worrying about you?"

"No, not anymore. What about you?"

"Just my mother. My father died when I was little."

"How does she feel about you being in Africa?"

"She's always worried, but she knows this is what I want to do."

"What you're doing, it's a pretty selfless act."

"Is it? I mean, why are we really here? To fulfill some inner need to justify our existence? To make a difference? The world thrives on selfishness, Aden." She turned her head to watch Garang and the other men. The guards had joined the inspection of the weapon. "Everyone has their motives."

Chapter Eleven

JUBA AND SFF VILLAGE, SOUTH SUDAN

BISHOP HAD SET up a basic office in the safe house. He sat on a folding chair, his laptop open on a cheap plastic table. The little shack Mirza had rented suited their needs despite the meager facilities. It had an enclosed garage for the Wildcat and was a distance from the town center and most of the local activity.

His first business was to email Mitch the equipment order. From Addis Ababa in Ethiopia, Mitch immediately confirmed he had most of the gear and could make the delivery. With that in order, all Bishop needed was to wait for Mirza to get back from his search for another vehicle.

As Mirza scoured the city for a four-wheel drive, Bishop used his laptop to pull up imagery of the coordinates Garang had given them. His computer had already connected through the satellite node in the Wildcat and downloaded the latest regional imagery direct from the Bunker's servers.

The SFF base was a small village on the bank of a river. A dirt track ran through the center of fewer than thirty grass huts. Bishop noted a cleared area in the middle that looked like it was used for soccer; a potential landing zone for Dragonfly. The village was isolated enough that the aircraft could approach without attracting undue attention. He sent a quick follow-up email to throw in a couple of soccer balls into Mitch's delivery.

The river cut through what looked like half of a massive crater. Millions of years ago a meteorite must have slammed into the earth at an angle, creating a ridge of high ground to one side. Over the years weather had broken down the other side of the crater until all that was left was a half ring of rocky ground that bumped up against the river.

Bishop marked the image on his screen, using a program to place defensive symbols on the graphic. The river was a natural obstacle protecting the western flank. The rocky outcrops that horseshoed the eastern flank provided excellent early warning and defense. The only infiltration points into the natural fortress were the openings that the river had cut into the basin and the track that followed it. He could see why Garang and his men had chosen this village as their base of operations. A small group of fighters could easily defend it against a larger force.

Mirza returned after an hour with a new Hilux pickup. Finding a decent truck had been easy since he'd been willing to pay a premium.

They went north immediately, Bishop in the Hilux, Mirza in the Wildcat. They paid little attention to the obvious poverty as they drove out of Juba and into the African grasslands. Buildings were mostly shacks and the cars on the dirt roads were barely serviceable. There was no sign of oil money in this part of the country.

Bishop led as they approached the village. His iPRIMAL was mounted to the dash with Velcro, keeping him on the route. A mile out they rounded a bend on the sandy track and halted at a checkpoint. Armed guards confirmed they were in the right area and they were waved through.

From the track the high ground that ringed the village was even more dominant. Rock outcrops jutted into the skyline and ran down a ridge toward the river, flattening out where the rough dirt track followed the riverbank.

Bishop brought the Hilux to a crawl as they drove through the gap between the high ground and the river. He scanned the ridge; sure enough, there were defensive positions covering the approach. He could not see fighters, but he knew they would be there, ready to turn the pass into a killing zone.

The village looked the same as the others they had passed through. Mud-walled huts, thatched roofs, dust, chickens running free, and cattle penned in yards constructed with branches.

Children gathered to welcome the new arrivals. Twenty or so malnourished kids swarmed the two trucks yelling "*Kawaja! Kawaja!*" the local word for foreigners. The commotion brought some of the locals from their huts. Tall Africans clad in bright robes approached cautiously. For a medium-size village there were remarkably few people. Bishop guessed that most of the villagers had left the area; those who remained were probably families of the SFF.

A fighter clad in camouflage pants and boots, bare chest laden with bandoliers and talismans, waved for them to stop. Bishop pulled the Hilux in next to three older, battered pickups and the SFF Unimog truck. Mirza parked the

Wildcat alongside and both of them got out. Garang, Jonjo, Jess, and a few others appeared from the largest of the huts.

"Two trucks; this is a good sign," Garang said as they alighted.

Other SFF warriors spilled out of the shacks and joined their leaders. They were a mixed bunch; some wore camouflage uniforms, others wore tattered jeans. Many had talismans hanging from their necks and gold bands around their wrists. They carried the usual weapons: worn AKs, PKMs, RPGs, and G3 assault rifles.

The PRIMAL pair carried their AK-104s slung. Bishop was wearing a simple chest rig containing a half dozen magazines and grenades. Mirza opted for a lower-profile satchel. Bishop called it a man bag.

"The Toyota is for your men." Bishop tossed the keys to the SFF leader.

He caught them with a grin, strode over to the truck and looked into the tray. The smile faded. "Is this a joke? It is empty. Where are the weapons?"

"Inbound." Bishop pointed out to the east.

On cue, Dragonfly roared around the ridgeline and swept low over the township. Every set of eyes was on the aircraft as it circled wide and began its approach.

Mirza trotted out onto the soccer field, smoke grenade in hand. He dropped the canister on the ground and it spewed out a stream of thick green smoke.

"Your pilot is mad. There's no room to land here," yelled Garang, waving his hands.

Bishop smiled.

Mitch brought Dragonfly in hard and fast. The giant propellers tilted skyward as it crossed the river. The downwash whipped debris into the air as it swooped down onto the soccer field. A wall of dust lashed the watching villagers and SFF fighters. The blades flattened the instant the wheels hit the dry grass. Mitch cut the engines and the cloud of dust settled as the black props gradually spun slower.

Fighters and villagers alike ran to the edge of the field, cautious of the sinister-looking blades.

The side door slid open and Mitch jumped down into the dust. He was dressed similarly to the other two PRIMAL operatives. A compact P90 submachine gun hung from his shoulder, a matching FN Five-seveN pistol on his hip. A cream-colored scarf was wrapped around his neck, the end cast over his shoulder.

Mirza stepped forward to greet him. "Welcome to Abyei District, Mitch."

"Thank you, my good man."

Bishop greeted the bearded PRIMAL pilot and all-around tech-head with a handshake.

Garang and his fighters tentatively walked over.

"This... this is amazing!" Jonjo broke the ice as he patted the side of the gray tilt-rotor. "What is it called?"

"Oh, she's a humdinger alright," Mitch said. "We call her Dragonfly." Mitch shook the young African's hand. "We'll have to get you up for a flight."

Bishop introduced Mitch to the group, explaining the role that the aircraft would play in their operations against the Janjaweed. Most of the villagers gained enough courage to approach the aircraft but they stood at a respectful distance as the SFF and the PRIMAL operatives talked.

Mitch noticed some of the youths creeping closer and he broke away from Bishop's briefing, climbing back into the cabin. He returned a few moments later with a large cardboard box. Reaching inside he pulled out a soccer ball and rolled it toward the children. They squealed in delight and he gestured for them to take the box. Within seconds children were kicking soccer balls around the field.

"What about our weapons?" Garang asked suspiciously. "Or is it just toys?"

"Keep your panties on, old chap, we've got your kit," responded Mitch as he effortlessly picked up a heavy case and deposited it on the ground.

The rest of the PRIMAL team helped him unload the aircraft, handing the plastic cases and wooden crates out through the side hatch, stacking them on the field. By the time Dragonfly was empty there were two piles, one of wooden crates and the other rugged black plastic cases.

Mirza dragged one of the plastic cases clear of the pile and opened it. The SFF men gathered around as he removed a SA-24 surface-to-air missile from the protective foam.

"Igla-S, very easy to use. Very deadly to all but the fastest aircraft," explained Mirza. "I can teach you how to use it in a matter of hours."

"A gift from one of our friends in the Ukraine," added Bishop.

"Can it kill a helicopter?" asked Garang.

"It'll blow the sucker clean out of the sky."

"Very good. What else did you bring?"

"This pile is for you, my good man," pointed out Mitch. "Four PKMs, a handful of RPG launchers, ten new AK-104s, and a bucket load of ammo. I've got a few bags of gear in the back as well: chest rigs, radios, and the like."

"And the other plastic boxes?"

"Ah, that's something special." Mitch opened one of the boxes.

Garang peered inside with a frown. "Plastic plants?" He looked up. "You brought us plastic plants."

Mitch pulled the 'plant' out of the box. "It's not a plant, it's a UGS: an unmanned ground sensor. This smart little weed uses a whole bunch of sensors to tell us where the bad guys are."

"So you plant these near roads and they tell you where the Janjaweed are moving?" asked Garang.

"On the money, champ. Your men do the planting and we monitor them from back here."

Mitch opened another box and pulled out a laptop. He powered it up and showed Garang the interface.

"I dropped a sensor at the border yesterday. This one is pretty similar, a little tree with a sensor-activated camera. It pinged through these images this morning."

Mitch scrolled through the pictures; the quality was sharp. The sensor had orientated itself toward a river crossing where a track sloped down into the water. The camera was able to capture stills of vehicles as they slowed to ford the shallow creek. The images showed a variety of trucks and four-wheel drives, most of them laden with Janjaweed warriors.

"Stop!" Garang jammed a finger at one of the images. "It's him! That fucking murderer!"

The screen showed a jeep bristling with machine guns, crossing the creek. In the passenger seat a man had stood to guide the driver. His face could be clearly seen above the windshield. Garang's hand shook as he continued pointing. "That motherfucker, his name is Sagrib. He beheaded our chief and had me beaten."

Bishop glanced at Mitch. "We're going to need more firepower."

"I've got plenty of stock in Addis Ababa. I'll do another run. Got some new toys that should do the trick." Mitch was using a Lascar hangar in the Ethiopian capital to stockpile equipment and fuel for the operation. "In the meantime there's a fifty cal in this lot for the Wildcat," he said referring to the M3M .50 caliber machine gun. Once mounted on the Wildcat's custom roll cage the rally car would be turned into a formidable reconnaissance and fire support vehicle.

"Sounds good, we need to keep it light and mobile. These guys don't have the vehicles to go head to head with that!" He pointed to the heavily armed jeep on the screen. "Ambushing and dismounted ops are going to be the key."

Bishop looked up and caught the eye of Jess. The doctor had been hanging at the rear of the group, silently watching the unloading of the weapons of war. "Throw in some medical and humanitarian supplies as well. We need to earn the trust of the villagers. Clean water would probably be a good start."

"Roger. If I get airborne now, I'll be able to come back in under darkness. I'll grab some cam nets and arm up Dragonfly as well."

"Good call, I think it's going to get a little hairy around here." Bishop looked at Garang; the man was still fixated on the photo of the Janjaweed leader.

WORD of the arrival of new weapons and equipment spread rapidly and Garang's meager force grew as Dinka warriors returned to the village. With over thirty SFF fighters, there were now enough men for the PRIMAL team to train and begin defensive preparations.

Over the next few days Mirza took a group through the deployment of the unmanned ground sensors. It was a simple process of driving the camouflaged camera stem into the ground and burying the seismic sensors. The men were fast learners and were soon deploying across the countryside to install the devices.

Next he ran Jonjo and one of the other fighters through the SA-24. They stood on the soccer field going through the firing drills as Mirza coached them on how to engage aircraft. Once Mitch returned with the tilt-rotor, he would get them to practice tracking a live target. If they were going to go up against an attack helicopter they needed to have their drills squared away.

As Mirza prepared the men, Bishop and Garang reviewed the village's defenses. The SFF had already constructed the basics; machine gun pits sited on the high ground covered the main approach. Eventually Bishop would get them to dig alternate locations. More important was improving their early-warning capability. They deployed a number of the more sophisticated acoustic and optical sensors capable of detecting movement out to the horizon. The high ground around the village provided a perfect vantage point for the solar-powered devices.

"Will this thing be able to detect a helicopter?" Garang asked as he helped clear an area among the rocks.

"Definitely. The acoustic sensor will pick up any vehicle sounds and slew the hi-res camera to get visual," Bishop explained as he snapped the pole-mounted sensors into the briefcase-size base station.

"Impressive, but I think I will still rely on eyeballs."

"That's smart. Nothing is as reliable as well-trained men."

They finished installing the device and started the short trek that would take them down the ridgeline back into the village.

"So what brought you to Africa?" asked Bishop as they walked.

"My father was born here. He moved to America when I was a boy."

"Whereabouts?"

"I grew up in Detroit but never really fitted in. After school I joined the army. Did a tour in Iraq then got home and didn't know what to do next."

"Yeah, I know what that's like."

"I saw a show on Discovery Channel about what was happening here. My father always wanted to come back but he died when I was in Iraq. He told me stories about this land, the people, the wealth. It was only a matter of time until I left America and returned to help my people claim what is rightfully theirs."

"So now you've got a cause and a beautiful woman."

"Ha! Jess, she's a dreamer and that's all. Women like her are easy come and easy go."

"Fair enough. You're committed to the cause and that's what counts in my book."

"Yes, I am." He paused as they reached the bottom of the hill. "One thing I haven't asked you, Aden. Once this is over and we have won, will the CIA be able to facilitate meetings with the oil companies?"

"When we have defeated the Janjaweed we will have set the conditions. It will be up to your government to negotiate but rest assured you will not have to look for the oil companies; they will come, hat in hand."

Garang contemplated Bishop's words in silence as they followed a goat track through the grassland at the edge of the village.

"More fighters have joined us." Garang nodded toward two rusted four-wheel drives parked at the edge of the village. "Word of our CIA friends has spread!" He strode ahead to meet the new arrivals.

Bishop's brow furrowed. In the last day another ten men had arrived, swelling the SFF ranks to nearly forty warriors and six vehicles. His primary concern was how easy it would be for an enemy spy to slip in and report to the Janjaweed before they were ready.

His iPRIMAL buzzed in his pocket. He pulled it out and activated the alert on the screen. It was one of the sensors located ten miles to the north. The 'plant' had detected vehicles and gunfire. He scrolled through the images; they showed two white UN vehicles crossing a creek. Windows on both vehicles were shattered.

Another alert buzzed in. More gunfire. The image showed two heavily armed Janjaweed jeeps.

He checked the digital map; the UN vehicles were heading south. Whoever was chasing them was not far behind. Within the next twenty minutes they would be forced to cross a river only five miles from the SFF camp; an opportunity for a snap ambush.

He sprinted into the village. "Mirza, mount up! Garang, we've got Janjaweed to the north."

The SFF leader snapped out a few commands and men with their new chest rigs and weapons sprinted toward their vehicles. A PKM machine gun mount had already been welded to the roll bar of the new Hilux.

Bishop briefed them using a stick to draw a diagram in the dust. He and Mirza would lead in the Wildcat with Jonjo riding shotgun. Mirza would man the M3M heavy machine gun now fitted on top of the modified Land Rover. Garang and a team of his best fighters would bring up the rear in the Hilux. Jess would be with them; the UN patrol looked like it was shot up pretty bad.

Once the quick orders were complete Bishop gave a nod to the SFF leader.

"Mount up!" Garang ordered and his men ran for the Hilux, throwing tins of ammunition into the tray. Jess and her medical kit were bundled into the back.

As Bishop made to climb up into the Wildcat, Garang grabbed him by the arm. "Is it him?" he said with a crazed look.

"I couldn't tell. I doubt it. More likely to be one of his patrols."

Bishop swung into the seat of the supercharged Land Rover and turned the ignition. Glancing in the mirror to make sure the Hilux was behind him he revved the engine and dropped the clutch, sending the Wildcat racing down the track in a cloud of dust.

Chapter Twelve

ABYEI DISTRICT, SOUTH SUDAN

"UN CALL SIGN, this is a friendly call sign. Do you read me?" Bishop keyed the transmit button on the steering wheel of the Wildcat as he fought to keep the four-wheel drive on the sandy track. He checked the mirror; the Hilux was keeping pace.

"Unknown call sign, this is Victor Forty-Four. Identify yourself," a Dutch accent broadcast. Bishop could make out yelling and gunshots in the background.

"Victor Forty-Four, we are friendlies located to your southwest. We are moving to establish a security position at the river crossing to your due south. Please confirm you are able to make it that far."

There was a pause before Victor 44 responded. "We've got no idea who you are, but if you can get these bastards off our tail we would be very grateful, *ja*."

"Victor Forty-Four, can do. You just get here alive."

"We will try!"

The track Bishop was following hit the main route and he spun the wheel, sending the Wildcat sliding around the corner. The big V8 roared and the tires gripped the dirt, sending them racing toward the river crossing.

The dirt road was little more than a pair of sandy wheel ruts that snaked through the grass down into the shallow waterway. Larger trees and shrubs dotted the banks, providing concealment for the ambushers. Bishop turned the Wildcat off the track and parked it so Mirza would have a clear line of fire. He dismounted, flagging down the Hilux.

"Garang, you and your men position on the other side of the track. Cover the river crossing. Wait for us to fire and then hit them with everything you've got."

The SFF leader nodded, directing his driver to mirror the position of the Wildcat.

Jess jumped from the back of the vehicle and Bishop jogged over to her.

"Jess, you need to be prepared to treat any casualties."

"Of course." She pulled the medical backpack from the tray of the Hilux. Bishop drew his Px4. "You know how to use one of these?"

"Sure do." She took the pistol, thumbed the safety off, and pulled the slide back to check that a round was chambered.

He handed her his holster. "I'm not saying you'll need it. But if you're out here in the thick of it you need to carry."

"Garang never let me have a gun. 'Only men are warriors. Women look after children and the animals,'" she mimicked.

"Garang doesn't get out much. The deadliest operative I know is a woman."

Jess gave him a curious look, clipped the pistol holster onto her belt, and shouldered the heavy medical pack. Bishop watched her for a few seconds as she started off down the track at a trot.

Gunfire broke the serenity of the African bush. In the distance there was a loud explosion and a thin stream of smoke rose into the air.

Garang's four men fanned out across the bank, seeking cover among the vegetation. A fifth soldier manned the PKM machine gun mounted on the back of the Hilux. They all focused their sights on where the track entered the river on the far bank.

The Wildcat was also parked behind bushes, hiding the vehicle except for Mirza manning the .50 cal machine gun. He cleared and reloaded the M3M, checking to make sure the rounds would feed correctly. Jonjo was breaking off branches from the surrounding trees and placing them on the Wildcat's roof to aid in the concealment.

Bishop took a position on the flank. "Mirza, hit the lead Janjaweed vehicle as it slows for the creek."

"Roger."

The scream of a diesel engine at maximum revs filled the air as the first UN Land Cruiser sped down the track and splashed into the river crossing. Close behind it was a second white four-wheel drive.

As the second UN vehicle hit the shallow water, two heavily armed jeeps appeared hot on their tail, the Janjaweed gunners firing long automatic bursts. Heavy caliber rounds snapped through the bushes and kicked up dirt. One of the wing mirrors on the Hilux tore off sending the PKM gunner diving into the scrub. Another bullet punched through the windshield.

The UN vehicles miraculously made it across the

narrow ford as the first of the Janjaweed jeeps entered the water after them. Mirza lined up the red-dot sight on his heavy machine gun and depressed the butterfly trigger.

The big gun roared, sending a stream of Raufoss rounds slamming into the first jeep. It shuddered under the impact as the high-explosive incendiary bullets shredded the occupants, rending limbs from bodies. An RPG rocket screamed from the bank, detonating as it hit the bonnet. The fuel tank exploded, consuming the jeep in a ball of fire as the remainder of the SFF unleashed their weapons it.

The driver of the second Janjaweed vehicle reacted instinctively, wrenching the steering wheel sideways to avoid the carnage. The jeep bounced in the wheel ruts before the front wheels jammed in the ditch. It flipped then slid on its side.

His immediate reaction kept the six-man crew alive. They all got clear of the wreck before Mirza could bring his machine gun to bear.

"Switch targets!" Garang screamed at his men as they continued to pour automatic fire into the first burning jeep. "Switch targets!" He jumped up onto the Hilux and racked the action on the PKM. He unleashed a long burst into the flipped jeep. The thud of Mirza's heavy .50 caliber joined the angry rattle of the lighter weapon as Mirza concentrated his own fire on the jeep. It exploded into a ball of fire as the exposed fuel tanks ignited.

The Janjaweed were not as ill-disciplined as the SFF fighters. They quickly realized their predicament and made for the thick vegetation that lined the riverbank. The men ran low and fast, dashing for cover.

Bishop spotted them from his position at the flank of the ambush. He dropped one with a snap shot from his AK before they disappeared into the bushes.

"Tangos right flank!" he bellowed as the Janjaweed began to fire back. He returned a burst from his AK and scrambled for cover.

Mirza tried to swing the heavy machine gun around to engage but it was too late. The Janjaweed had pushed to the edge of the water and were under the depression of the barrel.

It was Jonjo who responded first. From his position near Bishop, he lobbed a grenade across the water. It exploded in the bushes, silencing two of the Janjaweed.

Jonjo sprinted to a better position, ignoring the bullets cracking through the air. He lay prone and fired methodically, his suppressed AK spitting rounds into the remaining Arab raiders. Bishop fired controlled bursts from a knee, covering Jonjo's movement and adding to the weight of fire smashing the far bank.

Mirza grabbed his AK, jumped down from the Wildcat, and bolted forward to join them.

Bishop, Mirza, and Jonjo blasted away for another full minute before all movement on the other side of the river ceased.

"Cover me," ordered Mirza as he waded into the shallow water, AK in his shoulder. Jonjo joined him, both steadily wading across the river, weapons ready. At the other side they patrolled the bank, looking for someone to take prisoner. There was no one left alive. Jonjo checked the bodies and stripped weapons and ammunition from them, throwing it in a pile.

"Good work." Mirza placed his hand on the boy's shoulder.

"None of them are him."

"Sagrib? We didn't think he would be here. Not enough men."

"We need to kill him, Mirza. He is evil."

"We'll get him, Jonjo, don't you worry about that."

Jonjo nodded as he reloaded his AK-104. He looked thoughtfully at one of the dead Janjaweed, the man's face splattered across the ground from a headshot.

"How is the new AK?" Mirza asked.

"Amazing. Sight is so accurate." Youthful excitement overcame his disappointment at not killing Sagrib. He shouldered the rifle again and practiced looking through the advanced optic.

"OK, let's go back. We need to help Bishop and the doctor."

"Wait." Jonjo pulled a plain necklace over his head and held it out to Mirza. It was a simple talisman, a length of hide cord with a bullet hanging from it. "Take this."

"What is this for, Jonjo?"

"You have it. This will protect you from Janjaweed evil."

Mirza looked at the necklace, unsure what to say.

Jonjo pressed the talisman into his hand. "You gave me the AK. I give you this in return."

Mirza accepted the gift and dropped it over his head. It hung around his neck, the bullet cold against his skin. "Thank you."

The boy turned and waded back into the river. "Come. We do not want to keep the doctor waiting!"

Back on the other side, Mirza ordered Jonjo to help Garang maintain security. Bishop was already supervising their reorganization, ensuring the SFF reloaded and kept watch for any Janjaweed follow-up force. They had been fortunate; there had been no SFF casualties. Once they were satisfied with the security, Mirza and Bishop jogged up the track to where the two UN vehicles had stopped. Jess was there, tending to the wounded men.

"What's the situation, Doc?" Bishop asked, placing his AK on the bonnet of the UN Land Cruiser and pulling on a pair of rubber gloves.

Jess was working furiously on one of the men, the contents of her medical kit strewn on a patch of grass. "We've got two dead in the rear vehicle. The driver's a little shook up but not badly wounded." She pulled a tourniquet over the shattered arm of one of the men and closed it with a twist of the handle. "There's two more in the back. One of them is shot up pretty bad."

Bishop wrenched open the rear door and found one uniformed man sitting next to another who was slumped forward in his seat, blood pooling at his feet.

"I can't stop the bleeding," said the soldier.

"Mirza, give me a hand with this guy." Bishop eased the unconscious body out of the vehicle. Mirza grabbed his legs and they sat him on the ground.

Bishop spoke in a monotone as he worked. "Gunshot wound, upper chest. Clean in, clean out. Going to need a valve." Bishop sliced the man's shirt off with his knife as Mirza rummaged through Jess's medical kit.

It took ten minutes to stabilize the survivors. The final tally was two dead, two badly wounded, and three with minor injuries.

"What happened?" Bishop questioned the Dutch UN patrol commander. The rank on his shoulders identified him as a Major.

"We were part of a standard observations patrol, conducting assessments of the villages. We started with three Land Cruisers and a light armored vehicle. This is all that is left, *ja!*" He spoke quickly, adrenaline still coursing through his veins.

"Where did you hit the Janjaweed?"

He gestured to the two destroyed jeeps. "They shot at us on the outskirts of the village. The armored vehicle got hit first: no survivors. They had too much firepower so we withdrew."

"Can you show me the village?" Bishop asked as he unfolded a map.

"*Ja*, this one here," the UN officer pointed out a village to the northeast.

"How many men?"

"At least a hundred. They had more of the jeeps, maybe ten. They also had technicals and some trucks."

Jess interrupted, "Major, you need to get these people to medical aid as soon as possible."

"Of course. Thank you so much for everything you've done. Without your help we'd all be dead." The officer took Jess's hand in both his hands. He turned and shook Mirza's then Bishop's hands in turn. "Tell, me, who do you work for? I will ensure the UN gives you a medal."

"We don't work for medals," Bishop said. "But thanks anyway."

"OK, OK, I understand. Thank you again." The UN observer's men finished loading their wounded into their four-wheel drives.

The PRIMAL operatives and Jess stood by the road as the two shot-up Land Cruisers limped off down the track.

"Poor bastards," said Bishop. "That fucking blue beret is getting more people killed." He turned, slung his AK, and strode back to the creek.

"What were they doing out there without weapons?" Jess asked Mirza while packing up her medical kit.

Mirza crouched, helping her. "You don't want to get him started. Come on, let's get out of here."

"Well, I'm impressed by Aden. He handled the

wounded like a professional. If I didn't know better I'd think he was a paramedic," said Jess as they followed Bishop back to the SFF.

"He might be a trained killer but he could have been a doctor. Sometimes he cares a little too much."

"A liability in your line of work?"

"No, a necessity!"

As they loaded their equipment into the back of the Wildcat, Bishop sought out Garang. The SFF commander was standing next to the Hilux watching the Chinese jeeps continue to burn.

Bishop stood by his side. "Not a bad day's work. You did well today. You should be proud of your men."

"Except Sagrib isn't here. That bastard is still alive."

"True, but now we know where to find him."

Garang's head snapped from the burning jeep to Bishop's face. "Where?"

Bishop showed him the map and pointed with his knife. "This village here. I'm thinking we pay him a visit."

Chapter Thirteen

THE BUNKER, LASCAR ISLAND

THE WATCHKEEPER STUCK his head into the PRIMAL director's office. "Boss, we've got Bishop on vidcon."

"Be right in. Can you grab Chua as well?" Vance rose out of his chair and headed into the Bunker.

Despite being well after midnight, the operations center was bustling. In addition to Bishop and Mirza, PRIMAL had personnel deployed in Southeast Asia and Europe on separate tasks, all requiring support.

Vance sat in his command chair and a few seconds later Chua walked in and took a seat. The Chinese American intelligence chief had his usual energy drink in hand. Vance gave him a nod.

"OK, we're good to go," he said.

The watchkeeper took the call off hold and Bishop's face appeared on one of the main screens bolted to the Bunker's rock-hewn walls.

"Evening, boss," said Bishop.

"Bishop, how you doing, buddy?" asked Vance.

"All good. We'll have to keep this quick though; things are moving pretty fast at the moment," replied Bishop via his iPRIMAL.

"Is this linked to the UN vehicles?" asked Chua. The headquarters team was monitoring every ground sensor that the SFF fighters had planted around the border region. They conducted first-line analysis on the information before sending it to the field operatives.

"Yep, we made our first contact today. Ambushed the Janjaweed chasing the UN vehicles. Twelve Janjaweed EKIA along with two vehicles destroyed. Nil SFF casualties although I estimate about fifteen UN soldiers were killed."

"Poor bastards. At least you smacked up the Janjaweed," said Vance.

"Good job, Aden," added Chua. "I just got the official UN report. They lost thirteen. According to them they were ambushed by a rogue militia while conducting a humanitarian assistance mission. Interestingly they reported your presence. Quote: 'Unknown paramilitary contractors supporting local fighters provided invaluable assistance.'"

"The SFF made a good account of themselves. A little shaky but overall far more capable than I anticipated. Which is why I've decided on the next course of action."

"Go on," said Vance.

"The UN was hit at an outlying village. We've assessed it's likely to be the current Janjaweed forward operating base. The element that followed them up was small but the initial force was estimated as at least a hundred fighters and fifteen to twenty vehicles."

"More of the ChiCom jeeps?" asked Chua.

"That's what the UN officer said, although they're down two as of today."

"So what are you thinking, Bish? Raid and fade?" asked Vance.

"You know it. I want to hit them at dawn tomorrow. Smash as many of their vehicles as possible and bug out."

"You've only got forty men," said Chua.

"True, which is why we're planning on hitting them hard then withdrawing. Garang wants to assault the whole village and kill Sagrib. It's taken some convincing but he's agreed to just do the hit and run."

"Mission approved," said Vance. "But if it all turns to cactus I want you and Mirza out of there fast. Harsh as it seems we can always raise another unit of freedom fighters."

"Roger."

Chua jumped in, "Aden, if you've got time I want to give you a heads-up on the latest intel on the China side."

"Shoot."

"It's probable that the head of PETROCON, Han Zhu, has sent one of his agents into Sudan to equip and advise the Janjaweed. His assessed location is the PETROCON refinery at Abyei."

"That would explain the helo that hit Garang's boys."

"We don't have an ID on him yet, but I think he's going to be either MSS or PLA Second Department, seconded to PETROCON," Chua said referring to the two Chinese intelligence agencies. "I wouldn't be surprised if he was the same guy you had a run-in with on the *Tian Hai*."

"Yeah, he was definitely a pro, whoever he was. Had Second Department written all over him," said Bishop. "Thanks for the heads-up."

"That's about a wrap," said Vance. "If you need anything else just holler. Oh, and another thing, no crazy plans involving Dragonfly. That aircraft's worth a fortune and Tariq ain't gonna buy us a new one if you bang it up."

"No dramas. Mitch has made it pretty clear he's only flying logistics support on this one. Chua, I'm sending you the coordinates now. Any chance you can whistle us up some new imagery?"

"If there's anything recent you'll have it within the hour. If you can delay a few days I can see if we can schedule a pass with one of the Lascar flights."

"Negative, mate, we're punching in at first light. I've had a look at the stuff on the system; it's a few months old but it shows the general layout. We've come up with a basic plan already."

"I'll get the team on it now. Anything else?"

"No, that's it for intel support. Look, I've got to run. Mirza's knocked up a layout of the village and I want to take the teams through rehearsals. You guys got anything else for me?"

Vance and Chua shook their heads. The mission had advanced faster than they had anticipated. They would need to convene a planning meeting to make sure the overall mission had not changed.

"Get some sleep, Bish. You look like shit!" Vance added as they finished up the call.

"Cheers, love you too." He paused. "Hey, boss, you're losing a bit of size. What's the problem? HQ got you pushing too many pencils?" asked Bishop in his best Schwarzenegger accent.

Vance flexed his arm and a massive bicep strained against the fabric of his shirt. "How about you wrap up this mission and get back island-side so I can warm up on curls with what you max bench."

"Will do, Bishop out."

Chapter Fourteen

SFF VILLAGE, ABYEI DISTRICT

WHILE MIRZA and Bishop were out chasing the Janjaweed, Mitch had returned in Dragonfly and been busy at the village. He'd flown in solar panels, a generator, as well as a water purification pump. A team of local workers had wired the main SFF hut with power and converted another into a basic medical clinic, complete with an operating table. They had also planted more ground sensors on the road to the village, covered Dragonfly under camouflage netting, and stockpiled ammunition and weapons in one of the huts.

It was the new weapons that Bishop was most interested in. Mitch had delivered an ultra-long range sniper rifle for Mirza and an experimental grenade launcher for Bishop. They needed every advantage possible over the Chinese-backed Janjaweed.

"That looks pretty high tech," said Jess as she entered the hut.

It was midafternoon and Bishop had spent the last hour familiarizing himself with the latest delivery.

"Hey, Jess," he said absentmindedly, still engrossed in the new grenade launcher. It was a M25, a state-of-the-art support weapon that had only recently been trialed by front-line soldiers in Afghanistan. The launcher fired programmable 25mm grenades from a five-round magazine. With its integrated laser range finder and targeting computer, it could have been a weapon from a sci-fi movie.

"Probably a little too complex for Garang's boys." He put the launcher back in its case. "Might come in handy though."

"I just wanted to give you this back." Jess held out the Px4 pistol and holster that Bishop had lent her.

He checked it was loaded and holstered it back on his belt. "You know, we should probably give you a weapon of your own." He opened one of the crates and pulled out an AK-104. "Ever fired one of these?"

She shook her head. "Plenty of handguns but only hunting rifles."

He grabbed a handful of magazines from another crate and dropped them in an empty ammo tin. "I've got a spare ten minutes. I'll give you a quick lesson."

They left the armory hut and walked a short distance to where the SFF had set up a rifle range facing into the cliffs that surrounded the village.

"It's pretty simple." Bishop showed her where the key parts were located on the AK. "Cocking handle, safety, magazine release, and trigger." He ran her through the basic operating procedures.

"You ready to put a few rounds downrange?"

"Yeah, I think I've got the hang of it."

Bishop set up a target at twenty yards. He gave her two

full magazines and showed her the proper stance to compensate for the recoil of the weapon. "It's well balanced but will still kick." He reached around to show her how to hold it firm against the shoulder. "You need to be ready but not tense. That's the trick." His face was next to hers as he showed her how to line up the red dot with the target.

Bishop felt her press back against his body and for a moment he thought about kissing her.

The AK barked, snapping him out of the fantasy. The rounds smacked into the target and Jess laughed. "It's so easy."

He let her go and stepped back. She fired off another few rounds, sending them through the target.

"Try it full auto," he said.

The AK shuddered as Jess fired a burst downrange. She held her stance as she kept blasting the target, maintaining a firm grip. Bullets churned up dust until the weapon ran dry. Within seconds she'd removed the magazine and slammed home a second one. She re-cocked then kept hammering the target with short bursts until she was out of ammo.

"You're a natural," said Bishop.

She stood with the AK in her hands, a whisp of smoke leaving the barrel as she laughed. "It must be your teaching, Aden."

"Yes, thank you, Aden." Garang was standing behind them, his arms folded across his chest.

"No problem at all," said Bishop. "Jess, you can grab some more magazines and belt rig from the hut. If you want to throw a few more rounds downrange I'm sure Garang or one of his boys can help you out."

Garang gave the doctor a stern look as she smiled and wandered off with her new weapon.

"Women are not fighters," said Garang once she was out of earshot.

"She may not fight but she needs to be able to defend herself," responded Bishop.

"That is my job."

"Garang, you're not always going to be there. You've got men to lead, battle plans to make, orders to deliver. Everyone needs to be able to look after themselves to allow you to do your job."

The SFF leader sighed and sat down on a log. The excitement of the recent ambush had worn off and now he looked tired.

Bishop sat next to him. "What's wrong?"

"You say I have to lead men, make plans, give orders."

"Yes, you are a commander. These men need you to make the decisions."

Garang spoke more quietly. "I want to lead these men, I want revenge against Sagrib, but I don't think I'm right for this."

"You did great today—"

"No, you did great," interrupted Garang. "I was along for the ride. Last time I led my men, we were massacred."

"It's normal to have doubts, mate. The most competent warriors I've ever met have all had doubts. So far the odds have been stacked against you. Your enemy has had superior firepower and the element of surprise. That's all about to change."

"But what about the men? If they have doubts in me, then how can I lead them?"

"Well they're still here, so don't let them down."

"You're right," Garang said halfheartedly. "I suppose we need to get ready for orders?"

"Mirza's already got the men assembled." He gripped Garang's shoulder.

As they walked back they could see the SFF soldiers congregated around a model that Mirza had constructed out of rocks and dirt. They were sitting in their teams, laid out exactly how they would be during the fight. Although they were still dressed in an assortment of uniforms, now they all had the same equipment. South African–style assault vests were weighed down with ammunition and grenades. Their weapons were new, with modern sights bolted to their AKs and PKMs. Even the doctor looked the part with her AK and magazine pouches around her waist. The whole team looked professional and Garang's confidence grew. He felt ready to deal with whatever the next twenty-four hours would throw at them.

Chapter Fifteen

JANJAWEED FORWARD OPERATING BASE, THEPKENI VILLAGE, SOUTH SUDAN

THE TWO GUARDS had been on watch since midnight. Their backs against a tree, they sat wrapped in blankets to ward off the cold night air. From their position on the hill they could see for miles in every direction, from the smoldering fires of the village behind them to the star-lit plain that reached out to the horizon.

One of them stood, slung his rifle, and walked away to piss. As he relieved himself, he stared out into the distance. The first trace of dawn was on the horizon, a faint slither of light that would finally bring some warmth. He finished, rubbed his cold hands together, and picked up his AK-47. On his way back to the tree, he stopped. In the faint gray of predawn he could make out a small bird hovering near a bush. He watched it for a few seconds before continuing on his way.

A short distance down the hill two men lurked in the

shadows. Mirza was hunched over his iPRIMAL, watching the infrared feed from the Hummingbird drone. Jonjo crouched next to him, his suppressed AK-104 held ready.

"There's only two of them," Mirza whispered. "Forward slope of the hill. Under the big baobab."

Jonjo touched him on the shoulder to let him know he understood.

"Sledgehammer, this is Scalpel. Moving in for the kill," Mirza broadcast over the radio to Bishop and the SFF fighters.

They crept up the side of the feature. Jonjo led, his bush craft beyond anything Mirza had ever seen. The lanky African stalked like a cat, silent as he flitted from cover to cover.

They followed the rise up to where the micro-drone had spotted the two sentries. The robotic bird was now circling high above them, its tiny IR camera searching for additional hostiles.

The baobab tree came into sight and Jonjo raised his AK. Mirza flicked the safety off his suppressed pistol.

They were almost at the tree when one of the men shrugged off his blanket and stood.

Jonjo's AK snapped once and the sentry toppled over with a bullet hole in his head. The second man had been dozing. He awoke when his colleague hit the ground with a thud. Judgment clouded by sleep, he reached for his weapon and the young Dinka warrior shot him through the face.

The two scouts swept through the sentry point, continuing across the hill, cautious of additional guards. With nothing found Mirza keyed his radio, "Sledgehammer, this is Scalpel. Objective secure."

A burst of static confirmed Bishop had received the message.

Mirza lay on the forward slope of the hill, watching for any activity at the village. He could see the first morning fires, enslaved women cooking for their Arab captors. Two more Janjaweed wandered out to where their vehicles were parked. Technicals and jeeps lined up, ready for another day of killing and raping.

While Mirza maintained watch, Jonjo moved to the rear and waited for the rest of the men.

A few miles to the south, Bishop and the main SFF force jogged steadily in a long line. Every step took them further from their vehicles and closer to the village filled with heavily armed Janjaweed. The only noise they made was the thump of their boots in the dirt and the odd rattle from a weapon or ammunition. Every man was heavily loaded; in addition to their individual weapons and equipment, they carried two tins of machine gun ammunition each or a brace of RPG rockets.

Bishop had one of the SA-24 air-defense missiles slung across his back, his AK slung across his chest, and a tin of PKM ammunition belts in each hand. Despite the cool air, sweat was running down his face, drenching his shirt.

"Faster!" Bishop whispered urgently. They were taking longer than expected; first light had already broken and they only had minutes to get into position.

Garang, who was running next to Bishop, saw the signal first. A single red flash from the top of the hill. He aimed for it, lengthening his stride.

Jonjo signaled the column with another quick flash. Garang gave the order to halt and the men all crouched or knelt, facing outward. As rehearsed, Jonjo moved down to meet them, leading each of the teams to their firing positions. Within minutes there were three separate groups of ten men positioned on the ridgeline, each armed with two PKMs and three RPGs.

Bishop handed his SA-24 to Mirza; his ammunition had already been distributed among the machine gun teams.

"Any sign of movement?" Bishop asked.

"The village is just starting to stir. A few men have been working on the vehicles. I think Garang is right; the UN spooked them and now they're going to relocate."

Bishop looked out to the horizon. The faint glow had grown in intensity, a blue-gray hue washing over the rows of Janjaweed vehicles parked beside the village. He turned his head as Garang approached.

"We're ready," the SFF leader announced.

"OK, let's roll."

SAGRIB WAS ALREADY AWAKE, sucking back a cigarette as he absentmindedly kicked at a mangled body outside his hut. The girl seemed to stare up at him with blank, bulging eyes; her neck bore the mark of his hands. She was supposed to be a Dinka princess but what sort of royalty did not know how to pleasure a man, he thought. The Janjaweed warlord dropped the cigarette on the corpse and strode toward the middle of the village where more useful women were cooking breakfast.

As he walked, he pulled his satellite phone from his pocket and dialed Yang.

"Have my men arrived?"

"Good morning to you, Sagrib. Yes, your reinforcements arrived last night. They have the new buggies and the mortar ammunition." Yang sounded short of breath. He'd been interrupted during his morning training.

"Good. How many?"

"Nearly a hundred men; they've eaten almost everything we have."

Sagrib laughed. "The warrior must be strong if he is to kill. Send them to me as soon as they are—"

The sound of gunfire interrupted the call. Sagrib spun in the direction of the noise. Muzzle flashes lit up an entire ridgeline as gunfire poured into the vehicle park. A rocket detonated among the trucks and sent a huge fireball skyward.

"Sagrib, what is going on?" Yang asked urgently.

"We're under attack. Send everything you have!"

"WE'VE GOT THEM ON THE ROPES!" screamed Garang over the blast of the machine guns and RPG rockets being fired. "We should push down into the village and finish them!"

"No." Bishop shook his head. "That's not the plan. We hit the vehicles then we get the hell out."

"We can finish this now!"

A massive ball of fire rolled into the sky as another Chinese-built jeep detonated under the hail of fire coming from the SFF positions.

"That's exactly what he wants, Garang! Right now you've got him outmatched and his trucks are burning. But he still has at least eighty men in that village armed to the teeth and spoiling for a fight. You leave this hill and get bogged down in the village and you'll die here."

Garang clenched his teeth. He knew Aden was right. This raid had achieved its goal; most of the Janjaweed vehicles had been destroyed. It would take weeks for them to replace the rows of technicals and jeeps burning in front of them. Rounds snapped through the air above them as if to reinforce the point. They needed to withdraw before the Janjaweed could mount a resistance.

He turned to the SFF fighter acting as his radio operator. "Bring the vehicles forward!" The man relayed his order and three miles to the south their convoy started up, leaving the concealment of a thicket of trees to rumble across the plain.

Back on the hill, Bishop and Mirza continued to scamper between the groups of fighters, offering words of encouragement and advice.

"Shorten your bursts."

"Lift your point of aim."

"Increase your rate while they reload."

"Fire another rocket."

For every passing minute their ammunition dwindled while the return fire from the village increased. In an effort to take cover the SFF fighters started to slide back over the crest of the hill, reducing their visibility and the effectiveness of their weapons.

Down in the village the Janjaweed fighters had formed a skirmish line. Using what they could for cover, they returned fire and bounded forward. The sun was rising now and their shots became more accurate as the sky became light.

On the other side of the hill the SFF convoy approached: the Wildcat, two pickups, and the Unimog truck. Jess was driving the PRIMAL vehicle. As the first men descended the hill she swung out of the cab.

"Is anyone wounded?" she yelled over the continuing gunfire from the cover team still on the hill.

Men piled into the first vehicle, shaking their heads. "No, miss. Everything fine."

She repeated the question as Garang and the main body of troops jogged down the hill and climbed into the Unimog.

"Everyone is fine, woman," Garang yelled. "Get in the truck." He pushed her into the back of his Hilux as his driver started the engine.

Mirza, Jonjo, and Bishop were the last to pull back off the ridge. The two PRIMAL operatives placed book-size objects on the ground as they withdrew. Jonjo covered them, lying close to the ground, firing at the advancing Janjaweed. Almost every shot missed as he snatched at the trigger, but it slowed the enemy's advance.

"Jonjo, let's go." Mirza tapped the young fighter on the boot.

They scrambled down the hill and leaped into the Wildcat. Garang and the rest of the men had already left. Mirza swung the .50 caliber machine gun to the rear of the ring mount, covering the hill behind them. Jonjo sat on the bench seats at the rear, the SA-24 placed on the other seat, his AK held ready.

Bishop gunned the Wildcat and it churned the sand, bashing a path through the dry grass and shrubs as he followed the tracks of the rest of the convoy.

In the turret Mirza pulled his iPRIMAL out of his vest and activated the detonator app. Four devices were active; he selected them all and touched the red fire button.

The ridgeline disappeared in a cloud of dust as the custom directional mines exploded, thousands of pellets blasting into the advancing Janjaweed. The first line of raiders fell to the ground and the dust cloud obscured their vision.

In the Hilux, Garang sat in the tray beside Jess and other soldiers. He grinned as the hill detonated. "Victory!"

He pumped his fist in the air as the other men in the truck joined the chant. "Victory!"

Jess sat in silence, the wind whipping at her long brown hair.

Without warning, sounds like the beating of massive drums filled the air and gouts of dust intercepted the lead truck. Heavy caliber rounds smashed into it, tearing men apart and shredding the tray where they sat. The pickup skidded to a halt as the rear axle broke off from the chassis. A rocket streaked across the sky and exploded in the cabin, flipping the wreck with a massive fireball.

The helicopter gunship roared over the convoy and swung in a wide arc. Garang's driver swerved to miss the burning pickup and slammed into an ant nest hidden by the long grass. The mound of compact earth stopped the Hilux dead, sending the passengers flying.

The big Unimog truck also skidded to a halt. Panicked SFF pushed and shoved as they leaped out and scattered into the grass.

Bishop skidded the Wildcat 180 degrees. Mirza opened up with the .50 caliber machine gun but the gunship was flying way too fast. It banked, maintaining speed for the next pass.

Jonjo jumped out, the SA-24 in his arms, running through the pre-firing drill that Mirza had taught him. He shouldered the long tube and activated the missile's seeker.

The helicopter had almost finished its turn and the SA-24's heat-seeking warhead had a clear line direct to the hot engines. It picked up the thermal signature, announcing a lock with a high-pitched squeal.

Jonjo took a deep breath and squeezed the trigger. Nothing happened.

The gunship was coming straight for him. He could see flashes as pod-mounted machine guns fired.

He pumped the trigger frantically.

A hand reached over his shoulder and flicked off the safety bail.

Explosions of dust tracked toward him as he squeezed the trigger once more. The rocket leaped skyward a split-second before someone slammed into him, pitching him into the ground as heavy-caliber rounds cut through the air where he was standing.

The pilot of the helicopter reacted on impulse, pushing the stick sideways as the missile streaked toward him. It flew directly under the helicopter and detonated. Fragmentation was thrown forward and out, missing the airframe. The blast damaged the tail rotor, sending them spinning sideways.

Alarms wailed as the pilot fought to keep them airborne. Beside him Yang adjusted the straps of his safety harness and gripped the sides of his seat.

To the pilot's credit, he managed to push the helicopter another two miles before he put it down. They slammed into the ground with a crunch, forcing the control stick up and through the pilot's chest. Yang's seat collapsed, as it was designed to do, taking some of the force out of the impact. Despite a searing pain in his back, he managed to extract himself from the wreckage. As he made to abandon the ruined aircraft, the pilot lifted his head. Blood oozed from his mouth as he tried to talk.

"Thank you for keeping me alive," Yang said in Mandarin. He drew his pistol and shot the mortally wounded pilot in the head. He limped from the wreck, making for the smoke of the burning village and the safety of Sagrib's forces.

Back at the convoy, Mirza had lifted Jonjo from the ground and dusted him off. The young warrior had come away unscathed.

Bishop picked them up in the Wildcat and drove up the track to the SFF vehicles.

Jess was standing in shock, staring at the destroyed pickup, watching it burn. The air was filled with the stench of burning flesh, bodies cooking in the intensity of the fire. Fat dripped from exposed bones.

"For fuck sake!" exclaimed Bishop. He grabbed her by the shoulders and bundled her into the back of the Wildcat. "Jonjo, talk to her. Now where the hell is Garang?"

Bishop found him next to the Hilux. He was sitting in the grass, his fists clenched on his knees. He glanced up as the Bishop approached.

"Another seven men dead," Garang muttered. "The oil companies better come good on this, Aden."

"There aren't going to be any oil companies if you don't get your men together. That helicopter isn't going to be here alone, Garang. More Janjaweed are on the way."

The SFF leader didn't respond. He dusted himself off and issued orders to what was left of his fighters. The men, who had scattered into the grass, reappeared and piled back into the remaining vehicles. It was a far more subdued group that drove south.

Chapter Sixteen

PETROCON OIL REFINERY, KURDUFAN DISTRICT, SUDAN

"SIR, I have some unfortunate news. Someone is providing covert support to the rebels." Yang stood in the vehicle park of the refinery using his satellite phone.

"Yes, continue," replied Zhu.

"The Dinka have been armed with modern weaponry. Today they attacked the Janjaweed forward operating base and destroyed most of their vehicles. They also shot down the helicopter."

There was a pause as Zhu contemplated the information. "I should have anticipated this. It is possible that the CIA or MI6 have become aware of our activities and are attempting to balance the conflict. Do you think this support is coming from the same group involved in the destruction of the *Tian Hai*?" The Chinese businessman's tone was flat, devoid of emotion.

"It is possible."

There was another pause. "Hmmm. Tell me, Yang, do you think that this venture is still economically viable? Can we still force the rebels south and secure the oil fields?"

"The only thing stopping us is the Dinka rebels and we easily outmatch them. Even if the CIA is involved they can do little to stop us short of sending in the Marines."

"There's no chance of that. In Africa the Americans are timid. They would not move without UN endorsement, and our position on the UN Security Council precludes that."

"If we can locate the Dinka base, we can crush them and guarantee success. The Americans would be powerless. Omar has many more men and equipment is cheap. We will quickly replace his losses. Our objectives can be achieved."

"Excellent. Our intelligence has already located what they believe to be the rebel stronghold. As for manpower, I will speak to Omar and arrange for more of the Janjaweed to be sent south. Additional weapons and vehicles will also be made available. Is there anything else you need?"

"No, sir. Once we have reinforcements the Janjaweed return to an offensive. Their chief, Sagrib, is highly motivated toward the destruction of the Dinka, especially the one they call Garang."

"Yes, Garang..." Zhu contemplated. "The American Dinka certainly leads me to believe that the CIA may be involved. We cannot let them defeat us, Yang. Much is at stake. China needs oil to grow. Without it our great nation will wither like a plant without water."

The call ended and Yang limped back to the accommodation. His back spasmed as he walked. This mission had taken a harsh toll on his body; first the knife wound to his leg on the *Tian Hai* and now his injuries from the helicopter crash.

Yang clenched his jaw and his fists as he stiffly ascended

the steps. He would make the men responsible pay, of that he was sure. This morning's convoy had already brought five of the new fast attack vehicles, shipped in from China, bristling with machine guns. With the other four-wheel drives and trucks Omar would send, the Janjaweed would regain their mobility. The SFF raid will have achieved nothing. Rearmed with vehicles, weapons, and intelligence, Yang was sure Sagrib and his band of cutthroats would make short work of the Dinka.

SFF VILLAGE, ABYEI DISTRICT

It had taken two days for the beaten-up convoy to make its way back to the village. They had looped south making sure they crossed back over their own tracks to confuse anyone following them. Overnight they had hidden their vehicles on a thickly vegetated riverbank, half the men sleeping while half watched for the Janjaweed. At daybreak they had followed the river north and driven into their home base.

The men were exhausted by the time they arrived but Garang would not let them rest. They cleaned weapons and reloaded magazines as others pulled guard duty. Jess tended to the wounded and Garang disappeared into one of the huts. Sitting on his stretcher, he opened his notebook, adding the names of the men killed to his growing list.

"No one tells you about this part," said Bishop from the doorway.

Garang dropped the notebook on the stretcher. "We are losing more men than are arriving. Soon I will run out of fighters, and long before we defeat the Janjaweed."

"More men will come. Word will spread of your victory."

"Will it be enough? The Janjaweed are fanatics; they love to fight. My men are farmers and boys. They have had enough of war. I have had enough of war."

"As long as the Janjaweed do not fear you, then you will have war. They will come and they will rape, murder, and burn until you flee. Then they will chase you and take more. It can only end when they are defeated."

"We can't beat them, Aden. There are too many. Up north where they live, there are thousands."

"That's crap, Garang. Today you gave them a bloody nose. You smashed their trucks and shot down their gunship! Word of this will spread. Your army will grow and we will support you. The Janjaweed are bullies; hit them hard enough and often enough and they will break."

Bishop left the SFF commander to dwell on his words and walked back to the grass hut that served as their accommodation. Mirza was sitting out front on an empty ammunition tin inspecting a sniper rifle. One of their recent deliveries, the .338 Accuracy International would give Mirza the ability to out-range the Janjaweed machine guns. In front of him a compact burner was boiling a kettle.

"Brew?" he asked as Bishop approached.

"Yeah, mate, sounds good," he replied as he ducked into the hut to get his mug. He reappeared with it a few seconds later, grabbed an empty crate, and sat down opposite his friend.

"Between me and you, I've got some doubts about Garang." Bishop started to pull apart his own weapon.

"Why is that?" asked Mirza.

"Sometimes he's highly motivated, but only when things are going well. He takes a few hits and all of sudden doesn't seem to have his heart in it. I get the feeling he's looking for an easy way out. His lust for Sagrib's blood might not be enough."

"His men fought well though. You can't deny he played a part in that."

"True. I'm not saying he's not capable, it's just... he's not as committed as I would like."

"He doesn't have as much to lose as the rest," pointed out Mirza. "He's here as a volunteer. The others are as well, but if they don't fight they run or they die. Garang is here because he wants to help. He's the best we've got to work with."

Bishop started cleaning his AK.

Mirza continued, "I think you're a little biased."

"Biased! I'm not biased. How the hell am I biased?"

"Easy, soldier." Mirza grinned. "Everyone can see that you like his girlfriend."

"What? Jess? It's not like that. I just don't like the way he treats her."

"Because you like her."

"No, because... ah, fuck. Yes, I like her. So what? But don't think for even one second I would jeopardize this operation over a woman."

Mirza looked taken back. "Did I say you would? I just think you should go easy on Garang. He's giving it his all and the SFF performed well today."

The little kettle started to whistle.

"Some of them better than others. That kid Jonjo's a star player."

"He's an excellent soldier. I just hope he gets a chance to be something else when all this is over." Mirza took the kettle from the burner and turned off the gas.

Bishop passed him his mug. "Let's hope this gets to a point where it can be over."

WHILE MIRZA and Bishop drank their tea, ten miles away a Janjaweed scout stopped his motorbike at a track junction. He was checking the ground for tracks, looking for a particular type of sign, a wider-than-usual wheelbase with a particularly aggressive tread. The morning sun made his job easier. The light hit at an angle and cast shadows highlighting the pattern. He knelt to study the marks, his fingers tracing the outline of each rut. He stood, wiping his hands on his trouser leg. It was not what he was looking for.

Twenty-four hours had passed since the attack and still they had found nothing. Janjaweed scouts had scoured tracks and creek lines searching for any sign of their enemy. The Dinka convoy's wheel marks had gone south and disappeared into the hundreds of wheel ruts at a river crossing.

The radio he had looped over his handlebars squawked as someone transmitted. He strode back to the bike to listen to the message. Sagrib had provided a grid reference for the enemy base. He checked a map; the village was not too far, about ten miles south. He jumped back on the bike and kicked over the engine.

THE NEXT DAY the villagers had put together a feast to farewell the fallen and celebrate the SFF victory over the Janjaweed. They had slaughtered a cow and constructed a fire pit at the edge of the soccer field. Huge earthen pots sat on a bed of coals while the aroma of stewed beef heavy with spices wafted across the village drawing warriors, women, and children alike.

Garang had given his approval for alcohol and Mitch had produced a few cartons of beer. The men sat together in groups under the trees, drinking beer, eating bowls of stew, and relaxing.

"This is good grub," Bishop said between mouthfuls. He was sitting with Garang, Mirza, and Jess.

"Very good." Mirza nodded.

"The women in this village, they cook well. You don't see them trying to be soldiers," said Garang.

Jess dropped her bowl on the ground and stormed off.

They sat in silence, eating and drinking their beer. Garang finished, excused himself, and went over to sit with his men.

Mirza finished and stood. "I'm going to take some food to Mitch." The PRIMAL technician was busy with Dragonfly, fussing over some of the communications gear.

Bishop was left on his own. He finished mopping up the juices in his bowl with a slab of dense, unleavened bread, and wandered over to thank the women for the food. Then he opened another beer and headed toward the medical hut.

"You don't have to make excuses for him," Jess said as he entered the clinic. "He speaks his mind."

"That's not why I'm here."

She glared at him. "Really? Then why did you come over?"

"I wanted to apologize for how I treated you back when the truck was burning. I shouldn't have been so rough. It's just... I didn't think you needed to see that."

"I don't get you, Aden. On one hand you teach me to use an AK. On the other you try to protect me from seeing the destruction they cause." She placed the surgical equipment she was sorting down on the operating table and walked toward him.

Even in the cold sterile lighting of the medical clinic she looked beautiful. Her face was dirty, her hair a mess, but Bishop still couldn't think of anything other than kissing her.

The iPRIMAL buzzed in his pocket and he checked it. It was a message from Mitch; one of the ground sensors was active. "Jess, I've got to run. We can continue this later, OK?" He leaned forward and pecked her on the cheek before leaving the hut.

He jogged across to the edge of the soccer field where Dragonfly was parked. It sat under camouflage netting, hidden from prying eyes. Mitch had set up a workstation under the wing: plastic equipment cases with a laptop on top of them.

"Bish, mate, we've got a problem." He didn't look up from the screen.

"What is it?" asked Bishop as he ducked under the camouflage netting.

"Unwanted company."

Bishop looked over his shoulder at the screen. What he saw were the ugly features of a Janjaweed raider. The man was looking into the lens and talking on a radio.

"Can you jam that radio?"

"Negative, old man. These things are pretty low-tech." Mitch's fingers danced on the keyboard as a number of alerts jumped up on screen. "He's not alone. I'm getting movement on two of the ground sensors as well."

"Damn. They know we're here."

"It appears so. Mirza's rounding up the fighters. I hope to God they haven't had too much to drink."

"OK, our number-one priority is to get the civvies out. If the Janjaweed get their hands on those women and the kids, it will be on our heads. How many can you fit in Dragonfly?"

"Maybe fifteen at a push."

"Do two runs, wheels up in ten minutes. Put them down somewhere safe and keep the bird at a distance. If it gets too hot, we'll bug out and regroup later."

"Listen, Bish, I've got the gun pod up and running. I'd be better use in close support."

"Negative, civvies are the priority, including Jess."

"Roger, understood. I'll drop them out at Kaljak. It's been abandoned since the raid."

"Good idea. How long do you think we've got?"

"Probably less than an hour."

"That's cutting it fine." Bishop turned to leave. "Oh and Mitch, time to let that fucktard know he's on candid camera." He nodded toward the screen.

Mitch smiled and typed in a command. The feed from the camera turned to static. "Job well done." He shut the laptop and started packing up the rest of his equipment.

Bishop nearly ran into Jess as he ducked back under the camouflage netting.

"What's going on?" she asked.

"The Janjaweed have found us. I need you to work with Mitch and sort out the evac of the civilians and wounded. Can you do that?"

She nodded and he set off again, looking for Garang and Mirza. They had precious little time and he wanted to prepare the best reception he could for the Janjaweed.

SAGRIB THREW his radio on the ground. "Useless Chinese junk!" One minute he was talking to one of his scouts as clearly as if he were standing next to him, and then nothing. It did not matter anyway. The man had relayed his message. He had found another of the strange devices: the CIA robots. The Chinese information was good. The Dinka were definitely hiding in the village.

He grinned as he thought of the impending destruction. Over the last forty-eight hours Yang had resupplied him with more ammunition and vehicles, replacing his losses from the last Dinka raid. Omar had also sent him a number of trucks loaded with more Janjaweed. Now he had an army of one hundred and fifty fighters and nearly twenty vehicles.

It would have been better to have more of the new gun buggies, he thought. Yang had only been able to deliver four of the fast attack vehicles and Sagrib looked forward to putting them through their paces. After mortaring the village, he would assault it, the heavily armed buggies leading, killing anyone who was left. He doubted the American and his men would put up much of a fight; the dogs would run and his men would be ready to catch them.

"Start up!" He ordered his driver forward and the long convoy moved along the track that would lead them into the village. The gun buggies led; with their heavy weapons they would smash through any defenses. Next came the mortar teams in a Chinese dump truck, its suspension sagging under the weight of the ammunition. Bringing up the rear of the convoy were the technicals and jeeps that carried the bulk of his raiders. They would clear through the village, mopping up the remnants of the American's militia.

At the front of the convoy Sagrib grinned. It was time for payback. It was his turn to rain destruction on the Dinka.

Chapter Seventeen

SFF VILLAGE, ABYEI DISTRICT

"THERE'S TOO MANY OF THEM." Garang watched the approaching Janjaweed convoy through a pair of high-powered binoculars. He, Bishop, and a four-man team were in the first of the security positions above where the track passed between the river and rocky high ground. Mirza, Jonjo, and another team of SFF fighters were further along the ridgeline. Behind them, on the soccer field, Jess was coordinating the evacuation of the last of the women, children, and wounded. Mitch had already flown one group out, dropping them at the abandoned village.

"They must have been reinforced," Bishop observed, watching the dust cloud through the scope on his AK.

"We need to pull back now. Your plan is not going to work!" Garang said.

"You want to run? I can guarantee that your man, Sagrib the headhunter, is out there looking for you, and you want to run?"

Garang dropped the binoculars to his side, his square jaw clenched as he contemplated the opportunity to kill the Janjaweed warlord.

"If you want to run, Garang, we need to go now. Once their heavy weapons are in range, we'll have to commit." Bishop didn't lift his face from the scope.

The SFF men watched their leader with questioning faces.

"No, we fight."

"Roger." Bishop reached down to the switch of his radio. "Mirza, you are free to engage."

"Acknowledged."

Through his magnified scope Bishop could see the details of the vehicles on the track. Heavily armed buggies led the convoy, a pair in front and one on either flank, easily keeping pace on the rough terrain. As they approached the dominating ridgeline they slowed, machine gunners scanning the high ground.

"Ground crew, this is Dragonfly. I'm five out for the final load." Mitch's radio message blasted in through Bishop's headset.

"Dragonfly, you have to haul ass. We've got a hundred-plus tangos descending on our position."

"Acknowledged, old man. I've got throttles to the stops. Will be coming in hot and fast. Jess, are you ready for extraction?"

There was a pause then Jess's feminine voice joined them on the airways. "Yes, Mitch, we're ready. I've got a total of fifteen here not including me."

"Jess, this is Aden. Things are going to get really ugly. Make sure you are on that flight."

Bishop pushed the evacuation of the civilians from his mind. He needed to focus on slowing the Janjaweed advance.

There was a sharp crack of a high-velocity bullet as Mirza fired his .338 sniper rifle from behind them on the ridgeline. Down on the track one of the Chinese buggies swerved off the road, its driver shot through the chest. The long-range weapon fired again and the gunner collapsed on top of his heavy machine gun.

The Janjaweed responded by blazing away at the high ground with everything they had. Rounds smashed into the hillside all around the SFF men. Splinters of metal and shards of rock sizzled through the air as they hunkered down in their sandbagged pits.

"I think you got their attention," said Bishop over the radio.

"Yes, sorry about that."

The fire slackened off then stopped. The Janjaweed trucks continued their advance, following the buggies, all the machine gunners vigilant for another attack. The formation converged as the convoy reached the narrow gap between the river and the ridgeline.

"OPEN FIRE!" screamed Garang, depressing the trigger of his PKM. His men opened up with rockets and automatic bursts, sending a stream of lead down onto the Janjaweed.

Bishop fired his AK between two rocks as the Janjaweed responded with even heavier fire than before. Chinese heavy machine gun rounds smashed into the SFF positions. The men had prepared well, digging into the rock with shovels, using sandbags to reinforce, and camouflaging the positions with rocks and vegetation.

Next to Bishop a Dinka fighter with an RPG sat up to fire a rocket and a round hit him with a wet slap. He disintegrated as it impacted, spraying his remains across the rest of the terrified fighters.

In the background Mirza's rifle boomed time and time again, spitting high-velocity rounds with lethal accuracy. Bishop hunkered behind his rocks and shifted his view from the immediate battle to the rear of the convoy. Through his scope he watched a large truck swing off the track. Men piled out the back of it, carrying equipment. It was well outside of their weapons' range, at least three miles away.

The convoy of Janjaweed had slowed to a standstill, but the weight of return fire began to overwhelm the SFF defenses. The heavy machine guns on the Chinese-built gun buggies outranged the SFF weapons, and their large-caliber rounds smashed through the rock and sandbag protection of their positions. Mirza and Jonjo's group were getting hit particularly hard; higher up, their position was more exposed and easier to identify. Only the bravest of the SFF fighters were still returning fire. After the death of the rocketeer, most did not dare to raise their head above cover.

"Ground crew, this is Dragonfly. I'm two minutes out and coming in fast," Mitch broadcast.

"Roger, Dragonfly," Bishop said. "Things are getting pretty heavy here. You need to be in and out sharpish."

"Not real keen to be on the ground long, old man," responded Mitch.

Jess's voice came through on the radio. She was waiting at the soccer field, the remaining women and children with her. "We're ready to go, Mitch. Just get her down and I'll do the rest."

"Roger. Coming in hot."

SAGRIB GOT behind the heavy machine gun mounted to his buggy and swung the long barrel up at the high ground. The enemy sniper had killed his gunner, forcing him to take over. He depressed the double triggers and the QJZ heavy machine gun rocked the buggy as it unleashed a volley of rounds. His men were blasting away at the rocky ridge, chewing up rounds. They needed to suppress or clear these positions so he could push forward into the village. He stopped firing to lift his radio to his face. "WHERE THE HELL ARE MY MORTARS?" he screamed.

"Firing now," was the reply from the mortar line.

Three large explosions blossomed out of the bush to the right of the convoy, well short of the intended target. Shrapnel whistled over Sagrib's head. "Idiots," he muttered.

"Add a hundred, walk the rounds onto the target," he transmitted to his Chinese-trained mortar crew.

The next volley of bombs were still short, but in line. He grinned. The mortars would walk forward and push the Dinka scum from the high ground down into the village, pounding everything to smithereens. His men would sweep forward and clean up what was left.

"MORTARS!" screamed Garang. Dust mushroomed up on the grassy plain in front of them. "We need to withdraw!"

He made to stand but Bishop held him down. "We're not going yet. They still need to adjust and we need to buy Mitch more time."

Another volley of bombs erupted, edging closer.

"Mirza, make ready to pull your team out," Bishop transmitted.

The sniper's .338 boomed again from up the ridgeline. "Mirza here. Good to go when you are."

Down on the track the Janjaweed vehicles had slackened their fire. The gunners were conserving their ammunition, waiting for the mortars to finish the job. Bishop's team continued to engage the vehicles. Out of rockets, they were limited to bursts of AK and PKM fire, inaccurate compared to Mirza's precise .338.

"Jess, this is Dragonfly. Thirty seconds out," Mitch's voice came over the radio.

None of the fighters on the ridgeline could hear the tilt-rotor as it descended on the village. The noise of gunfire blocked it out.

"Make it snappy, Mitch. We need to pull out," Bishop yelled into his mike.

Another volley of high explosives landed nearby. Dust and smoke swept their position, obscuring them from the Janjaweed below.

"All teams pull back," ordered Bishop.

Garang and his men did not need to be told twice. Under the cover of the smoke and dust, they turned and scampered from the high ground. They followed a goat track that wound down toward the back of the village and up to the defensive positions they had prepared at the high ground to the rear. Mirza's .338 boomed for a final time as his group pulled back, dropping behind the ridgeline.

As the SFF withdrew, Mirza and Jonjo broke away, running down toward the first line of huts. Bishop did the same thing, hitting the edge of the village hot on their heels. Dragonfly was on the soccer pitch, its giant propellers beating the air as Jess hurried the final villagers into the hold. The downwash of the rotors lashed her with dust as she threw the last child through the door and dove in behind him.

Bishop sprinted into the first cluster of huts where Mirza, Jonjo, and a four-man team were waiting. "Take cover," he screamed, sliding into one of the hastily dug foxholes.

The tilt-rotor lifted off as the first mortar rounds hit the edge of the village. The blast wave shook the aircraft and shrapnel sliced through the air. For a split second it lingered in the air, almost as if it would fall, then with a roar the blades tipped forward and it accelerated across the river. Tracer fire arced after it, falling short as it gained speed and disappeared over the horizon, trailing a thin line of black smoke.

"See ya soon, guys," broadcast Bishop as he hunkered down in the bottom of his shallow hole.

"Keep your head down, old man," responded Mitch before he was out of radio range.

"THEY'RE RUNNING," transmitted Sagrib to his mortar team. "Increase your rate of fire. Drop everything you have!"

Mortar bombs whistled overhead, landing inside the Dinka village. Dust and smoke ballooned up out of the bowl of death as the high explosives pummeled it.

Between blasts Sagrib could hear the sound of aircraft engines. He slewed his gun from the ridgeline in the direction of the sound. A strange aircraft raced out of the smoke. He thumbed the triggers of his machine gun and sent a stream of heavy-caliber shells racing toward the target. The airplane gathered speed and disappeared over the treetops.

The Americans had fled, he thought, leaving the Dinka to fend for themselves.

As the Janjaweed mortars pounded the little village, Sagrib prepared his vehicles for the final assault. His three remaining gun buggies would lead. Bristling with heavy weapons, they would clean up what the mortars had missed. Next would come the dismounts; almost a hundred Janjaweed would sort through the scraps.

He grinned as the mortars rained down hell on the village. In the dust he could see mud huts exploding as they were hit. He imagined the shrapnel slicing through the bodies of Dinka women and children. Today was a good day, he thought.

BISHOP'S DAY was not going so well. He was lying in the bottom of his foxhole as high explosives slammed into the earth around him. The explosions threw shrapnel into the mud-brick walls, the blast blowing the flimsy structures apart.

"Garang, any chance you can get a shot on those tubes?" he screamed over the radio as a bomb exploded near him, showering everything in dirt.

"Negative. They are out of range. Even from the other side of the ridgeline we couldn't reach them."

More mortar rounds rained down on the village as Bishop, Mirza, Jonjo, and the other SFF men weathered the turmoil and the earth shook. They could scarcely believe the amount of ordnance the Janjaweed was throwing at them.

"This is less than pleasant." Mirza still sounded deadly calm.

"I'm beginning to think this part of the plan sucks balls," replied Bishop between blasts.

"You always have such a way with words," joked Mirza.

Jonjo looked at the two like they were mad.

A scream filled the air as one of the SFF cracked. He jumped out of his protective hole and sprinted away.

Bishop cautiously peered up and swore. A mortar bomb plowed into the earth in front of the man, flinging him through the air like a rag doll. He landed in a crumpled heap.

It was Mirza who leaped from safety and grabbed the casualty by the shoulder straps of his vest. He dragged him backward toward his foxhole. Another bomb exploded, slamming Mirza into the ground, knocking him unconscious.

———

AS MIRZA LAY IMMOBILIZED the men on the mortar line were preparing to drop another brace of rounds down their tubes. The three Chinese-built 82mm mortars were lined up in a clearing three miles from the village. The Janjaweed crew was being supervised by a pair of Yang's Chinese contractors. They helped make aiming adjustments while the Arabs dropped the soft drink-bottle-size rounds into the tubes.

"Fire!" screamed one of the contractors.

Bombs slid down the tubes, hit the spigot at the bottom, and detonated with a loud thump. The projectiles launched skyward and within a few seconds the bombs landed inside the village.

The Janjaweed mortar team worked efficiently, unloading the bombs from the dump truck, preparing the charge bags and fuses, then passing them down the line to fire. Consumed by the task at hand, ears deafened by the constant firing, none of them noticed the predator sneaking in behind them.

The 7.62mm minigun that hung from Dragonfly's nose was a recent modification. The aircraft was designed to be executive transport, not a gunship. Mitch had added the pod more to facilitate hot extractions than any intent to hunt targets on the battlefield, but today, hunt it did.

Belching flame, the minigun raked the mortar position with tracer and lead. A long burst danced across the mortar tubes and their crews, chewing men into mince. A second burst tore the Chinese truck to shreds, detonating the stacks of mortar bombs it carried. The explosion was massive. In the blink of an eye the entire mortar crew was obliterated. A massive blast wave rocked the tilt-rotor before it banked hard.

"Good shooting, Jess. How much change have we got left?" Mitch asked the doctor, who was sitting in the aircraft's copilot seat. "Number should be in the bottom right of the screen."

"Five hundred, give or take a few."

"Enough for one more pass." Mitch tipped the stick forward. "We're going in hard and fast. It's up to you to make them count."

Jess nodded, focusing her attention on the targeting camera's screen. Her finger pressed the trigger gently, taking up the slack. She had been surprised by how simple the system was to use. It had taken literally seconds for Mitch to explain it. She simply pulled the trigger and the ballistics computer ensured the bullets landed at the red crosshair; not dissimilar to the video games she'd played back home. She'd never been that good at them but she was making a reasonable showing, enabling Mitch to concentrate fully on flying.

SAGRIB WAVED HIS MEN FORWARD, leading the assault from his gun buggy. He'd lost communications with the mortar team, but it didn't matter. They had done their job; the village was a smoking ruin. His gun buggies were leading, foot soldiers fanning out on either side of the track. The pickups and jeeps brought up the rear. The whole formation moved forward at a fast trot so the dismounted fighters could keep up.

"Behind us; an aircraft!" warned one of the men. Sagrib spun his machine gun to the rear. A sound like a swarm of giant mechanical bees filled the air. Rounds stitched the ground and the tilt-rotor thundered over. One of the jeeps shuddered as the line of bullets smashed through it, splattering the crew across the surrounding fighters. Sagrib tracked the fast-moving aircraft, his heavy machine gun bucking as he sent automatic fire streaming toward it. The small plane seemed to lurch. Then it was gone, out of range.

Sagrib surveyed the damage. Despite the overwhelming firepower, the aircraft had achieved little. One of his four-wheel drives was knocked out of action and no doubt the mortar crew was dead, but he still had most of his foot soldiers. He kicked the back of his driver's seat and yelled, "Keep going!" The formation surged on relentlessly.

"MIRZA, WAKE UP! WAKE UP!"

He felt like he'd been slapped in the face with a bag full of hammers. His brain hurt, even more than the time Bishop had forced him to drink shots in a bar in Thailand. His eyes blinked open and he was greeted by Jonjo's concerned expression.

"What happened?" He tore the radio headset off. The sophisticated buds had protected his ears from the blast but now they were broken.

"Mortar, caught you in the open."

"Is your man alright?" Mirza hauled himself to his feet checking his body for holes.

"He's alive but we might be in trouble. The Janjaweed are coming!" Jonjo pointed toward the noise of approaching vehicles and automatic gunfire.

"Mirza! Quit slacking off and get back in the fight," screamed Bishop, shooting his AK. He was crouched behind the remnants of one of the huts firing single, aimed shots.

Mirza grabbed his weapon from the dirt and pulled back the cocking handle, checking there was still a round in the chamber. He ran over to Bishop's position. As he orientated himself, he could see the village was a total shambles. Most huts had been flattened, thatch roofs blown off, pieces of mud-brick walls all that remained of the simple dwellings. The scene looked like a battlefield from a war movie.

Jonjo followed, and when they reached Bishop he unslung a bulky weapon and handed it over, along with a bandolier of magazines.

"Thanks, mate," Bishop said as he inspected the M25 'Punisher' grenade launcher. The forward team was now down to just Bishop, Jonjo, and Mirza. The other SFF fighters in their group carried their injured man to the rear to join Garang and the main body of fighters.

"What happened to the mortars?" Mirza asked as they waited for the enemy.

"Mitch and Jess smashed them with Dragonfly," said Bishop.

"Jess? When?"

"While you were sleeping."

Mirza shook his head in disbelief. "Only you can arrange for us to be saved by a beautiful woman!"

The growl of engines grew louder and an increase in gunfire grabbed their attention. They positioned their weapons on the remnants of a thick mud-brick wall and waited.

A line of foot soldiers came first; dark-skinned Arabs clad in a motley array of camouflage uniforms, wielding everything from AK-47s to G3s and Uzis. They had moved to the front of the formation, clearing the wrecked huts methodically, crouching low, running from cover to cover.

The skirmish line was followed by three heavily armed gun buggies and a column of battered trucks.

Rounds snapped through the air as the Janjaweed fired at shadows. They were two hundred yards from Bishop's position when he ranged them with the Punisher's high-tech sighting system.

Bishop fired five grenades in quick succession and the two others opened up with their AKs, spitting suppressed rounds at the Janjaweed.

The Punisher grenades airburst above the forward line of Janjaweed, spraying them with a hailstorm of shrapnel. Men collapsed screaming as tiny fragments of metal tore into their skin. Mirza and Jonjo's accurate shots sent the rest scrambling for cover.

"Go, go, go!" ordered Bishop as he loaded another of the chunky magazines into his weapon.

Jonjo withdrew first, Mirza covering him with controlled bursts.

Two of the Janjaweed buggies pushed forward, their gunners opening up. Rounds stitched the ground around Jonjo as he sprinted for the cover of the next line of huts.

Bishop launched a grenade at a gun buggy. It exploded short, kicking up dust and debris. The gunner swung his machine gun around until he was hit by a burst from Mirza's AK.

"We need to get the hell out of here!" screamed Bishop. Lines of Janjaweed had already cleared through the first huts and were pressing forward. One of the armed buggies had moved around to the flank and threatened to cut them off.

Bishop ducked as rounds slammed into what was left of the mud wall they were using for cover. He felt the tug of a bullet passing through his pant leg.

Mirza crouched alongside him and changed the magazine on his weapon. To their rear Jonjo began firing. Bishop launched four more of the explosive shells from the M25, pulled a smoke grenade from his chest rig, and lobbed it over the wall. "Let's go!"

FROM HIS GUN buggy Sagrib fired his machine gun into the billowing smoke, hoping for a lucky shot.

"Keep going, you lazy swine!" he screamed at his men. "They're trying to get away."

More smoke began spreading from deeper in the ruined village. The entire basin was rapidly filling with a thick cloud. There was no doubt in Sagrib's mind; the Dinka were trying to slip away. He jumped down from his vehicle, unslinging his AK, and jogged forward with the first line of men. Other Janjaweed fell in behind, ready to reinforce their leader.

His men fired at shadows in the smoke, shooting trees and damaged huts with savage bursts of fire. They encountered no enemy and picked up their pace.

Sagrib and nearly sixty fighters surged forward like wolves on the trail of a wounded deer, desperate for a kill. Behind them their vehicles kept pace, machine gunners scanning for targets.

The Janjaweed cleared the last line of ruined huts as the smoke started to dissipate. Sagrib halted his men. There was no sign of the Dinka villagers or fighters.

Vehicle tracks led into the tall grass and onto the sandy track that went through to the other side of the high ridge. Dust hung in the air and the growl of a four-wheel drive could be heard further down the track.

"Bring up the trucks." Sagrib waved his men forward. Janjaweed vehicles accelerated down the track; the buggies, technicals, and jeeps all bunched up.

Out on the flank, one of the foot soldiers stopped to scan the high ground. A sound had drawn his attention, the sound of metal scraping on rock. He shaded his eyes from the sun. In the shadow of a boulder was a shape that looked like a man. The shadow moved. The Arab raised his weapon and a single shot drilled him between the eyes.

The ridgeline came alive with muzzle flashes as Garang's men opened up. Janjaweed fell like stalks of wheat under a farmer's scythe as 7.62mm rounds cut through their ranks. RPG rockets streaked through the air to slam into the trucks, setting fire to ammunition, fuel, and flesh.

One of the jeeps reversed, accelerating away in a cloud of red dust. The gunner and occupants fired long automatic blasts at the SFF positions. The jeep looked as if it would escape, until a rapid burst of heavy machine gun fire slammed into the bonnet. It ground to a halt as another burst ripped into the cabin and the driver exploded into a spray of crimson.

With a rumbling V8 the Wildcat emerged from a patch of vegetation. Thin trees were pushed to the side as Bishop maneuvered it to another firing position. Mirza was manning the M3M machine gun and ducked a branch as they left the concealment of the trees. He fired the rapid-fire .50 caliber, blasting the Janjaweed jeep once more. The Raufoss rounds tore into soft metal, the incendiary bullets setting plastic and nylon alight. Within seconds it was ablaze, and any surviving occupants were running for their lives.

"Stand and fight!" Sagrib cried out to his men. "Fire back at the Dinka pigs!"

Overwhelmed by the ferocity of the ambush, many of the raiders turned and fled. One group held their ground using a truck as cover, trying to suppress the Dinka positions. Hopelessly exposed, they died as automatic fire continued to riddle the remaining vehicles.

In a matter of seconds the battle had turned against the Janjaweed. Sagrib fired the last of his bullets into the hillside and ran back into the ruined village with the remainder of his men. At least half his fighters were still alive, those outside the Dinka killing zone. Sagrib knew that without his leadership they would flee, but under his command they could still regroup, withdraw, and fight another day. The Chinese could supply more guns and vehicles while Omar would send reinforcements.

He made it as far as the first hut when his legs were knocked out from underneath him, sending him face-first into the dust. The Janjaweed warlord rolled onto his back and looked down in horror. His right shin was shattered, his foot attached with shreds of flesh and cloth, the boot and severed foot sitting at right angles to his leg. He rolled onto his stomach and started crawling, leaving behind a thick wet trail in the dirt.

"Cease fire! Cease fire!" Garang's voice echoed across the high ground. The SFF guns fell silent and once more the village was still. Only the crackle of burning vehicles and feeble cries of the wounded could be heard.

The Dinka warriors rose from their ambush positions on the high ground. They chanted in their local tongue as they walked down through the killing ground. Flitting through the smoke like wraiths, they used their bush knives to dispatch the wounded raiders.

"Once more we dance into the jaws of death, only to escape and live to fight another day," Bishop joked from the driver's seat of the Wildcat.

"Some a little closer than others." Mirza rubbed his forehead where the blast had slammed him face-first into the ground.

Jonjo laughed in the front seat. "Nothing to fear. I told you the talisman would protect you." He grinned as he jumped out of the truck and moved down the track to where the Dinka were gathering, their chants filling the air.

Mirza reached for the bullet that hung from his neck. Despite his body heat it still felt cold to the touch. He stared at the pack of men jumping and chanting at the edge of the village.

"We need to get them together and leave, Bish." Mirza's voice was calm. "We may have won this battle but the war is far from over and this is the first place the next Janjaweed army is going to look."

"Too right. I'll get Garang. You organize the drivers." Bishop got out and made for the chanting throng of Dinka. As he got closer, he noticed they had gathered around a single body. He shouldered his way through.

Lying in the middle, a look of rage on his waxen features, was Sagrib.

Garang was there, chanting with the rest of his men. His face was contorted into a mask of rage and hatred. Bishop grabbed him by the shoulder.

"Garang, we need him alive and we need to go," Bishop yelled into his ear.

"NO, HE DIES HERE!" Garang screamed at Bishop.

"He has intel. We need to get it out of him." Bishop grabbed the muscular African by his vest and shook him. "You give me thirty minutes and I'll have enough info to take this to the next level."

Garang contemplated the words. He looked across at Jonjo. The young soldier was the only Dinka warrior who had remained calm. While the others chanted, he stood silently staring at the Janjaweed warlord.

"Very well, he comes with us. Bring the vehicles."

Bishop strode into the circle of Dinka to where Sagrib lay. Despite his mangled foot, he was still conscious. He spat as the PRIMAL operative inspected his wound. Bishop leaned forward and punched him in the face, knocking him out. The Dinka fell silent, watching as Bishop worked a tourniquet over the Arab's wound and tightened it, cutting off the flow of blood.

"Grab what weapons you can. Burn the rest," Garang ordered his fighters. "We're leaving!"

Chapter Eighteen

KALJAK VILLAGE, ABYEI DISTRICT

THEY HAD CHOSEN the village of Kaljak as a makeshift base because it was abandoned. The Janjaweed had hit it once and it was unlikely they would return. In the time since Garang and his men helped evacuate the village, Mother Nature had conducted a thorough cleanup. Hyenas had dragged away the corpses of the dead villagers and vultures had stripped the flesh from the bones of the crucified missionary. It was almost as if she had known the SFF would need a new home now that their hideaway had been compromised.

The tilt-rotor had arrived first, dropping two loads of evacuees from the SFF village. Mitch and Jess left them under the protection of a small security detail before returning to launch their attack on the Janjaweed mortars. Damaged by ground fire, Dragonfly had limped back to the new base and landed heavily. Mitch had immediately gone to work to repair the damage.

It was late afternoon when the Dinka convoy rolled in. Wheels bounced over the old craters carved by Janjaweed mortars as the trucks pulled in next to what used to be the marketplace. Villagers gathered, trying to catch a glimpse of a father or a brother, wanting to know who had managed to get out alive.

Jess appeared from a hut, her hair up and hands covered by rubber gloves. "We're ready for the wounded."

Men carried the critically injured into the makeshift surgery. There were three with significant gunshot and shrapnel wounds, including the man Mirza had saved. Another five had superficial injuries that the doctor would treat later.

"Aden, you're OK!" Jess's eyes lit up when she saw him.

"Only because you and Mitch came back," said Bishop as she gave him a quick hug.

"It was all Mitch. He insisted."

"Regardless, the two of you saved our lives. If you hadn't cleaned up those mortars, all of us would have died back there."

Two of Garang's men lifted Sagrib from the back of the Wildcat. Jess saw the injured man and gestured for them to bring him into the clinic.

"Not him." Bishop shook his head. "Bring him with me. Mirza, find me a chair."

"What are you going to do to him?" asked Jess.

"We're just going to have a chat."

Jonjo and Garang made a move to follow. Bishop turned, waving them away. "You make sure your men have secured the village."

"No. I want to watch him die," replied Jonjo.

"You'll get your chance. Garang, keep everyone away, especially Jess. She doesn't need to see this."

Garang nodded.

Two Dinka warriors dragged the Janjaweed warlord by his shoulders, letting his shattered leg drag in the sand, his hands zip-tied behind him. He hurled abuse at the two men in his native tongue. Bishop led them around the corner to a bloodstained wall, the site of the crucifixion.

Inside the hut, Mirza appeared with a wooden school chair and the two men dropped Sagrib onto it. The warlord glared at his captors, scanning the faces of the two Dinka. His lips parted in a toothless grin as the guards dropped their eyes. His glare focused on Bishop and his grin faded. The white man met his gaze with a cold, unblinking stare of his own.

"So you are the CIA pig who leads these dogs?" He spat his words.

Bishop drew his combat knife from his chest rig, leaned forward, and drove the blade into Sagrib's injured leg. The Arab screamed as the knife ground against his thighbone.

"Listen to my words very carefully, scumbag, because this is the first and last time I'm going to tell you. Answer my questions and that is all. Mouth off again and I'll give you more pain than you can ever imagine." Bishop pulled the knife from the man's leg and wiped it on the pants. "Tell me who you're reporting to."

"Fuck you, CIA pig!"

"I warned you, Sagrib." Bishop turned to his partner, who was sitting against a low wall. "Mirza, can you grab the tools from the truck."

Mirza nodded and walked toward the Wildcat. Bishop took a handful of thick zip-ties from his rig and laid them on the ground in front of the captive. Mirza returned a few moments later with a tool kit.

Bishop laid the box on the ground and sorted through it

methodically. The kit was designed to keep a truck running no matter what the circumstances. It held all sorts of useful equipment including the tool that he was looking for, a cordless grinder.

"Zip-tie his thighs." Bishop removed the grinding part from the power tool and replaced it with a circular cutting blade.

Mirza placed the zip-ties around Sagrib's legs. The Arab kicked out and Mirza drove his elbow into the thigh, at the same time drawing the improvised tourniquet tight.

Bishop held up the power tool in front of Sagrib's face and thumbed the trigger. It spun up with a sinister hiss.

"The tourniquets will stop you from bleeding to death. Once I've finished cutting off your legs, I'm going to start on your arms. Once I've finished there I'm going to hand you over to the doctor. Now, she's a compassionate woman; she will save your life. But then you will be given to the villagers and you will spend the rest of your life groveling for food like a pig, unable to take your own life. You will be forced to live in filth like a dog."

The warrior's eyes grew wide and for the first time in his life he felt fear. According to his faith, if he died fighting the infidel he would be rewarded with unimaginable riches. However, living his remaining years like an animal, groveling for scraps in a Dinka village, would condemn him to an eternity of hell.

Bishop continued, "Answer my questions and I'll give you the death you want. I'll shoot you myself. It will be quick."

Sagrib held his lips firmly shut but his eyes betrayed his growing panic.

"How did you find our camp?"

Bishop started the circular saw and the faint smell of

burning ozone wafted up from its electric motor. He moved it closer to the Arab's knee and the blade ripped through the filthy desert fatigues.

Still Sagrib said nothing.

He inched the spinning blade closer and it sliced into skin. Sagrib grunted as his flesh parted. The blade sprayed a fine mist of blood.

"The Chinese snake, Yang," Sagrib hissed.

"How did he know where to find us?"

"The Chinese have agents all through the south. One of them found it. I don't know how."

"Tell me more about Yang. What does he look like?"

"He's Chinese, small, a fighter. I don't know, they all look the same."

"So now you work for the Chinese?"

Sagrib spat in the dust. "No, I work for Omar. The Chinese work for us. They bring us guns and we give them oil."

"How many more Janjaweed does Omar have?"

Sagrib started laughing, cackling like an animal. "That's why it doesn't matter if you kill me. He has thousands more. He fills the Janjaweed pockets with gold and they kill anyone who stands in his way. There are hundreds more men like me, thousands more warriors of Islam. We cannot be beaten. It doesn't matter how many men the CIA sends, it will not be enough."

Bishop stared at the Arab for a few seconds before he wiped the grinder on the man's pants and placed it back in the tool kit.

Sagrib waited, anxiously hoping for a gunshot that would end his pain.

Bishop closed the toolbox and made for the exit.

"Shoot me," Sagrib begged.

He continued out the door.

"You promised me you'd shoot me!" Sagrib screamed. "I told you what you wanted. Give me a warrior's death!"

He stopped and turned back. The Janjaweed warlord's face was a mask of hatred mixed with intense pain.

"I lied." Bishop turned to the guards. "Give him to the villagers. Let them decide what to do with him."

He walked away from the screaming Arab.

Mirza stepped in beside him. "So what now?"

"Now we cut off the head."

Chapter Nineteen

KHARTOUM, SUDAN

"WE'VE HAD A MINOR SETBACK." Omar was sitting at his desk in the PETROCON tower, talking into his speakerphone as he drummed his thick fingers on the desk. It had taken him an entire day to summon the courage to make the call. It was now midmorning, the day after the ambush that wiped out Sagrib and his men.

"You call it a minor setback?" Zhu's voice hissed through the speaker. He'd already been briefed by Yang on the failure.

"The Janjaweed followed up on your intelligence."

"Which was accurate."

"Yes, but they were ambushed by a larger force and now most of my men are dead, including Sagrib."

There was silence before the Chinese oil executive replied. "I send you weapons, vehicles, and intelligence, and still you cannot crush a group of old men and children.

Omar, I am beginning to think that you are wasting my time."

"I will fix this problem, Zhu. I've already gathered more men. I can replace Sagrib. All we need is more equipment. The Dinka must be destroyed. Sagrib's men will have killed most of them already. There will only be a handful of the dogs left. It is Allah's—"

"Omar!" the Chinese businessman interrupted. "What you need to understand is that China does not care for your petty war or your religious ranting. Do not think for one minute that this is anything more than a business transaction. China needs oil and we will negotiate with whoever has it. At this stage it would seem that is not you."

Omar swallowed nervously. "We will have the oil, believe me. I've sent for more Janjaweed, twice as many as before. I just need more guns, more vehicles, and more intelligence."

"More, more, more! Your little war has already cost China millions, Omar, and for what? So far the amount of oil that has been pumped out of your little country pales in significance to the price of a merchant ship, a brigade's worth of armor, toys for your Janjaweed, and a helicopter."

The Sudanese minister's jowls wobbled as he shook his head. "None of that is my fault. How was I to know the CIA would help the Dinka? You told me there was no chance of that."

Zhu remained silent.

Omar continued, "I have sent for twice as many men. We cannot fail."

Still the Chinese businessman said nothing.

"Given the extra costs I would be willing to offer a cheaper price on the oil."

Finally the Chinese businessman's voice emitted from the speakerphone on Omar's desk.

"You will offer a lower price and China will remain committed to this venture. I have already ordered replacement vehicles. They are on the way to the refinery. Your men will report to Yang there and will work for him directly. Ensure they understand this. I will not have production delayed through the incompetence of another of your religious fanatics."

"And equipment?"

"It will be supplied. Ensure your men do not fail us again, Omar."

The speaker emitted a beeping tone. Zhu had terminated the call.

KALJAK VILLAGE AND PETROCON OIL REFINERY

Garang and most of the fighters had a well-deserved twenty-four hours rest before recommencing operations. The PRIMAL team worked nonstop. Mitch completed multiple resupply flights with Dragonfly. Bishop and Mirza, with the assistance of Jonjo, were busy conducting reconnaissance and planning future operations. The next focus was the Chinese oil refinery and logistics base nearly fifty miles away.

Five thousand feet above the oil refinery an eagle soared on a thermal updraft. During the day the empty steel pipes trapped the heat of the sun. In the cool of the evening they released that energy in the form of a column of warm air.

The eagle used the natural elevator to climb into the sky, conserving his own energy reserves as he searched for prey.

As the bird conducted a lazy turn, something caught his eye. He peeled off to investigate, swooping down to fly directly above a small aircraft.

The intruder's sensors were orientated toward the ground. A tiny, yet powerful camera swiveled in a gimbal mount as the aircraft cut a slow circle in the air.

The eagle gave the strange creature a few moments before deciding it was neither small enough to eat, nor large enough to be a threat. He turned away, returning to his own hunt.

Nearly fifty miles away, Mitch was controlling the electric drone from his laptop. A cable linked the computer to the satellite communications suite in the Wildcat. A crowd had gathered around the tailgate of the vehicle, watching the high-resolution feed.

"So many," Jonjo said as the camera revealed the rows of gunned-up trucks parked inside the Chinese refinery. Activity in the base was high; armed men were busy loading the vehicles and moving between the buildings.

"Are you surprised?" Garang snapped. "Omar has called up more of his men. With the Janjaweed eating from his hand and the Chinese providing the metal, he has a never-ending army."

"We can fight them!" declared Jonjo. He looked toward his leader. "We already destroyed a force five times our own, yes?"

"Without more men we cannot fight that." Garang jabbed his finger at the screen.

Bishop said nothing. He turned and gave Mirza a grim look.

"We're nearly out of battery power, team. Any last-minute requests before the fat lady sings?" asked Mitch.

"Can you give us a quick scan of their defenses?" asked Bishop.

"Got less than a minute. I'll pull in real tight and give you a bit of a geezer."

The blurry shapes in the image gained clarity as the UAV banked and closed with the refinery. Within seconds they could make out the refinery's improved defenses. The outer perimeter bristled with heavy machine guns, additional sandbagged fortifications reinforcing the fence line.

"Bugger. We're nicked," Mitch said.

Everyone watching could make out the muzzle flashes that lit up the screen as the refinery guards spotted the drone and opened fire.

"Little Nellie's all out of juice," he declared.

"Kamikaze?" asked Bishop.

"Why not! Our plastic fantastic deserves to go out with a bang."

Mitch pitched the little aircraft forward and it dove toward the refinery, shuddering as a round clipped its wing. Mortally wounded, it started to barrel roll, corkscrewing as it fell from the sky. Mitch maintained control and a spinning shot of a group of Janjaweed fighters came into view. They were all staring up at the camera. They grew in size as the drone plummeted toward them.

Jonjo laughed as their faces filled the screen, looks of terror and confusion painted on hard Arab features.

Then the screen went blank as five kilograms of aircraft slammed into the men.

The crowd of SFF men watching cheered. Jonjo slapped Mitch on the back.

"We injure two and a hundred more replace them." Garang's harsh tone cut through the joviality.

No one noticed Jess standing at the back of the group. She stared at Garang with sad eyes. She'd joined them in time to see the Janjaweed army that had assembled at the refinery and she had watched Garang cut down Jonjo's enthusiasm.

As the group dispersed, Jonjo brushed past, ignoring her. She waited until the other SFF had moved away and approached the three **PRIMAL** men still standing at the back of their truck.

"He's right, isn't he?" she asked Bishop.

Mitch closed the laptop and gestured for Mirza to join him. Jess waited for them to wander back toward Dragonfly before she continued, "They can't win, not without more help."

Bishop took a second to reply, noticing the doctor seemed to look more beautiful the dirtier she became.

"Where there is a will, there is always a way."

"It's the will that I'm worried about."

Bishop noticed she was still carrying the AK he had given her, slung over her shoulder. "What do you mean?"

"He is changing, Aden. The will isn't there anymore. I'm worried he's giving up."

"You need to keep him focused, Jess."

"How can I do that when he won't even look at me, let alone talk to me?"

"Combat does funny things to people. Believe me, I've seen enough of it to know. He might seem a little distant but I don't think he's about to throw in the towel."

"Aden!" Mitch yelled from Dragonfly's open door.

"Look, I've got to check in with my HQ but I'll be around later if you want to talk some more."

"OK." Jess smiled and Bishop couldn't help but return the gesture. Then he turned on his heel and jogged toward the aircraft and a videoconference with the Bunker.

Chapter Twenty

KALJAK VILLAGE, ABYEI DISTRICT

"WHAT'S the time over there, team?" Vance's voice filled the cabin of the PRIMAL tilt-rotor. Dragonfly was still on the ground in Kaljak with Mitch, Bishop, and Mirza sitting in the cabin, using the aircraft's communications package to establish the videoconference with the Bunker.

"Bit after seventeen hundred," replied Bishop as he unwrapped a protein bar.

"So by my calculations it's been forty-eight hours since I've heard from you. Too busy to drop me a line and tell me what the hell's going on?"

"Sorry about that, Vance, but we've had some issues at this end," he said between mouthfuls. "After the defensive operations we bugged out to Kaljak and since then we've been trying to get things sorted."

"No problem with that. What I don't like is getting my blue force info from my intel guy. Chua's got enough on his plate trying to track down this Yang asshole without having the ops staff leaning over his shoulder every five minutes."

"Yeah, OK, I get it. We'll keep you up to date."

"Damn straight you will. Just because you're always going in all guns blazing doesn't mean you can't find five minutes to dial home."

"Hey, I wasn't the one blazing away. This time it was Mitch who saved the day," replied Bishop. He grinned as the PRIMAL pilot leaned out of the camera view and started shaking his bearded face making a chopping motion with his hand.

Vance raised his voice. "How the hell did he do that? Pretty damn sure I told him to keep that bird out of trouble."

"All good," Bishop said. "He just got the villagers out on time. Meant that Mirza and I could unleash hell on the Janjitards."

"Hmmm, why is it I think you're spinning me more shit than a senator at a congressional hearing?"

"Scout's honor," said Bishop.

"I suppose you're not going to sell them out, are you, Mirza?"

"I would prefer not to be placed in that position, Vance."

"Well, the screens here are telling me Dragonfly's running green across the board, so you can't have run it that close to the edge."

"Course not, boss," added Mitch. "Babied her all the way." Vance did not need to know about the bullet holes or emergency repairs he had done.

"Moving right along, Chua and I saw the feed from the refinery. Looks like they're building up for another push."

"Yep, too big for us to deal with," Bishop said. "We'd be playing Whac-A-Mole for a full month trying to deal with those bastards."

"My thoughts exactly, Aden," added Chua. "My team thinks there are at least two to three hundred new fighters at the refinery. PETROCON also has four of their aircraft inbound to Khartoum. They're shipping in a ton of gear."

"Puts the SFF up shit creek without a paddle. How long will it take the Janjaweed to build up?" asked Bishop.

"Depends on a few factors. Firstly, if they're keen they can move in over the next twenty-four using what weapons they have. However, I think it's more likely they'll wait for all the gear. Give them a few days to break it out and knock over basic training and you've got a week."

"Not a lot of time. Any hope of the UN bolstering their forces to counter them?"

"Nope, the Chinese vetoed the last call for an increase in troop numbers. Current forces are insufficient."

"Excuse me, gentlemen," Mirza interrupted. "What about this Omar character that keeps coming up? The Janjaweed commander we questioned said he worked for him, and Garang thinks that he's the man behind the whole campaign. Chua, you also mentioned him during our initial briefing."

"Excellent point, Mirza. My source in Khartoum tells me that Omar is running a covert operation. He's got the unsanctioned support of the government as they cannot afford to be publicly associated with his actions."

"So, Omar's running his own government-endorsed black ops with support from PETROCON," said Bishop.

"That's my assessment. I'm about to launch an op into China to follow up on the PETROCON side of the house.

We're stretched pretty thin at the moment but I think Saneh can handle it."

Bishop raised an eyebrow at the mention of the Iranian's name. "More than capable."

"So what would happen if we took this clown Omar out?" asked Mitch.

"It would build on our current strategy," said Vance. "The Janjaweed buildup could be disrupted, buying us more time. And it would send a clear message to the corrupt fat cats in PETROCON headquarters."

"So what are we waiting for?" asked Bishop.

"Chua is sending you a target pack on his office building, Chinese-built, of course. Not the most detailed deck but you'll get the basic layout."

"Garang's been inside," added Mirza. "He was with the Dinka chief when he was beheaded. Should be able to give us an idea where to find Omar's office."

Bishop nodded. "And let's not discount ambushing the prick on his way to work. Our time frames are tight but we can still get creative." He glanced at his watch. "If we punch out now, we can be in Khartoum by midmorning tomorrow. I reckon we should go by road. That frees up Mitch to fly in more kit for the SFF."

The pilot nodded in agreement.

"Mirza and I will roll into town, recon the key locations, and come up with a plan," continued Bishop.

"Mission approved," confirmed Vance. "Chua and I will be working it from this end. Do you have all the gear you need?"

"I've got light assault rigs on board along with some other bits and pieces that the lads might find a use for," said Mitch.

"OK, let's get it done. Oh, one other thing, Bish. What happened to that Janjaweed commander you captured?"

"He's hanging around with the locals, and I mean that in the most literal sense possible."

"I WANT TO COME WITH YOU," Jonjo said as he helped Mirza load equipment into the back of the Wildcat. It was early evening and the night air was already filled with the cries of predators on the hunt. The two men worked in the faint glow of the vehicle's interior lighting, stacking the equipment cases between the truck's bench seats. The large .50 caliber machine gun had already been removed.

"You are needed here," replied Mirza.

"One more fighter here will not make a difference. I want to kill Omar. He killed my chief and my friends."

Mirza finished with the last of the plastic cases and turned to face the young African warrior. "Jonjo, this isn't about revenge. It is about survival. With you here, Garang and the other men have the best chance of surviving."

"What about you and Aden? Who will make sure you survive?"

Mirza laughed. "Keeping Aden alive is my full-time job."

"Then who will look after you?"

Mirza stroked his short beard as he thought. "We look after each other. He just seems to attract more trouble. You need to take care of Garang and your men."

At the mention of the SFF leader Jonjo dropped his eyes and kicked at the tire of the Wildcat.

"What's wrong? You don't think Garang needs you?"

"Garang treats me like a child."

"He looks to you like a younger brother. He is proud of the man you will become but cautious that it happens too fast. He's also carrying a great responsibility. He needs your help now more than ever."

Jonjo nodded. In the faint lighting Jonjo studied the Indian. With his beard, Asiatic features, and broad smile he looked nothing like Garang. Yet he was more of a warrior than Garang would ever be. He was the man Jonjo aspired to emulate.

While Mirza and Jonjo were talking, Bishop, Jess, and Garang sat under the baobab tree next to Dragonfly. Bishop was running them through the plan while sipping warm tea from a chipped enamel mug.

"You need to maintain the momentum, Garang. If you back off now, the Janjaweed will regroup and come back stronger than ever."

Garang shook his head. "I disagree. We are the ones who need to consolidate. We have dealt our enemy a great blow. Now we need to gather more supporters and share the burden of the war. If you are successful in Khartoum, that will be enough pressure to keep the Janjaweed at bay until I have more fighters."

"The men are starting to trickle in. You've already replaced your losses. Mitch will continue to fly in weapons and you have the men to train them. You need to maintain the momentum."

"No, we need to rest," insisted Garang.

"Listen to Aden," Jess said earnestly. "We've achieved so much. It would be stupid to let that go."

"Shut up," snapped Garang. "What makes you think you know anything of strategy?"

"Garang, there's no need—" Bishop started.

"Enough. I have made my decision. We will conduct

patrols while you are gone but we will not seek out the Janjaweed until we are stronger. I don't want to hear any more of it." With that he stormed off into the darkness, leaving Bishop and Jess sitting alone.

"He's lost his will to fight," she said.

"We've seen a lot of fighting these last few days. Maybe he just needs a break."

"No, he's losing the fire he had before. That's what drew me to him." She looked close to tears. Bishop wanted to hold her but she rose from her seat. "Good night and good luck, Aden." She gave him a sad look and walked off toward her own hut.

Bishop downed the rest of his tea and made his way over to where Jonjo and Mirza were talking next to the Wildcat. "Mirza, you good to roll?"

"Everything is ready."

"Alright, Mitch is going to fly out for more weapons. Garang is going to try and rally extra fighters. Jonjo, Garang's going to need your help to get them trained on the gear that's coming in."

The young soldier nodded and trotted off into the darkness.

"What, no good-byes?" Bishop asked.

"He wanted to come with us," Mirza said. "He understands his place is here with the other fighters. Doesn't mean he's happy about it."

"Kid's a jet in the bush but I think he might be out of his depth in Khartoum." Bishop opened the passenger door to the Wildcat and climbed in.

"I agree he is of far more value here, for now." Mirza took the driver's seat and switched on the headlights. He turned over the supercharged V8, slipped it into gear, and they began their journey north.

They slowed at the SFF checkpoint, waving to the pair of sentries before heading into the darkness. Behind them a pair of hyenas reared up on their hind legs, snapping at the body that hung from a tree. Sagrib's corpse turned slowly until its bulging eyes faced the set of red taillights disappearing into the distance.

Chapter Twenty-One

KHARTOUM, SUDAN

THE WILDCAT probably wasn't the best choice for covert ops in Sudan's capital, reflected Bishop as they drove into Khartoum. Although from a distance the Land Rover did not attract attention, close up it was evident it was a high-performance vehicle with an unusual number of antennas. Bishop checked the pistol stashed in his door pocket. If any Sudanese security forces pulled them over, he was ready to fight. The weaponry they were carrying in the back would be certain to land them in jail if discovered.

Mirza drove them directly into the business district. The medium-rise buildings and paved roads of downtown Khartoum were a change from the south, the first real city they had seen since arriving in East Africa. Fortunately the early morning streets were quiet and they pulled into their hotel without incident.

"Khartoum Palace, hey? This place is a goddamn dump." Bishop dropped his gear in the middle of the hotel room after checking in. The violent action disturbed a family of cockroaches. They scurried under the faded, salmon-colored lounge.

Mirza surveyed the worn carpet and peeling wallpaper. "Grass huts and Africa's finest night-time skies; we've been a little spoiled, Bish."

Bishop laughed as he parted the curtains on the shoe-box-size room's only window. "Maybe I'm being a little picky. We're paying for the view anyway, aren't we?"

From twelve floors up their 'four-star' room had a commanding view of what passed for Khartoum's business district.

"Bit of a one-dog show," Bishop observed, pointing out the PETROCON building that towered over the surrounding structures.

Mirza dumped his gear and joined him at the window. Chua had recommended the hotel because it had an underground garage and it provided excellent observation of their target's last known location, the PETROCON office building.

"Certainly doesn't fit in," said Mirza as he turned away from the window.

"Has to be at least fifty stories," said Bishop. "Tinted glass, sloped roof. Probably got a decent security system. It's going to be a pain in the ass to get inside."

Mirza returned with a tripod and camera fitted with a powerful telephoto lens. He set it up next to the window, adjusting the tripod so the lens nearly touched the glass.

"According to Chua's source Omar hasn't left the building in the last few days."

Mirza looked up from one of the equipment cases he had started to unpack. "I guess we won't need this then." The case contained a long green tube: a 66mm rocket launcher. The PRIMAL operators had planned to use it to ambush Omar's limousine.

"Never know when you're going to need some extra bang, Mirza. Don't want to be the guy that rocks up to a rocket launcher fight with a rifle."

Mirza laughed as he shut the case and pulled a laptop from one of their drag bags. He opened it on the room's battered desk and synched it with the camera. Bishop looked over his shoulder as he brought up a satellite shot of the target location. The camera feed appeared in the top corner.

"Front door is the only way in, Bish."

"Not keen for any *Mission Impossible* antics onto the roof?"

Mirza gave him a look that summarized his low regard for Tom Cruise's on-screen stunts.

"Yeah, I thought so."

"Garang said there was an underground garage filled with service vehicles. If we could get our hands on one, it might make the infiltration a little easier." Mirza flicked through the floor plans Chua had included in the target pack until he reached the one for the basement levels.

Bishop leaned over his shoulder. "Good idea. Then we bang up the service elevator to floor thirty-six, slot Omar, and take the same route out. Five minutes in, five minutes out, and we're gone."

Mirza changed to the floor plan for the thirty-sixth floor. It was exactly how Garang had described it. Elevators opened into a foyer that led to a conference room. A side door linked it to a large office: Omar's office.

"Now we know why he never leaves." Mirza zoomed in on the layout. "Bathroom, bedroom, staff quarters, kitchen, dining hall; he's got everything here he needs."

"They probably bring the girls up the elevator from the basement."

"The girls?" Mirza asked.

"Fat cats like Omar always have girls. Girls and guards. But they won't be a problem. The last thing Omar expects is a direct attack here in Khartoum."

"It could work."

"Trust me." Bishop grinned. "It'll work."

Chapter Twenty-Two

KHARTOUM BUSINESS DISTRICT, SUDAN

THE BEGGAR RAISED his head as people passed, shook his tin cup, and slumped forward again. His kind was common in the city. Years of devastating civil war and drought had driven people from their farms and into the poverty of the under-resourced capital. The developing oil industry had so far benefited only a few. Some new buildings were the only evidence of the riches being pumped from the oil fields to the south.

It was early morning, still dark, and the foot traffic passing the beggar was only a trickle. Most were workers heading to the city's construction sites. Underpaid and overworked, the laborers had nothing to spare for the homeless.

Gathering his tattered robes, the man hauled himself to his feet and started off down the street. A slow ambling hobble aided by a gnarled walking stick, one last link to the farmlands he had fled.

He tapped his mug against the windows of the cars

parked on the street, wailing in Arabic. He spotted a white utility van and stepped up his pace. The oil companies paid their workers slightly more than most thus offered a better chance for a streetwise beggar.

"Coins, coins," he chanted, tapping his mug against the passenger-side window of the van.

The driver awoke from his nap with a start. "Go away," he yelled at the bearded vagabond.

Not to be dissuaded, the beggar hobbled around the front and out onto the street. "Coins, coins," he continued, tapping his mug on the window.

The driver looked at his watch and shook his head. He still had half an hour until he had to return to work.

"OK, OK." He wound down the window and fished in the center console for a handful of change. "Here—"

The aerosol spray hit him directly in the face, a full dose entering his airways. Before he could respond, he slumped forward, unconscious.

Mirza caught the man's head, resting it gently against the steering wheel as he removed the keys from the ignition. He tossed the cup and cane into the gutter and shrugged out of his robes, revealing blue coveralls. Donning the unconscious worker's cap, Mirza unlocked the sliding door on the van and climbed in, locking it behind him. He checked the driver's breathing and pulled him into the back of the van. After zip-tying the worker's hands and feet, he placed him on his side and jumped into the driver's seat. Seconds later Mirza was guiding the PETROCON van through Khartoum's early morning traffic.

Bishop met Mirza in the hotel's underground garage. He was dressed the same: blue coveralls and a baseball cap.

"Where's the driver?" asked Bishop as he loaded their gear into the back of the van.

"He's fine. I found him a nice spot down by the river to sleep it off."

"You know there's crocs in the Nile, right?"

Mirza grabbed one of the cases and froze, giving a concerned look. "Crocs? Like crocodiles?"

"Yeah, chomp, chomp," Bishop used his fingers to represent a crocodile's jaws.

Mirza looked shocked.

"I'm just screwing with you, Mirza. He'll be fine."

Mirza shook his head and swung back into the driver's seat as Bishop slammed the side door shut.

They left the garage and rejoined the morning flow of traffic.

Bishop used the iPRIMAL strapped to his wrist, inspecting the building plans once again. "Chua's target pack said that entrance security was light. Card access to the parking."

Mirza held up the driver's pass.

"Good work!"

It was a short drive from the hotel to the PETROCON building. Situated on the eastern bank of the Nile, the huge structure towered over the surrounding buildings. As they approached Bishop moved to the back of the van, staying out of sight as Mirza brought the vehicle up to the security checkpoint that guarded the ramp to the internal basement parking. He lowered his window and swiped his pass on a proxy pad. It flashed green and the flimsy boom gate rose into the air. An armed guard in an air-conditioned box gave a wave as the van drove down the ramp.

"Can I have a look at that pass?" Bishop asked as Mirza drove them through the garage and down another ramp.

"Sure." He handed it to Bishop, who started laughing

"What is it?"

"The guy in this photo looks nothing like you." Bishop chuckled. "For starters, he's black; second, he doesn't have a beard, and third, he's got a shaved head. This is going to be easier than I thought."

They parked the van on the lowest level. Mirza backed it in between two other PETROCON vehicles, in close vicinity to the service elevator. Once parked he joined Bishop in the back and proceeded to don his equipment.

Over their coveralls they wore lightweight body armor. The basic ballistic-plate carriers held everything they would need to fight into and out of the building: magazines, grenades, pistol, knife, radio, and medical kit. Additionally Bishop's rig had a backpack attached, carrying explosives, just in case they needed to breach.

"You good?" Bishop asked as he actioned his suppressed MP7 and pulled a neck wrap up to cover his face.

"G to the G," answered Mirza. He carried the same suppressed submachine gun but unlike Bishop he didn't wear a cap or face wrap, preferring a Nomex balaclava to hide his face. Both men used discreet earpieces and wore reflective glasses. Their outfits served to protect their identities as well as provide protection from the noise and debris expected from Close Quarters Battle.

Bishop opened the sliding door and they walked across to the elevator. Mirza swiped the card and the doors opened. Inside the stainless-steel box, the single CCTV camera's red light blinked off, the jammer on Mirza's vest completely overwhelming the CMOS sensor.

"Mirza, we've got a problem." Bishop stared at the control panel. His finger extended, hovering over the buttons.

"Floor not listed?" asked Mirza as the doors closed.

"Correct."

"Let me have a look." A multi-tool appeared from a pouch and he swiftly removed the screws that held the stainless-steel panel in place, exposing the circuitry. Despite having limited experience with technology when he joined **PRIMAL**, the former Indian Special Forces soldier had adapted quickly, showing a flair for breaking security systems. Working with the team's resident break-and-enter guru, Kurtz, he had quickly become a highly proficient covert entry specialist.

"It's here, just doesn't have a button." He snapped a lead into the bottom of his **iPRIMAL** and activated a purpose-built app. He clipped a pair of alligator clamps to the circuitry. There was a lurch and they started moving.

"Good work!"

The elevator raced skyward, the numbers counting up at high speed: 25, 26, 27, 28...

"I've got left and center, you go right," Bishop said and they pushed to either side of the sliding doors. Bishop slipped a distraction grenade from his vest.

Both men waited silently. Chinese music filled the elevator. Birds whistled and some string instrument wailed.

30, 31, 32, 33, 34, 35...

The door opened and Bishop flung the canister through the gap. It detonated as it sailed through the air, the first of the nine bangs echoing through the hall.

The two **PRIMAL** operatives rushed out into their allocated arcs.

Bishop's MP7 snapped as two guards armed with AKs filled his optic. The red dot danced from head to head as he fired, toppling the men like bowling pins. He moved forward in a CQB stance, legs shoulder-width apart, body hunched over. The voice of his first urban combat instructor echoed in his head, "Slow is smooth, smooth is fast."

"Clear!" Mirza announced on the radio.

"Clear," Bishop echoed.

Mirza covered the door to the conference room while Bishop zip-tied shut the other set of doors and dragged one of the dead men back to the elevators. He opened the doors of one and dropped him half-inside, trapping it on that floor. The elevator they had arrived in was already fixed; Mirza's adjustments had seen to that.

"Unlocked," Mirza announced.

Bishop joined him at the conference room door, switched out his magazine, and gave a nod.

Mirza turned the handle and popped the door. Bishop slid straight through, clearing the center and right-hand side of the long room as his partner came through behind him, mirroring his action.

They moved swiftly across the boardroom to the door that led into the office. Confused yelling could be heard from the other side.

"Breach," whispered Bishop, swinging the backpack off his shoulder. He pulled out what looked like a thin roll of rubber matting, peeled off a protective layer, and stuck it onto the door. A tiny chip in the center of the mat flashed blue as he slaved it to the iPRIMAL strapped to his wrist. He stepped to the side and activated the charge.

The explosives ripped the heavy door off its hinges and threw it into the plush office of the oil minister. It smashed through a desk and sliced into the opposite wall.

The armed guards in the room flinched, firing wildly in every direction but the gaping doorway as they sought cover from flying debris. One of their shots shattered the huge window behind the remains of the desk.

Mirza shot both of them as he entered. "CLEAR!"

Bishop scanned the room. "Where the fuck is he?"

Mirza pointed toward the door at the back of the office.

Bishop kicked it in, bursting into the politician's adjoining apartment.

They had found Omar. The fat oil minister stood wrapped in a silk robe, holding a scantily clad woman by the neck, a silver pistol pressed against her temple.

"Who are you people?" Omar's voice wavered.

The PRIMAL operatives moved deeper into the room, circling around the expensive furnishings, weapons fixed on their target, looking for a clear shot.

"Stop moving or I'll kill her," Omar said.

"Let the girl go!" Bishop's tone was menacing.

Omar sneered, "So you can kill me?"

Bishop's MP7 spat a single slug. It entered the minister's face through the right eye, tumbled and sprayed the contents of his head across the polished marble floor. A split second later the grossly overweight carcass hit the floor with a wet slap.

"He put it so succinctly," said Bishop, ignoring the screaming woman. "Now let's get the hell out of here."

They raced back the way they came. Both elevators were still trapped.

"Can you take us direct to the garage?" asked Bishop as they entered the elevator.

"I think so." Mirza attached his iPRIMAL to the control board.

"You think so? Going to be pretty untidy if we stop on the ground floor and all the guards waltz in. This elevator's only rated for fifteen..." He tapped the specification plate with the suppressor of the MP7.

The doors closed and they dropped, the numbers counting down from thirty-six.

35, 34, 33, 32, 31, 30...

"No change to the plan. We get into the van and we drive out nice and slow," said Bishop.

22, 21, 19, 18, 17, 16, 15...

"Bish..."

12, 11, 10, 09, 08, 07

"Yeah, mate."

05, 04, 03...

"I really hate this elevator music."

Bishop laughed as they passed ground floor and reached the bottom level. The doors opened and the garage looked exactly the same as they had left it. They held their weapons at the ready and crossed the short distance to the van. Mirza dumped his gear in the back, slipped a pistol into his coveralls, and jumped into the driver's seat. Bishop stayed in the back, MP7 ready if they needed to fight their way out. The van's tires squealed on the smooth concrete as they drove up two levels and arrived at the security checkpoint.

The guard in the box was yelling into the phone, his hands waving animatedly. He took no notice of the van as Mirza swiped his access card and drove up onto street level. They crossed PETROCON's outdoor parking lot and joined the bustling Khartoum traffic.

Bishop glanced down at his watch. "In and out in ten minutes. I wouldn't be surprised if they still don't know what's going on."

He glanced back through the windows in the rear doors of the van. A helicopter was landing in front of the building.

Mirza looked concerned. "The Chinese are going to be all over this."

"Yeah, we need to get back to the hotel fast and ditch the van."

Mirza drove a little faster, weaving through the traffic.

PETROCON TOWER, SUDAN

"Get me the chief of police." Yang stared coldly at the prostrated corpse of Omar. "And someone show me the CCTV shots of the men who did this."

Yang had been scheduled to meet with the Sudanese minister only minutes after he had been killed. He had flown in with one of the PETROCON helicopters only to be greeted by hysterical security guards and the news that Omar had been assassinated.

He walked through the apartment's open doors into the office with the dead body. The security door had been explosively breached, the guards outside dispatched with precise headshots. Definitely the work of professionals, he thought.

"Sir, this is the only clear picture we have." One of the PETROCON guards approached with a piece of paper in his outstretched hand.

Yang snatched it from him. It showed two men in blue coveralls and body armor: a tall, well-built man and a second, smaller operative, both carrying MP7 submachine guns. Although the screen shot was blurry and the faces were covered, the men and their weapons were unmistakably familiar. Yang's lip rose in a snarl as the picture brought back memories of another painful defeat. His instincts told him these two individuals had to be his assailants from the sinking of the *Tian Hai*. The tall one he had fought; the other one had disappeared over the rail before he could stop him.

Yang reached for his phone, dialed a number, and waited for it to connect.

"You did not give enough warning," he accused. "They achieved their mission. Tell me what I am looking for."

Yang listened intently for a full minute before replying. "This will be remembered. Keep me posted on any additional information."

He terminated the call with his source as a tall Arab dressed in a police uniform entered the office, an entourage of staff officers in tow. The chief of police surveyed the destruction wrought on the minister's office, frowned, and turned his attention to the Chinese man.

"Are you Mr. Yang?"

"Yes, sir. I represent PETROCON in all matters of security. As you are no doubt aware the minister for petroleum and energy has been assassinated."

The chief of police nodded. "You have very powerful friends, Mr. Yang. I have been ordered to place all my resources at your disposal."

Yang bowed his head. "Sir, that is not necessary. This clearly falls under your jurisdiction. This should be your operation."

The chief of police was slightly taken aback by the security consultant's deference. In his experience the Chinese could be some of the most arrogant and demanding masters. "Very well. Do we have any leads?"

"We do. I have just been informed that the men who did this are using a hotel as a safe house. A hotel somewhere in Khartoum."

"Khartoum has a lot of hotels, Mr. Yang."

"Yes, but how many hotels have an underground garage

containing a tan-colored, soft-top Land Rover sporting a number of antennas?"

"Give my men a detailed description and we'll have every police patrol looking for these terrorists within the half hour."

"Excellent. The PETROCON guards will be at your disposal should you need them."

"That will not be necessary," the chief replied curtly. He turned to one of his aides. "Put the SWAT team on high alert. Have every police officer in the city searching for this vehicle. I want every hotel, apartment, and parking lot searched now."

"Yes, sir." The chief's aide disappeared from the office.

"You had better stay close to me," said the chief. "Just in case your contact has more information that might be useful."

Chapter Twenty-Three

KHARTOUM PALACE HOTEL, SUDAN

BACK AT THE hotel the two PRIMAL operatives moved quickly to pack their equipment. They had changed out of their PETROCON coveralls and back into cargo pants and shirts.

Mirza moved to unplug the laptop that was hooked into the camera at the window. "Bish, we've got a real problem."

"What is it?"

"Company, and lots of it."

Mirza had focused the camera on the street below the hotel. It was crawling with cops with at least four patrol cars, and a pair of green armored vehicles now blocked the exit from the garage.

"Shit!" Bishop swore. "How the hell did they find us so fast?" He grabbed his armor out of a bag and threw it on.

Mirza did the same, then pried the 66mm rocket launcher from its case and slipped it over his shoulder. They checked their MP7s, hearing protection, and ammunition.

The rest of the equipment they left. The laptop and camera were already sanitized. Although they contained imagery for planning the Omar assassination, there was no other data that could be traced back to PRIMAL.

"Let's hit the roof. Any luck we can zip-line across to another building and get out that way," Bishop said. They had already prepositioned a rope and grappling hook launcher on the roof as part of their escape-and-evasion plan.

"Lead the way."

The pair moved cautiously out of their room and down the dimly lit corridor into the internal fire stairs. Moving up the stairs, it was only two levels to the top and they paused in the stairwell.

Bishop pushed the door open and peered out. The rooftop was empty and he scanned the city skyline before pulling back.

"Snipers?" Mirza asked.

"Not sure," Bishop said, wishing he had a longer-range weapon with a telescopic sight. The nearest building that overlooked the rooftop was over two hundred yards away, out of the effective range of their compact submachine guns.

"If they have their cordon in place, they should have snipers," said Mirza.

Bishop peeked out the door again. He could see their rope. It was where they had left it, attached to a railing on the rooftop's edge. A grappling hook launcher lay next to it, ready to be fired at the neighboring building.

"They should have a lot of things but they leave most of it up to Allah," Bishop muttered. "I'll run out and launch the hook. Once it's secure, follow me and we'll bug out."

"Ah, Bish—"

Bishop pushed open the door and rounds snapped through the air. He threw himself backward into the safety of the stairwell.

High-velocity projectiles punched through the door in a shower of splinters. The pair beat a hasty retreat down the stairwell as slugs ricocheted off the walls.

"Don't even think about saying it," said Bishop.

"It's OK, we'll find another way." Mirza patted the rocket launcher. "Or we can always make a way out."

"I reckon they'll be sending a team up. I'm not one for sitting around so let's meet them halfway."

They set off down the stairwell, weapons held at the ready. They were on level four when they heard boots on the stairs below.

Bishop pulled a concussion grenade from his vest and dropped it down the gap in the middle of the staircase. It took a second to hit the concrete floor at ground level. Enough time for some panicked yelling before it detonated.

The four Sudanese SWAT operators in the bottom of the stairwell were rendered combat-ineffective by the blast. Without hearing protection, the concussion punctured their eardrums, leaving them writhing in pain.

The wounded men stumbled back through the door into the foyer.

"We never seem to have much luck with stairs," joked Mirza as he prepped a demolition charge. The slab of C4 was hooked up to a short timer.

"Tell me about it. We always seem to be fighting up them, down them, and out of them."

Mirza adjusted the timer and lobbed the charge into the stairwell. The blast breached the door, throwing it into the hotel foyer. A wall of dust and debris followed it, hurling Sudanese police through the air like rag dolls.

Mirza and Bishop gave the blast a moment to clear before moving down the stairs and into the lobby.

They caught the remains of the SWAT team cold. Bishop's MP7 spat 4.7mm rounds downrange, killing two of them before they could return fire. The rest of the team turned and ran as Mirza's automatic bursts joined the fray.

They slid in behind the hotel counter as the SWAT team pulled back to their vehicles across the road. The lobby was deserted. Employees and guests in the vicinity had long evacuated and all that remained were empty casings, the blown-off emergency exit door, and the bodies of the dead policemen. Outside, someone screamed an order and all hell broke loose.

Mirza and Bishop hugged the floor as thousands of rounds lashed the ground floor of the hotel. Assault rifles, pistols, shotguns, and machine guns blasted away for a good ten seconds. Rounds snapped above the two men, shreds of glass and wood hitting them as they pressed as flat to the floor as they could get.

When it stopped a voice bellowed over a megaphone. "COME OUT WITH YOUR HANDS UP!"

"You think they've got any ammo left?" asked Bishop as he consulted the map on his iPRIMAL.

"YOU HAVE ONE MINUTE TO COME OUT WITH YOUR HANDS UP!"

"Shit's not looking good, Mirza. We've got solid brick behind us and half the Sudanese army in front of us."

Mirza was studying his own device and broke out in a broad grin. "I've got a connection with the Wildcat."

"Awesome. Maybe we can hook into the comms relay, give Vance a call, and let him know how screwed we are."

"No, you don't understand. Mitch built her from the

ground up. If we are in range I can drive it through my interface."

Bishop looked across shaking his head. "The two of you have been watching too many Bond movies. So what are you thinking? We use it as a distraction?"

"I'll drive it out then detonate the eighty kilos of HE under the front seats."

The smile disappeared from Bishop's face. "You telling me I've been driving around sitting on a shitload of bang? Fuck you, Mirza. People have been shooting at us."

"I'm sorry. It slipped my mind."

"So we use your James Bond gadget out front and the rocket launcher out the back. Mouse hole through to the other building and disappear in the chaos."

"YOU HAVE THIRTY SECONDS!"

"They're very impatient," commented Mirza.

"Let's not keep them waiting."

In the garage below, the dashboard on the PRIMAL vehicle lit up. A flashing green symbol appeared next to the rev counter and the V8 rumbled to life. The four-wheel drive reversed and bashed into the wall behind it. Then the gear indicator changed and it crept forward, turning away from the wall. The nose was now facing the ramp that led up the street.

"TEN SECONDS!"

The big V8 roared and the tires squealed on the cement as the four-wheel drive lurched up the ramp. It swerved haphazardly and scraped the handrail before bursting out onto the street.

The Wildcat appeared from the side of the hotel, next to the foyer where Bishop and Mirza were hunkered down behind the counter.

"You're not very good at this, are you?" Bishop jibed as

he watched the Wildcat's camera feed on Mirza's iPRIMAL.

The Sudanese started firing as soon as the vehicle appeared, riddling it with bullets. The firing continued as Mirza drove it in a wide circle.

As Bishop watched the camera feed, he spotted someone he thought he knew in the group of men clustered around the armored vehicles. On the small iPRIMAL screen it was hard to discern, but it looked like the Chinese guard from the *Tian Hai*.

Mirza had finally sorted out the control function on his iPRIMAL. He turned the mortally wounded Land Rover toward one of the armored vehicles and gunned the engine. Men fled as it approached.

"*Allahu akbar*," he announced as he tapped the touchpad.

There was a huge explosion and the screen when dead. A cloud of debris and dust blew into the foyer.

Mirza waited for the blast wave to pass over them, then jumped up on one knee. He extended the 66mm rocket launcher, set the warhead to 'breach', and aimed it down the corridor toward the rear of the hotel. There was a loud bang as he fired and the rear wall flashed in the dust.

Bishop led as they scrambled through the debris of the two explosions. He used the tactical flashlight on his MP7 to light up the rear wall. There was a hole the size of a trash can lid leading into the adjacent building.

Squeezing through the hole they appeared in the rear of a clothing store.

The store was closed but the light streaming through the front windows illuminated rows of women's dresses lining the racks.

"Not really my style," Bishop said.

"Perfect." Mirza grabbed a long black garment off a shelf and threw it to Bishop.

"What is it?"

"A burka!"

"You want me to wear a goddamn burka?" Bishop exclaimed as he examined the garment.

"Have you got a better idea on how we're going to get out of Khartoum?"

"No, you're right. This is genius."

They donned the burkas, the black shapeless outfits completely covering their combat rigs and weapons.

"Should I take my Oakleys off?" Bishop asked.

Mirza struggled not to laugh. His friend looked slightly ridiculous in the burka, the tinted sunglasses completely hiding him from view. "Keep them on, you're looking very fashionable," he said, knowing their disguises were unlikely to stand up to any close scrutiny.

They unlocked the front door and walked out onto the streets of Khartoum.

KHARTOUM PALACE HOTEL, SUDAN

Yang's ears were ringing and a trickle of blood ran down his face where a piece of shrapnel had nicked his skull. He was in better condition than the Sudanese SWAT team. The police had been decimated. Their bodies formed a broken trail from the foyer of the hotel back to the burning wreck of the car bomb.

The Sudanese were not letting anyone into the building until they confirmed that the 'terrorists' were dead; something that Yang knew was highly unlikely. The car bomb would have been a diversion and by now they would be long gone.

Once his hearing had partially returned Yang pulled out his phone and dialed his boss.

"What is the situation?" Zhu asked as soon as the call connected.

"They escaped."

"I expected as much, the Sudanese security forces are somewhat limited. So now both Omar and his Janjaweed pet are dead. I fear we have severely underestimated the American resolve to slow our influence in the region."

"I'm not convinced that this is the work of the CIA. From the security camera footage I think these are the same two men responsible for the *Tian Hai*. They have the same weapons, look similar, and match the descriptions my informant has provided. The *Tian Hai* and now the assassination of Omar exhibit audacity I would not expect from CIA agents."

"You sure it's the same men?"

"I know it is, and now I know they are also responsible for the recent setbacks involving the Janjaweed."

"This is from our new friend."

"Yes, he has proven most informative."

"Interesting. So if they are not Americans, then who are they? Mercenaries?" Zhu asked.

"I assume so but at this stage I don't know. The South Sudanese could not afford to pay for this level of capability. With your permission, I would like to investigate further." Yang's voice was level, but Zhu knew his thirst for vengeance was raging.

"You think the venture should continue?"

"Yes, Omar and the Janjaweed commander are replaceable. Our infrastructure and time are not. Despite the setbacks we are now well postured to increase our pressure on what remains of the southern rebels."

There was a short pause as Zhu considered his options.

"Has this become personal, Yang? These two men seem to be one step ahead of you at every turn."

The Chinese agent struggled to compose himself. The muscles in his neck bulged as he clenched his teeth. From the sinking of the *Tian Hai* to being shot down in his helicopter, Yang had never experienced such defeat in his life. His injured leg, stiff back, and now bloodied forehead were all constant shameful reminders.

"If I said no then I would be lying."

"Good, there is much at stake. Go forth and destroy these men, headquarters will provide anything you need." Zhu terminated the call.

Yang took a moment to focus his thoughts, then signaled for his driver. The young African drove his car to him through the police picket line where he'd been waiting. Yang gave instructions to return to PETROCON HQ and the waiting helicopter. He needed to get back to the refinery. South was where his two enemies would be heading, south to the oil and the battlefield. Already a plan was forming in his head as to how he would deal with the mercenaries.

Chapter Twenty-Four

KALJAK VILLAGE, ABYEI DISTRICT

THE BATTERED blue van had cost them ten thousand US dollars. Mirza had found it on the outskirts of Khartoum and paid the inflated price to convince the driver to part with it on the spot. They had fueled it from a hawker selling petrol by the bottle at the roadside and driven south.

The Bunker's operations team had planned a route for them, avoiding all reported border checkpoints. Bishop had managed to reestablish comms using his iPRIMAL. The data link wasn't strong but it was enough for them to receive GPS waypoints.

After thirty-six hours of travel, they arrived back at the new SFF village, nearly four days since they had left for the mission to Khartoum.

"I can't feel my butt," Bishop said as he climbed out of the van.

Mirza hadn't fared much better. He slowly pried himself from the driver's seat and immediately stretched.

A group of SFF fighters watched them suspiciously from the shade of a huge baobab tree. Bishop didn't recognize any of them, but he had a good idea where their weapons had come from. Sporting AKs with optical sights and PKMs that looked fresh out of the crate, it was obvious Mitch had been busy bringing in weapons for the new SFF recruits.

"Mirza! Aden!" Jonjo appeared from another hut and jogged toward them. He grabbed Mirza in a bear hug and reached out for Bishop's hand, pumping it wildly. "I was starting to worry!"

"No need to worry. The mission went off without a hitch!" Mirza extracted himself from the youth's grasp.

Bishop gave Mirza a sideways glance. "Yeah, smooth as silk. We even traded in the Wildcat. How have things been here?"

Jonjo talked as they strolled over to the shade of another tree and sat on a pile of ammunition crates. "Not well. Garang has been away, trying to bring men into the fight. Some have come." He gestured toward the newcomers under the baobab. "But not many."

"And the Janjaweed?" asked Mirza.

"They keep raiding the villages. We have ambushed some but the more we hit the more there are. Without the other militias to help us we are only delaying our defeat. In a few days we will have to abandon this village and move south."

"Where is Garang now?" asked Bishop.

"Recruiting. Should be back tonight."

"And Jess?"

"She's with the wounded. We have taken losses." There was a moment of silence before Jonjo continued. "Enough about us. What happened in Khartoum?"

"Omar is dead," said Mirza.

Jonjo's eyes lit up in excitement. "How? I want to hear about it!"

As Mirza told the story, Bishop walked over to the hut that served as the medical center. He nodded at the nurse who manned the desk in the waiting area. Continuing to the operating room, he ducked through the plastic sheeting that kept out the dust, and found Jess.

She was working on a soldier who had been shot through the upper arm. The man was heavily sedated and lying on a portable operating table. Bishop noted the lighting and other equipment that Mitch had provided. He grabbed a surgeon's plastic gown and shrugged it on. He cleaned his hands from a pump pack of hand sanitizer, donned gloves and a mask, and walked over to the table.

The slug Jess had pulled from the man's arm hit the tray with a clunk as she looked up. Bishop noticed the heavy bags under her eyes.

"You're looking a little tired there, Doc."

"Aden, you're back." She flicked a stray hair out of her face with the back of her gloved hand.

Bishop gave a broad smile. "Wild horses couldn't drag me away."

For a second the fatigue seemed to lift, then she focused back on the bullet wound.

"Let me close up for you." Bishop moved around to her side.

"Would you? I'd love to sit down."

Bishop took the plastic tray with the needle and sutures while she sat on a chair in the corner.

"Did things work out in Khartoum?" she asked.

"Yeah, things worked out OK." Bishop started to close

the wound, pressing the sides of the torn flesh together as he sewed. "How have things been here?"

"Plenty of wounded," Jess answered flatly.

"What about Garang?"

"What about Garang? I haven't seen him in two days. When I did see him he completely ignored me."

"I'm sure he's got a lot on his mind."

"Don't make excuses for him, Aden. He doesn't deserve them."

Bishop finished closing the wound and wiped it down. He dropped the sharps in a safety bin and stepped back from the table.

Jess got up from her chair to inspect the wound. "He's not going to be happy with that."

"What? Why?"

"Your stitches are too neat. The worse it looks, the more they like it. You know, boys and scars."

He laughed and Jess called out for her nurse. She gave a set of instructions and removed her garb. Bishop followed her lead and they walked back into the waiting area.

"You know, without you most of these men would die," he said.

"You mean without Mitch! That man's an angel. Everything I ask for he delivers."

"Without good people equipment is worthless."

"Tell that to Garang. All he cares about is being the big man. He—"

Jess's rant was interrupted by Jonjo bursting into the room.

"Garang called, he wants you and Mirza to come to Juba and meet with the other militias."

"Trying to rally more support to the SFF flag?" Bishop asked.

"Yes, he thinks that if you are there the others will join."

Bishop nodded and turned to the doctor. "You need anything from Juba, Jess?"

"Actually I wouldn't mind checking in with the hospital. I can also show you where the SFF safe house is."

"Sounds good. We'll run it past Mirza."

They left the clinic and walked over to where the other PRIMAL operative was inspecting a new AK under the shade of the baobab.

"Mirza, it's good to see you again," said Jess.

"And you," he said, smiling.

Bishop sat on a crate. "What do you think, Mirza? You up for a day trip to Juba?"

Mirza thought for a moment before replying. "I think you should go; any extra support could turn the battle. I should stay here and work with Jonjo and the others."

"Sounds like a plan. Jess and I will head to Juba. We'll take the Hilux. Jonjo, you and Mirza stay here and keep up operations against the Janjaweed. We'll only be gone two days. Hopefully we can get more tribes to join us. Any objections?"

There was silence from the group.

"Excellent. Jess, we'll roll in a few hours. I need to get a bit of shut-eye before I fall asleep on my feet."

JUBA, SOUTH SUDAN

"How far?" Bishop turned the Hilux off the main gravel road in the center of town.

"It's at the end of this street," Jess replied. The last time she had been to the SFF safe house was months ago, during a time she had shared hopes and ambitions with Garang. She was not looking forward to seeing him.

The safe house was on the outskirts of Juba within a group of high-walled compounds that lined the dirt street. The suburb was barely a step up from a shantytown, the basic buildings constructed with cheap concrete blocks, walls topped with broken glass to deter intruders. Trash filled the streets and the smell of burning plastic hung in the air.

Bishop parked a short distance down the street and placed a call on his iPRIMAL. Garang answered on the second ring.

"Are you close?"

"We're just down the street. Is everything OK?" Bishop asked.

"Yes, everything is good. The delegations will start arriving soon. I need you to be here to greet them. It's very important that you are here first."

"We'll be there in a moment." Bishop terminated the call.

"What's wrong?" Jess asked.

"Nothing. Garang seems a little stressed."

"Yes. A lot is riding on this meeting. Perhaps it would be best if I stayed in the car?"

"What? No, you're as much a part of this as me."

They left the truck and walked to the compound. Bishop had stashed his AK-104 and chest rig in a bag locked in the car. He covered his pistol belt with his shirt.

"This is it," said Jess as they approached a wall with a heavy metal door. She rapped on the door a few times and thirty seconds later it opened with a screech.

One of Garang's trusted fighters let them in. The man lowered his AK-47 and escorted them to the courtyard where the Southern Freedom Fighters' leader greeted them.

"Aden, thanks for coming. Is it just you?" Garang asked. "I thought Mirza was coming as well?"

"Yeah, Mirza and Jonjo are holding the fort."

Garang gave Jess a look that suggested she was not welcome. "We're leaving weapons outside, Aden." He pointed to a low wooden table at the entrance to the main building.

"Why?" asked Bishop.

"It's a sign of respect to the other leaders. My men outside will be armed but weapons won't be allowed in the room."

"Fair enough." Bishop took his sidearm from its holster, removed the magazine, and cocked it, catching the ejected round. The last thing he wanted was someone shooting him with his own pistol.

For a safe house it was relatively well furnished. A large rug covered the concrete floor, and comfortable-looking couches were pressed up against the walls.

"Jonjo tells me the mission in Khartoum was a success," said Garang as they sat.

"No problems; in and out quick. Omar has been eliminated."

"Well done. While you've been away we have been busy as well."

"Jonjo filled me in. Have you had any luck with the other militias?"

"Yes and no. They seem interested and promise big things but so far they have done little. I am hoping this meeting today will make them commit."

One of Garang's men opened the door and gestured for the SFF leader to join him outside.

"Excuse me, I will greet our guests." Garang left the room.

Jess waited a few seconds before speaking. "He's acting weird."

"Tell me about it." Bishop pulled out his iPRIMAL and moved off the couch. "I should have brought Mirza." He peered out a window.

"Oh fuck—"

The door opened and a Chinese man burst into the room wielding a pistol. Bishop grabbed the weapon, pushed it skyward, and drove his fist into the man's face. The gunman collapsed and Bishop yanked the pistol from his grasp.

A shot fired as more men streamed in: Garang, two Chinese heavies, and Yang. Bishop staggered backward, dropping the gun. Someone kicked him in the head and he collapsed face down on the rug.

"ADEN!" screamed Jess, running toward him.

One of the Chinese thugs grabbed Jess's hair, dragging her away.

"Garang! You killed him, you fucking traitor," screamed Jess, struggling against her captor. "You sold us out, didn't you, you worthless coward—"

Garang slapped her savagely. "Shut up, bitch. I've saved us. The Americans were never going to give us the investment we needed. We would have lost. This way everyone will get rich."

Tears streamed down Jess's face as she continued to struggle against a vice-like grip.

"Where is the other one?" Yang asked calmly. "There are supposed to be two. You promised me both of them."

"The other one stayed with my men. He is not the leader. This one is the leader."

"Yes, but you promised both." The Chinese agent stared calmly at Garang like a snake watching a mouse.

"I will deal with him later. Without this one he is nothing."

Yang snapped an order at one of his men. The thug knelt next to Bishop's body and checked his pulse. He looked up at Yang and spoke in Chinese.

"He is still alive," translated Yang.

The guard rolled the body over.

"Hello, champ," Bishop said groggily, looking at Yang. "Fancy seeing you here." The bullet had hit Bishop in the upper left arm, punching through his flesh only a few inches lower than his shoulder. It was a straight in and out shot, unlikely to have caused much trauma.

"I knew it was you," spat Yang. "The *Tian Hai*, the ambush, the helicopter, Khartoum; it was all you!"

"Bingo! You're like a Chinese Sherlock Holmes, aren't you?"

Garang crossed the room and picked the iPRIMAL up off the ground. He inspected the screen with a frown. "He called someone."

There was a loud bang and the device detonated in Garang's hand. He emitted a blood-curdling scream as his fingers were shredded by the tiny charge inside the device. Plastic and glass sliced into his flesh. He dropped to his knees, clutching the ruined hand in front of him, whimpering.

"That's one reason to use hands-free," quipped Bishop.

Yang watched with disdain and gestured for one of his men to remove Garang. "Take him to the Bangladeshi hospital."

"What about my money?" Garang whimpered.

Yang took a silver briefcase from one of his guards and

thrust it toward the wounded SFF commander. "I should halve it, but as a gesture of goodwill I will let you have it all." Garang was shepherded out the door, holding the briefcase with his good hand.

Yang turned his attention back to Bishop. "I'm sure you think you are very funny. I can promise you will not be laughing when I am finished with you."

He turned to his two remaining men, switching to his native tongue, "Sedate them and load them both in the truck. The woman might end up being useful."

Chapter Twenty-Five

THE BUNKER, LASCAR ISLAND

"SIR, WE HAVE A MAJOR PROBLEM." The operations watchkeeper burst into Vance's office.

"Bishop?"

"The meeting's gone bad. Bishop activated his duress alarm. Shots have been fired."

For a big man Vance moved fast. He jumped up out of his chair and followed the watchkeeper into the operations room.

On the central screen a high-resolution satellite image showed the location of Bishop's iPRIMAL in downtown Juba, a mile west of the airport.

Everyone in the room was silent as they listened to the audio feed being transmitted live from Bishop's phone.

"Shut up, bitch. I've saved us. The Americans were never going to give us the investment we needed. We would have lost. This way everyone will get rich."

On one of the other screens voice recognition software confirmed the voice as being Garang's. Vance scowled. The ungrateful bastard had sold Bishop out.

"Where is the other one? There are supposed to be two. You promised me both of them."

Vance glanced up at the other screen. The software had captured the voice and was searching databases. The accent was clear: Chinese.

"The other one stayed with my men. He is not the leader. This one is the leader."

Thoughts raced through Vance's head. What the hell was going on? Was Bishop alive? The software still had not found a link to the Chinese voice.

"Yes, but you promised both."
"I will deal with him later. Without this one he is nothing."

"Big call, fucktard!" Vance growled. Mirza was not the sort of guy that anyone in the operations room would cross. Everyone knew the lightly built Indian was lethal, a quiet killer who would never give up until he completed his mission.

"He is still alive," the Chinese guy continued.

There was a collective sigh in the ops room.

"Hello, champ. Fancy seeing you here."

"I knew it was you. The Tian Hai, the ambush, the helicopter, Khartoum; it was all you!"

Clearly Bishop and this Chinese guy had developed a close working relationship, he thought. Vance glanced at the technician controlling Bishop's iPRIMAL and gave him a thumbs-up. The tech nodded back.

"Bingo! You're like a Chinese Sherlock Holmes, aren't you?"

Vance kept his thumb extended upward.

"He called someone."

It was Garang's voice, louder than the others, in close proximity to the phone's speaker. Vance dropped his thumb, turning his hand down. The technician hit the signal to detonate the explosive charge in the phone and the transmission cut.

"Intel! I want to know who this Chinese fucker is and I want to know yesterday," bellowed Vance.

"We got him, sir. His name is Yang Tan. CIA have him on file as PLA, Second Department."

"Alright, that makes sense. Now where are they gonna take Bishop? Back to Khartoum or over to the refinery? Someone get Chua in here. I want answers!"

"He'll be here any minute," said the watchkeeper.

"Good. In the meantime, let's get on to Mirza and give him an update. Then I want to know what assets we have nearby and how long it will take to get them in country. Mirza is gonna need back up. The recovery of Bishop is now our top priority, all other operations are on the backburner."

The staff were already busy at their terminals. They had been in this position before and knew exactly what needed to happen.

Vance turned and headed back to his office. He needed to place a few calls of his own.

Halfway to his door, he stopped. "One last thing. Someone come up with a plan to execute that goddamn turncoat. By this time next week I want Garang dead in a ditch somewhere."

SUDAN

Bishop's head was throbbing. The fact that it was bashing against the inside of a car window probably didn't help. As he slowly regained consciousness, he realized his feet were bound and his hands were firmly secured behind his back. He shuffled up into a sitting position and looked out the window at the landscape racing past.

"Our guest is awake."

The rough Chinese accent caught Bishop's attention and he glanced forward into the rearview mirror. Yang's reptilian stare glared back at him.

"Thanks for the wake-up call. How long till room service?" asked Bishop.

"You still think you are funny. That will change."

Bishop turned his head and realized Jess was sitting next to him, still unconscious.

"Jess." He shuffled over toward her. "Jess, can you hear me?"

"She'll be awake soon. She is not as big as you. The drugs will take longer. How is your arm?"

Bishop glanced at his left shoulder. It was wrapped in a heavy bandage.

"I took the liberty of closing the wound for you."

"Shit, makes me feel bad about sticking a knife in your leg."

"Somehow I doubt that, Aden."

"No, you're right. That was a pretty sweet move."

Yang went silent and Bishop turned his attention on the still unconscious doctor.

"Jess, wake up."

She groaned and opened her eyes. "Aden, Aden!" She panicked, struggling against the plasticuffs that bound her hands and feet.

"It's OK. I'm here."

He shuffled across to help her into a sitting position. Her hair was a total mess, a line of dried saliva marked her shirt, and her eyes were bloodshot.

"You OK?" asked Bishop.

"A little groggy. I think they hit us with Ketamine. How's your arm?"

"Ah, the beautiful doctor has decided to join us," interrupted Yang. "I trust that you are feeling well?"

"Go to hell!" snapped Jess.

"You really should be more pleasant. This may be our last opportunity to chat. I can assure you that when we reach our destination our interaction will be far more formal."

"What does he mean by that?" she asked.

"Means he's going to get rough," said Bishop quietly. "There's no need to bring her into this. She doesn't know anything about us."

"This I already know, but it would seem that you have

become quite fond of her. So maybe you should start talking."

Bishop stared out the window at the African savannah flashing by. It was mid-afternoon and the land was starting to cool. Soon the big cats would stir, preparing for darkness and the hunt. He turned his head to face the front and for the first time he realized there were a number of gun buggies escorting them.

"You already know who I work for. My agency isn't going to sit on its hands, you know. They will be looking for me. They know who you are and where I'll be."

"I doubt that very much. Mainly because I don't believe that you work for the CIA. I think you're a mercenary, a gun for hire. The question is, who has hired you?"

Bishop laughed. "You're a fool, Yang. What private contractor has access to the sort of support that's behind me? Face it, you fucked up snatching me and before you know it a SEAL team is going to be kicking in the door and making Swiss cheese of everyone who's not a hostage. Then we'll see who's the funny man."

Yang smirked in the mirror. "Yes, we will see."

The SUV slowed and Bishop instantly recognized the high fences, earthen berms, and fortified security posts of the PETROCON refinery. He had studied satellite imagery and drone footage but had not anticipated seeing it this close, in person.

The buggies in front of them passed through the chicane of concrete barriers, stopping to have their undersides checked by mirror-wielding guards.

When it was their turn, Yang wound down the window and snapped a set of orders to the guards. They waved the SUV through the checkpoint and into the compound.

They pulled up in front of a cluster of boxy buildings.

Yang and the driver jumped out, leaving Bishop and Jess alone.

"What happens now?" asked Jess.

"Nothing to worry about," lied Bishop. "They're after me, not you."

Footsteps could be heard approaching. "They won't hurt you, Jess. I promise."

The doors were wrenched open and they were dragged out. Bishop landed on his side, his legs still tied together. A hood was slipped over his head and he was forced to his feet. He heard the snick of a knife slicing through the plasticuffs at his ankles. Strong hands guided him forward.

"This is where it's going to get really fun," Yang hissed in his ear.

"Why? Because you get to play out all those homoerotic fantasies bouncing around in your sick little head?" Bishop's voice was muffled in the hood. He braced for the inevitable and when the blow landed, it lifted him off his feet and sent him sideways. He embraced the darkness and dropped to the ground unconscious.

THE BUNKER, LASCAR ISLAND

"OK, team, what've we got?" Vance walked into the conference room and dropped into the leather seat at the head. To his right sat Chua; to the left one of his operations officers.

"Good news," Chua started. "We have confirmation of Bishop's location. We pulled GPS coordinates and voice match off Yang's phone." Chua saw the quizzical look on Vance's face. "I pulled a few strings and got it covered by the NSA; no big deal. Anyway, Bishop is currently located at the PETROCON refinery."

"That's good news?"

"For now. My assessment is they're going to transfer him to the Chinese Embassy in Khartoum. Best guess, we've got less than twelve hours before they move him."

"Working with that time frame what options do we have to bang in on the target?"

"Nothing solid," reported the operations officer. "I spoke with Mirza last night and he doesn't have enough manpower to hit the refinery. His preference would be to interdict a road move."

"Makes sense. What about options to reinforce his team?" asked Vance.

"Aleks and Kurtz are both on a plane from Abu Dhabi to Ethiopia. Mitch is inbound and should RV with them around 1000 hours our time. If all goes well they should be on the ground with Mirza no later than 0600 hours local."

"Excellent work. Having those boys around will certainly give us a few more options. I want you and your team to work up a number of concepts. Let's run with an interdiction of a road move with a worst-case scenario if they try to chopper him out."

"I'm working on a third option as well, Vance," the man said. "A road move to the airfield up north and a fixed-wing flight into Khartoum."

"Good thinking. That's all for the time being. Give me a heads-up when the boys are on the ground."

"Will do, boss." The operations officer grabbed his folder and made for the door.

When he was gone, Vance turned to Chua. "So what's the go with China? You dig anything up on this Zhu guy?"

Chua nodded. "Saneh's been sniffing around in Shanghai. In between her time spent in nightclubs and shopping malls, she has actually uncovered something we may be able to use."

"Useful for the overall mission or recovery of Bishop?"

"Both." The intel chief pulled an A4-size blowup of a surveillance photo from his folder and slid it toward Vance. "It seems that Zhu has a son."

Vance picked up the photo. "Real ladies' man, hey."

The shot was taken in a nightclub, a polo-shirt-wearing Chinese youth cuddled up with what looked like a pair of very attractive European escorts.

"You thinking a straight out prisoner swap?" asked Vance.

"My preference would be to recover Bishop without having to give up the kid; then we could use him to influence Zhu to play nice with South Sudan."

"But we can always use the kid as a contingency."

Chua nodded.

"Good plan, I like it. My only concern is Saneh being on her own in Shanghai."

"She's very resourceful, I'm sure—"

"That's not the issue. A kidnapping has lots of moving parts. She'll need backup."

"Vance, with most of the team in Africa, we simply don't have the extra manpower."

"No doubt about it, we're stretched." Vance leaned back in the leather chair, putting his boots up on the conference table. "I know of one person available and I'm pretty sure he can speak Chinese."

Chua looked confused for a moment.

"Pack your dancing shoes, Chua. You're heading back to the motherland."

Chapter Twenty-Six

BAR CONTINIUM, SHANGHAI

THE STRETCHED Audi A8 limousine came to a smooth halt in front of the hotel, its powerful engine purring like a contented beast. A bellboy grasped the door and opened it, waiting patiently for the occupants to alight.

The legs that swung out of the vehicle caught everyone's attention, from the smartly dressed security guards to the concierge and patrons of the hotel. Long and graceful, yet defined and muscular, they announced a women who took great care in her appearance and physique.

The owner of those legs didn't fail to impress. She gracefully accepted the hand of the bellboy, letting him guide her onto the red carpet.

The woman was devastatingly alluring, dark and sultry, with the grace and poise of a dancer. Her high cheekbones, dark eyes, and long brown hair suggested an Eastern European, or perhaps Middle Eastern heritage.

She was dressed in the most couture of outfits, a classic

mid-length black dress that revealed her ample cleavage. Six-inch heels accented her toned legs.

From the other side of the vehicle a pair of blondes appeared. Beautiful, but not striking like the brunette, they joined her on the red carpet that led inside the foyer. In a Michael Bay movie they would have been filmed in slow motion: a hair flick, a coy smile, pure sexual energy.

They strutted to an elevator at the side of the lobby, guarded by a sharp-suited doorman.

"Welcome to Bar Continium." The doorman smiled charmingly over his clipboard. "Can I have a name for the list?"

The brunette pursed her lips. "Aneke Krisko." Her accent was rich with Slavic inflections.

The doorman checked his list. "I don't seem to have you here."

"Are you sure?" She reached into her handbag and took out a business card. "Perhaps you are confused with the spelling?" She smiled suggestively.

The doorman glanced at the handwritten phone number on the card. "Ah, yes, here you are. Aneke plus two. This way, ladies."

They rode the mirrored elevator from the foyer to the 135th floor. When the doors opened the three women stepped into a wonderland of glamor and pumping music.

The Continium was Shanghai's newest and most exclusive nightspot; its clientele, the rich and privileged of Mainland China. Businessmen, generals, politicians, and their sons; a male-dominated environment where a woman's company came at a price.

The three females strode across the plush carpet, drawing the eye of almost everyone. The brunette led them around the dance floor filled with awkwardly gyrating men and svelte models, and up into one of the booths that ringed the club's floor-to-ceiling windows.

No sooner had they sat, the drinks began to arrive.

Their waiter first offered them a bottle of champagne. "Compliments of the gentleman in the suit." Next came a bottle of top-shelf scotch whiskey, accompanied by a selection of sodas, green tea, and ice. "Compliments of the man over there, Mr. Zhu. He would like you to join him."

The brunette dismissed the offerings, sending the waiter scurrying with a flick of her hand. In her thick accent she ordered a round of Cîroc vodka on ice.

The three girls chatted, drank, and enjoyed the dazzling view of the city. Far below them the lights of Shanghai sprawled along the Yangtze River. They were oblivious to the scowls they commanded from the female competition around them. Other escorts fought for the attention of their clients as the three newcomers continued to attract stares.

A waiter appeared with a tray of drinks, one of everything the cocktail list had to offer. "Mr. Zhu has asked me to tell you to not be so fussy. You make it hard for him to get your attention."

The brunette smiled. "You can tell Mr. Zhu that my friends and I would very much like for him to join us."

The waiter nodded and disappeared to pass on the message.

A few minutes later two men approached the booth. A short, portly Asian wearing a white polo shirt with a popped collar grinned at the three women. A taller, rougher man sporting a shaved head and a loose-fitting suit tailed him.

"You must be Mr. Zhu," said the brunette, inviting him to sit beside her.

"You can call me Ping," he replied.

"I'm Aneke. Thank you ever so much for drinks. Your friend is also welcome to sit with us."

Ping addressed the second man and he sat between the two blondes. They snuggled in either side of him and he grinned.

"You prefer brunettes, yes?" Aneke purred, placing her hand on Ping's leg.

"Yes, yes, of course," he stammered. "Blondes are so last year."

Aneke gave him her undivided attention for the next half hour. They talked, she laughed at his attempts at humor, and they drank.

"You know, my father is a very powerful man," said Ping.

"Is that so? He must be very proud to have a son like you."

"Yes, he is very proud. I am already a senior manager in the company."

"And so young? That is impressive."

Aneke continued to stroke his ego, letting him spill his life story as he drank. She regulated her own intake, sipping from cocktails as he guzzled.

The other man, the bodyguard, refrained from drinking. Aneke gave him a smile and he returned it, clearly enjoying the attention of the two voluptuous blondes at his side. His hands roamed over their bodies as they smiled and laughed.

"I'm going to powder my nose," Aneke whispered, her lips gently caressing the lobe of Ping's ear. "Would you like to come?"

"Yes, yes."

"I'm going to take him away for a moment. Is that OK?" she asked the guard.

His brow furrowed and he made to stand up. Ping

waved his hand, assailing him with a torrent of Mandarin. The guard remained seated.

"It's OK," Ping explained. "He works for my father. Big muscles, little brain." He laughed as they left the booth and circled the dance floor. Ping had his arm around the brunette's waist.

They passed the elevator and the bar, making their way to the corner of the club where the restrooms and private function areas were located. The clientele loved karaoke and the Continium pampered to their needs in elegance and style. Individual booths lined one side of a corridor, soundproofed, decked out with expensive furnishings, and serviced by scantily clad waitresses.

It was still early in the night and most of the booths were unoccupied. Aneke slid back the door on one and peeked inside. It was empty. She grabbed Ping by the hand and dragged him in, closing the door behind them.

The room was themed in blue. Plush carpet covered the floor and velvet blue armchairs clustered around a low glass table. There was a bar in the corner and a huge flat-screen television bolted to one of the windowless walls.

"You like to sing?" Ping giggled as he slumped into one of the chairs.

"No, I like to dance," said Aneke, lifting her foot onto one of the soft chairs. Her dress rode up her thigh, exposing the top of her pull-up stockings. She smiled seductively as she slipped her fingers under the top of the stockings and pulled out a small plastic bag filled with white powder.

Ping smiled as she emptied the package onto the glass table. He took out his wallet and handed her a black AmEx credit card. She used the card to form thin lines of powder on the glass. Ping watched her closely as he rolled a hundred-yuan note into a tube.

"Ladies first," Ping offered Aneke the tube.

"*Nyet*, you go first. I need it to make you sober for what I have in mind." She bit her lip suggestively.

Ping smiled and leaned forward, the tube clutched between his thick fingers. Inhaling loudly, he sucked an entire line into his nose.

Grinning, he slumped back into his chair. "Good stuff. You should try."

"I will soon, my dear," Aneke said, reaching up to brush a strand of long hair from her face as she watched him.

Ping smiled again as the euphoria of the drug washed over him. His head slumped sideways as the chemicals relaxed his muscles.

"Target is under. Meet you at the service elevator in five." The brunette had dropped her Slavic accent as she spoke into her phone. Her English was naturally tainted with a Middle Eastern flavor.

"Come on, big boy." She helped the heavily sedated Ping out of his chair. The drug running through his system was designed to make him passive, not completely immobile.

She checked the hallway was empty before guiding the inebriated playboy out of the karaoke room and back toward the restrooms and the service elevator.

"Where are we going?" Ping's speech was slow and slurred.

"Downstairs, sweetie."

A staff member stopped in the corridor, eyeing the pair suspiciously.

"My friend he has too much to drink, *da*. I take him home now."

The waiter nodded and disappeared.

She reached into her bust and pulled out a security

swipe card. The doors to the service elevator opened and she guided Ping inside.

"Hey, you! STOP!"

She stabbed the close button with her finger as Ping's security guard spotted them. He sprinted down the corridor toward them, reaching under his jacket for a handgun. The doors closed with a second to spare. The elevator shuddered as he slammed into the doors.

"Chen, we've got a problem. The guard, he's onto us," she spoke calmly into her phone.

"OK, I'm downstairs. I'll keep an eye out."

Above the door the floor numbers lit up as they dropped. Like a toddler, Ping watched them, enthralled with the flashing numerals.

When they reached the ground floor, the doors opened to reveal a service corridor. The brunette led Ping to a loading bay where the hotel's deliveries arrived. The Audi was parked alongside large industrial bins and piles of boxes.

"Hands up, whore!" a man shouted from the loading bay. His English was halting but his intent was clear. His pistol pointed directly at the brunette's face.

Slowly she raised her arms.

Ping, grinning like an idiot ambled forward and hugged his bodyguard.

The pistol stayed aimed at her as the guard grabbed Ping with his other hand. "What did you do to him?"

"He'll be fine; just a little drug."

A Chinese voice piped up from behind the guard. Another man had joined the party. This one was dressed in a tailored black suit complete with a chauffeur's cap. He was shorter than the guard and lightly built.

The two men conversed in Mandarin and the guard

seemed to become more comfortable with the situation. He backed away from the brunette, pushing Ping along with his free hand. Once he let go of Ping, he reached into his jacket, pulling out his phone to make a call.

The smaller man moved in a flash. He grasped the guard's pistol and snapped the wrist backward.

The guard was caught by surprise but reacted quickly. Using his superior size and strength, he launched forward, ignoring the crunching sound that his wrist made as the chauffeur bent it back even further. He lifted the smaller man off the ground and charged ahead.

He made it a few steps before collapsing to the ground, the chauffeur pinned beneath him.

The brunette's worried look turned into a smile as she noticed the syringe sticking out of the guard's neck. The plunger was fully depressed.

"Hey, Saneh, could you lend me a hand?" The chauffeur was trying to leverage himself out from under the dead weight of the slumbering guard.

"Chen, you took your sweet time." Saneh helped push the two-hundred-pound guard off Chua, PRIMAL's chief of intelligence.

He extracted himself and stood brushing the dust from his suit. "Sorry about that. I had some trouble backing the car in." He gestured to the rear fender of the brand-new Audi. It had a large dent in it.

"Didn't I say we needed something smaller? You men and your toys. You're just as bad as Bishop." She strode across to where Ping was sitting on the steps that led from the dock down to the garage. "Come on, Ping, let's go." She helped him to his feet and opened the door of the Audi for him.

Chua was already in the driver's seat by the time she

joined him in the front of the car. Ping was stretched out in the back snoring. They pulled out of the loading dock and onto the street.

"The Lascar flight is prepped and ready," said Chua. "As soon as we get to the airport we'll make our boy comfortable and get airborne. Short stop in Hong Kong to pick up his buddy and then straight to the island."

"Excellent," responded Saneh as she slipped out of her heels and replaced them with a pair of plain black flats. "Any news on Aden?" she asked with a hint of concern.

Chua shook his head. "No, nothing new. He'll be fine. You know Bishop's always popping up at the worst possible time having escaped by the skin of his teeth."

"Don't I know it." Saneh sighed as the streets of Shanghai flashed by. "Don't I know it."

PETROCON OIL REFINERY, KURDUFAN DISTRICT, SUDAN

"They have my son."

The satellite link between the two phones was crystal clear, allowing Yang to detect the slight quaver in his employer's voice, something he had never heard before.

"Who?" he asked calmly.

"Who do you think, Yang?" Zhu yelled. "The American scum who are trying to destroy us. They took him from a nightclub in Shanghai. My men have searched the city and found nothing."

Yang forced himself to remain calm. "If they have him he will already be out of the country. I will put word out to all my contacts but I doubt they will help. These people are professionals. They will contact us shortly."

"Will they hurt him?" Zhu asked softly.

"No. They are going to offer us a trade. Your son for the man we captured."

"How can you be so sure?"

"What other reason would they have to take him? They know that if they hurt him, then you will become even more focused on destroying them. No, they will offer a trade."

"This is true. If we must trade your prisoner, so be it. I will spare no expense to have Ping returned. If required I will burn South Sudan to the ground."

Yang had no doubt that Zhu was willing to do exactly as he promised. In their culture they planned far into the future of generations yet to come; sons ensured the family's ongoing prosperity. The intelligence operative understood that a son was the most valuable thing a powerful government official could have; however, the thought of trading Aden made him furious.

"I need time to interrogate the prisoner before any trade is made," Yang said.

"I have already requested an interrogator from Second Department. He will arrive in the capital tomorrow. You are to move the prisoner to our embassy in Khartoum."

"That is not necessary. I am more than capable of extracting the information we—"

"Enough! You are a capable agent but you are not an interrogator. This man will wring every piece of information possible out of this Aden. He will experience pain like he has never felt before. Xinhai will make him sing like a bird and I will have my son returned."

"Xinhai." Yang smiled at the name of the notorious

interrogator, a man known throughout their intelligence community as The Butcher.

"The commander of Second Department is family. He promised me the best."

"And Xinhai is just that," Yang agreed reluctantly. "He will pry every detail from our prisoner. We will soon know who he is working for."

"Yes, and once my son is returned, then you will take this enemy apart piece by piece. Guard the prisoner with your life, Yang."

"I will ensure he is delivered in one piece. What do you want done with the girl?"

"Dispose of her as you see fit." Zhu terminated the call.

Yang placed his phone down on the plastic folding table that served as his desk. Aden's organization had displayed a capability far beyond his expectations. They had reached into China and shown the audacity to take action. There was no doubt in his mind; he was not dealing with a government agency. This organization had the potential to be far more dangerous.

Chapter Twenty-Seven

ABEYI DISTRICT, SOUTH SUDAN

"I WANT to help you rescue Bishop." Jonjo was driving the pickup as it bounced along a rutted bush track. Four SFF fighters were huddled in the tray, wrapped in blankets to ward off the early morning cold.

"You're already helping. The more Janjaweed your men kill, the fewer we'll be up against." Mirza was sitting next to the young warrior in the cab as they drove toward the extraction point. As a precaution against possible Chinese informants, they reduced the new SFF recruits' exposure to PRIMAL's tilt-rotor aircraft.

"I know the ground better than anyone," continued Jonjo.

"True, but you're responsible for the lives of nearly a hundred men now. You cannot simply run off and leave them. They need you."

The SFF ranks had continued to grow and although Jonjo was only seventeen the militia relied heavily on him.

Another SSF veteran had stepped up to replace Garang but it was Jonjo who was leading ambushes and exacting a heavy toll on the Janjaweed patrols.

"This is the clearing, Jonjo."

The bush thinned out and Jonjo stopped the truck.

"Promise me you will come back," he demanded. "We need your help."

"I'll come back, my friend. I just need to make sure Aden is OK."

"Yes, I know. You're his guardian angel."

"In a way, yes."

Mirza jumped out of the truck with his sniper rifle and grabbed his equipment from the men in the back. They clambered over each other to shake his hand and wish him well. Throwing his gear over his shoulder, he strode into the clearing.

"Mirza," Jonjo yelled after him. "Remember to wear your talisman."

The PRIMAL operative gave him a thumbs-up and the truck sped off.

Dragonfly came in low over the treetops, its giant props hammering the surrounding trees with their wash. The gray tilt-rotor touched down and the side door slid open. Two men clad in camouflage fatigues and chest rigs jumped out, weapons held at the ready. They moved to either side of the aircraft, scanning for threats.

Mirza keyed his headset. "Dragonfly, this is Mirza. Permission to board?"

"Permission granted."

Mirza emerged from the bushes, walked swiftly to the side door, and clambered in. As he secured his gear under the nylon webbing seats, the armed men climbed back into the aircraft, sliding the door closed behind them. They dropped into the seats securing themselves for takeoff.

The engines roared and Dragonfly lurched into the air. It gained speed before the giant blades pitched forward and the flight smoothed.

"Hey, Mirza, *gut* to see you again." One of the men leaned forward, offering his gloved hand. He was tall and lanky with straw-blond hair, hard features, and a thick German accent.

"Good to see you too, Kurtz." Mirza and the former GSG 9 policeman were firm friends, training together regularly in the arts of covert entry and electronic surveillance.

"I also am glad to see you, comrade." The other man grabbed Mirza by the hand and pulled him out of his seat embracing him in a bear hug. Aleks was former Russian intelligence but sporting a shaved head and heavy beard, he looked like the type of man you'd find clad in a heavy flannel shirt swinging an axe on an Alaskan pine plantation.

Both men had been recruited on a previous PRIMAL mission. Under the leadership of Bishop they had thwarted the attempts of a Ukrainian arms dealer to deliver a WMD into the hands of Iran's most fanatical leaders. Both men had joined PRIMAL under Bishop's recommendation and they loved him like a brother.

As Dragonfly climbed into the morning sky, Mirza briefed them on the situation. The newcomers had arrived from a people-smuggling mission in Europe, one that had been put on hold given the current situation.

Aleks poured coffee from a thermos and they clustered around a tablet as Mirza outlined the key locations and events of the previous seven days.

At the end of the brief, the cockpit door opened and

Mitch joined them. "Righto, lads, we ready to get this show on the road?"

"Who... who's flying aircraft now?" A look of concern passed over Aleks's features.

Mitch laughed. "Keep your alans on, mate. She can fly herself." He pulled a rugged case out from under the seats and sat on it. Mirza handed him the tablet. He selected the aircraft's network and opened the intelligence package the Bunker had sent him.

"I wish we were here on better terms, lads, but it's not the case. Let's get right to it. They're holding Bishop at this oil refinery." He zoomed the map in. "Last night we intercepted a call between Yang and his boss indicating they're going to move him today to Khartoum. Their plan is to scoot down to this airfield, rendezvous with a flight, and transport him up north." Mitch traced the route from the PETROCON facility down to a short dirt strip approximately fifteen miles southwest of the refinery.

"Do we have any other intel confirming the move?" asked Kurtz.

"Sure do. There's a flight banging into the airfield today at 1030 hours." He pulled his iPRIMAL out of the thigh pocket of his flight suit and checked one of his notes. "A Fokker 50 scheduled for a touchdown and then onflight to Khartoum. Matches up with their plans. I'll also have a UAV watching the refinery to confirm any movement of prisoners." He turned his attention back to the tablet. "Our intel guys are assessing that a full road move would leave them exposed. That's why they've opted for a short trip to the airfield. They know that once he's in the air, we've run out of options."

"That's a valid assessment," added Mirza. "The SFF have ambushed a few convoys on the northern route."

"*Da*, it makes sense to me," said Aleks. "So where are we going to hit them?"

"The airfield, chaps. We've got a little under an hour to fine-tune the plan and execute it. Not much time, I know, but this will be our best opportunity to recover Bishop."

"Clocks ticking, *ja*. Nothing like a bit of pressure to bring out the best in us," added Kurtz.

"For Bishop, lads," said Mitch.

"For Bishop," they echoed.

Chapter Twenty-Eight

KURDUFAN DISTRICT, SUDAN

"TIME IS 1015 and you have a green light. Good luck, lads," Mitch's voice came over the radio.

Kurtz was the first out of the door, followed by Aleks and Mirza. Dragonfly was flying at maximum altitude, and at twenty five thousand feet they were breathing oxygen as they plummeted toward their target. The PRIMAL team had practiced this type of insertion hundreds of times. They swiftly stabilized themselves as they reached terminal velocity, belting toward the earth's surface at well over a hundred miles an hour.

They tracked in a line as they fell, each of them watching the dial on their altimeter as they approached 'pop' height. Kurtz deployed his chute first, prompting the other two operators to do the same. Under canopy they spiraled down toward the airfield.

"Breaking away!" Kurtz announced as he guided his canopy out of formation.

"As am I," confirmed Aleks.

The pair had identified their positions on either side of the runway with Mirza heading deeper, toward the apron.

Mirza overflew his intended drop zone then cut in sharply, corkscrewing down toward it. At the last moment he pulled on his toggles and touched down. In a few seconds he had shrugged out of his chute and collapsed the canopy. Working quickly he recovered his chute, stuffed it all into a camouflaged bag, and stashed it in the dry vegetation.

"Mike ready!" he announced over the radio as he unslung his sniper rifle and locked the folding stock in place.

"Kilo ready!" Kurtz's voice broadcast over his earpiece.

"Alpha ready," Aleks grunted.

"Roger, team. This is Dragonfly. I have visual on the target convoy, approximately four minutes out. Two trucks, three gun buggies, and one SUV." There was a short pause. "Oh, and Kilo, nice landing. I got that on camera. You OK?" Still at twenty-five thousand feet, Dragonfly was well out of visual range, but Mitch could monitor the situation through the surveillance pod.

"Screw you, Englander, what kind of *Dummkopf* puts up a fence in the middle of fucking nowhere," Kurtz replied.

Aleks's laughter filled the airways.

Mirza lay in a thicket of bush on a gradual rise near the end of the runway. In his camouflage outfit he was almost invisible, the pattern blending seamlessly with the surrounding terrain. Aleks and Kurtz would be doing the same, searching for the best piece of ground to target the approaching vehicles. All three were armed with sniper rifles; Mirza with his bolt-action .338 and the others with semi-automatic G28s. Together they covered three sides of the runway and the apron. The only area they did not block was the runway stretching away to the south, but the lack of cover would be fatal for anyone trying to escape that way.

"I have the Fokker on scope. Five minutes before it lands," Mitch said. "Remember, the two detainees are in the SUV." He had used a UAV to monitor the loading of the prisoners at the refinery.

The suppressed barrel of Mirza's sniper rifle peeked through the grass. Through the telescopic sight he had a clear view across the hard-packed earth of the runway. He glanced down at his iPRIMAL and noted the position of Kurtz. The German was almost directly opposite him. He would need to watch his fire.

"I have visual," reported Aleks as he looked through his sniper scope.

Within seconds the convoy sped onto the apron. The three gun buggies moved into a defensive posture with the SUV parked in the middle. Machine gunners in the turrets pointed their heavy weapons outwards. Other guards jumped from the trucks and formed a security screen. The Chinese security contractors went through the motions but weren't expecting a threat. Any vehicle approaching would be easily detected and apart from a few basic shelters, the airfield was empty. In the distance the engines of the Fokker could be heard.

Mirza scoped the black SUV. Through the heavily tinted windows he could make out the shape of two people in the backseats. Both had hoods on their heads. "I confirm, package is in the SUV. Neutralize the gunners first, then drivers, then engines, foot mobiles last, acknowledge."

Kurtz and Aleks each confirmed.

"Fokker touching down in thirty seconds," added Mitch.

"On my count." Mirza took up the slack in the trigger. "One, two, three!"

The rifle bucked in his shoulder as the .338 Lapua Magnum round exited the rifle. Almost simultaneously the gunners in the three gun buggies collapsed, their heads exploding.

One of the perimeter guards heard a round snapping past his head and dropped to the ground, firing a burst from his weapon.

Still hidden, the three PRIMAL snipers continued to engage. Bullets hit the bonnets and side panels of the three gun buggies. Holes appeared in the driver's-side window of the SUV. The airfield became alive with the sound of automatic gunfire as the Chinese guards blasted away, trying in vain to shoot at their hidden attackers.

Mirza switched his fire to immobilize the SUV, punching rounds into the front tires and engine block.

"Aircraft has touched down," said Mitch.

"Switch fire to dismounts." Mirza reloaded another ten-round magazine.

The PRIMAL operatives started engaging the guards. Two crumpled as they ran toward Kurtz's position looking for cover.

The roar of the Fokker 50's engines filled the air as the pilots reversed the thrust. The sight that greeted them was pure chaos.

Chinese contractors lay dead on the runway with the rest trying to find cover behind the crippled vehicles. Suppressed, surgical fire was hitting them from every angle, dropping them as they crouched behind their vehicles.

A quick-thinking buggy driver triggered his smoke discharger. It threw the smoke canisters down range with a loud thunk, then thick gray smoke spread out across the runway. It billowed up and around the Fokker. Its crew slammed on the brakes as hard as they could, terrified of what lay beyond the smoke. The engines screamed as they coaxed every ounce of reverse thrust from them.

As bedlam unfolded in the smoke, Mirza reached forward and calmly flicked his thermal imager over in front of his scope. It would take a few seconds to adjust.

The PRIMAL fire lapsed as Aleks and Kurtz changed their own scopes. In that time one of the guards managed to reach the heavy machine gun mounted on one of the buggies. He pushed the dead gunner's body out of the way and fired blindly into the smoke.

The 12.7mm armor-piercing rounds were designed to penetrate steel plate and made short work of the Fokker's soft aluminum skin. Two rounds slammed into the outside engine and the third, a tracer, tore a fist-size hole in its fuel tank.

The wing ignited and a sheet of flame shot into the air as the aircraft came to a complete halt, still a few hundred yards from the smoke-shrouded vehicles.

Their telescopic sights came online almost at exactly the same time. All three of them fired through the smoke at the white thermal outline of the gunner. The slugs hit him within the space of a second. His corpse slumped in the turret.

"Finish the rest, I'm closing in," announced Mirza.

"Acknowledged," said Aleks.

"I'm moving," spluttered Kurtz. "Smoke is everywhere."

"What the hell is going on down there, lads? Is there anything that isn't on fire?" asked Mitch.

"Wasn't us!" said Kurtz as he jogged into a new position.

The weight of Chinese return fire had dropped to almost nothing as Mirza trotted across open ground, heading for the vehicles. An infrared beacon pulsed on his armor, enabling Aleks and Kurtz to ID him through their sights. The smoke from the canisters was dispersing, replaced with haze and smoke from the burning passenger aircraft.

"That's the last of them," said Aleks as he placed a round through the forehead of the final remaining guard.

"I concur. I can see no squirters," reported Mitch from high above.

As he approached the vehicles, Mirza slung the sniper rifle over his shoulder and drew his pistol. He picked up his pace, moving directly for the SUV. The front window of the vehicle was shattered, the driver dead at the wheel.

When he almost reached the SUV the rear door on his side opened and a black-hooded figure stumbled out. One of the hostages had managed to get free. He could tell immediately it wasn't Bishop.

"JESS! GET DOWN!" Mirza screamed as he sprinted toward her. Behind her, in the SUV he'd spotted another figure armed with a submachine gun.

It happened in slow motion. Mirza was only a few steps away when the burst of fire hit her. She spun as the machine pistol fired at full automatic. Her body convulsed as bullets thudded into her.

She collapsed before Mirza reached her, his pistol still held ready. It jumped in his hand as he pumped the trigger. The .45 slug hit the Chinese guard square in the face as he climbed out of the SUV. The machine pistol fell from his hands as he toppled forward.

Mirza holstered his pistol and tore the black hood off Jess's face. She smiled up at him, blood oozing from her mouth and nose. "I knew you'd come. Bishop said you would."

"Dragonfly, I need evac now. Jess has been hit," Mirza

transmitted as he sliced open the back of her shirt with his hook knife. Tears formed in his eyes as he surveyed the damage the rounds had inflicted on her body. Blood flowed from no fewer than three entry wounds in her back and an exit wound in her lower abdomen.

He didn't look up as boots skidded to a halt in the dust next to him. Kurtz's rifle hit the ground with a clatter as the German tore his medical kit from his vest. "Bishop isn't here, Mirza."

"I know." Mirza had already packed the abdomen wound with wadding and was working frantically to stem the flow of blood from the wounds higher up in her back. He was kneeling with the American doctor sitting, slumped forward against him.

"Get a line in, Kurtz, or we're going to lose her."

"The bastards tricked us," Kurtz said as he opened the medical kit. "This whole show was a diversion." The lanky German inserted the catheter into the back of Jess's hand and hooked an IV bag to the insertion point. He held the bag high, forcing the fluid into her arm. Aleks arrived and held the bag, allowing Kurtz to focus his attention on sealing the other wounds.

"Mirza," Jess whispered between coughing fits. Blood was frothing at her lips. "Mirza, tell him I love him."

"You tell him, Jess. We'll get him back soon."

She shook her head as her eyes glazed over.

"No Mirza, you have to tell him." Her eyes closed and her head slumped forward over his shoulder.

"Kurtz, we're losing her." Mirza laid her down and tore an adrenaline shot from his vest. He plunged it into her chest and pressed the plunger home. There was a brief flicker of her eyelids then nothing.

"*Nein, nein, nein!*" Kurtz screamed. He pounded her chest

with his fist. "Don't fucking die on us. Don't you dare fucking die!"

"KURTZ, stop!" Mirza grabbed him by the shoulders. "She's gone, she's gone."

Kurtz leaped to his feet and stormed across to the SUV. He kicked the corpse of the man who had gunned down a woman he had never even known.

In the background the beat of Dragonfly's rotors could be heard and Mitch broadcast over the radio.

"Team, we've got a large convoy of hostiles heading your way. I'm on the deck in thirty seconds. Can I confirm that Bravo is not in location?"

"That's correct," said Mirza. "Bravo is not in our location. I have the doctor here but she hasn't made it." He made to pick up Jess's body.

Aleks stopped him. "You go, Mirza. I carry her." Mirza nodded his thanks and followed Kurtz to where the tilt-rotor touched down.

The big Russian slung his rifle and picked up Jess. He cradled her gently in his arms and walked to the waiting aircraft.

Behind them the Fokker burned, a dozen bodies littered the tarmac, and the six Chinese vehicles sat broken and useless, windows shattered and tires shot up. The Fokker's crew had escaped the flames and watched in silence as the three men and the dead body disappeared into the tilt-rotor. They shielded their eyes from the dust as it leaped into the air and disappeared into the distance.

NORTHWEST OF THE PETROCON OIL REFINERY, SUDAN

The two four-wheel drives raced along the main highway to Khartoum. Highway was a generous description for what was essentially a single-lane dirt track bulldozed through the Sudanese bushland.

The lead vehicle slowed as it approached a herd of cattle, the driver leaning on the horn. The cattle herder raised a fist as the four-wheel drives forced their way through his herd. Clear of the obstacle, the driver stomped on the accelerator and they resumed their breakneck pace toward the Sudanese capital.

In the backseat of the lead vehicle Bishop sat with his hands cuffed behind him, a black hood covering his head. It had been well over twelve hours since his capture and his body was letting him know it. His face was badly bruised, along with his torso, where Yang had used him as a punching bag. The gunshot wound to his upper arm throbbed; every bump sent jolts of pain through the injury. He fought hard to suppress even the slightest of moans, intent on depriving Yang of that small victory.

As he sat in silence his thoughts were preoccupied with Jess. He had not seen her since their arrival at the refinery and he hoped she was in the vehicle behind them. He knew if they had separated them, then she had very little hope of rescue.

A shrill ring tone snapped his thoughts back to the present. Sitting in the passenger seat, Yang took the call. A short conversation in Mandarin ensued. Bishop listened intently, hoping to pick up a word or two, or even garner the slightest information from his tone.

Yang terminated the call. "It would seem your friends

fell for my little deception, Aden. They attempted to recover you from the airfield, but you were not there apparently." Yang laughed. "Very unfortunate for you. It would seem the SEALs are not coming to rescue you anytime soon."

Yang and the driver laughed. Bishop sat in silence.

"What, no smart comment? No jokes, Aden?"

Bishop sat perfectly still, his mind racing. Was Yang trying to trick him? Had the team really fallen for a ruse? Had anyone been killed?

"I have a joke for you, Aden. What did your girlfriend say to the rescue team?"

Bishop was silent.

"Nothing, because she was dead!"

Yang's words hit Bishop like a kick to the chest. Grief coursed through his body. Tears ran down his cheeks, hidden by the black hood. He tasted blood as he bit down on his lip in a long, silent scream. Forcing his emotions under control he let out a breath and spoke.

"You're a dead man, Yang!"

Chapter Twenty-Nine

THE BUNKER, LASCAR ISLAND

"CHUA, we've got a fix on the number."

PRIMAL's intelligence officer leaped up from his desk. "Where is he?"

"Somewhere over central China, current ground speed nearly eight hundred clicks. Heading west." The intel analyst pointed to the blinking dot on his screen.

"Zhu's on his way to Sudan," said Chua, squinting at the monitor. "He'll be on the ground before we're ready." He had only been back in the Bunker for an hour, heading there immediately after his flight from Shanghai had landed.

"Time to throw out the bait," Chua said as he crossed the operations room floor. He knocked once on Vance's door and stuck his head in.

"Yes," Vance grunted from behind his desk. The PRIMAL commander looked grave. With Bishop captured and the recovery mission a failure, the stakes had never been higher.

"Zhu's on his way to Khartoum."

Vance stood up. "Let's put in the call. What's the latest on the team?"

They headed for the conference room.

"I spoke briefly to Mitch. They're taking it hard. Although it's Kurtz who's taken it the worst."

"Kurtz? Why?" Vance sat at the head of the table in the conference room. One of the technicians was already there with a laptop.

"Apparently the kid's fallen for a girl in Europe. She looks a bit like Jess."

"A girl from their recent job?"

"Yes, but I'm not across the details yet."

"What about Mirza?"

"He's OK. You know what he's like."

"Yeah, I pity the poor fucker that gets in his way now." Vance looked to the technician at the end of the conference table. "We good to go?"

"Yes, sir," the man replied.

"Let's get to it."

Chua picked the headset off the table, put it on, and gave the technician a nod. The speakers in the room came alive with the sound of a number being dialed. There was a pause, followed by a dial tone. The phone rang three times before it connected.

"*Zhè shì shuí?*" asked a voice on the other end.

"Mr. Zhu, the question I would ask is not who is this but why I am calling." Chua's voice was digitally altered; through the room's speakers it sounded distant and metallic.

"You have my son?" Zhu asked.

"This is correct, and you have one of my men."

"Yes, and you have already tried to recover him and failed."

"Zhu, I am not here to discuss the past, I am here to discuss the future. Do you wish to negotiate or would you prefer me to end this discussion?" Chua asked calmly.

There was a pause. "No, we will negotiate," Zhu said softly.

"Good. It is not my intent to harm your son in any way. I simply wish to return him to you in good health and receive my man in the same condition. Is this clear?"

"Do you know who you are talking to? I am—"

"I do indeed," interrupted Chua. "But do you have any idea who you are talking to?"

There was another pause before Chua continued. "I didn't think so. Now listen very carefully. Tomorrow morning you will be contacted on this number in Khartoum. You will have my man with you and we will conduct the swap. Is this clear?"

"Perfectly."

"Then I will speak to you soon. Have an enjoyable flight, Zhu."

The technician terminated the call. "Signal strength was strong, Chen. If they managed a trace, they'll be getting a small bed-and-breakfast in St. Louis."

"Good work, team," said Vance. "Let's just hope they take the bait. Chua, I'll leave you to brief Mitch and the boys."

KHARTOUM, SUDAN

Zhu sat in the Nile River Café of the Corinthian Hotel sipping green tea from his favorite china cup. He gazed out the windows of Khartoum's only five-star hotel, watching a barge nose its way down the Nile. Around him a team of suit-wearing bodyguards did their best to remain unobtrusive.

Yang entered the café and crossed the polished marble floor to stand silently at his master's shoulder.

"This china has been in my family for three generations, Yang." Zhu placed his cup down. "My grandfather took it from the belongings of a British officer in 1901. He passed it to my father, who passed it to me." Zhu switched his gaze from the windows to his subordinate's face. "Yang, one day I would like to pass it to my son."

Yang nodded. "Everything is ready, sir. The chief of police has men across the city. Our own people are with them to ensure there are no mistakes."

"And our hostage, Aden?"

"My men have him ready at the embassy."

Zhu wiped his mouth with the corner of a spotless white napkin. "Has Xinhai been able to make him talk?"

"No, not without injuring him. You gave strict instructions."

"Yes, I know. However, if today doesn't go as planned those instructions will change."

Zhu's phone beeped, indicating he had received a message. He read it and showed it to Yang.

I hope you enjoyed your breakfast. Please proceed to the roof of the hotel and await further instructions.

Yang spoke into a radio as Zhu rose from his chair. "Secure the roof. Alert all units that we have contact."

"I think it would be wise to follow their directions as much as possible," said Zhu as they walked to the elevators.

"I agree."

They exited the elevator at the top floor and took the emergency stairwell to the roof. Chinese personnel already manned all the doors and Zhu's bodyguards escorted him every step of the way. By the time they reached the top of the building, another security team had cordoned off the area. Security contractors armed with sniper rifles were positioned on all sides.

Zhu was breathing heavily from the flight of stairs and barely had time to catch his breath before his phone rang. He answered, putting it on speaker.

"Listen very carefully." It was the same metallic voice as before. "Southeast of your position is the Souq Arabi. You are to release my man at the western entrance in five minutes."

"And my son?"

"If you look due east of your position you will see a construction site with a large crane."

Zhu rushed to the edge of the building and peered out over the city.

"Yes, I can see the crane."

"Very good. If you look closely you will see that there are two men on the end of the crane. One of them is your son."

Sure enough, out on the arm of the crane were two figures.

The voice continued, "If Aden is not released within the time period, your son will fall from the crane. Four minutes and thirty seconds, Zhu." The voice hung up.

The two figures on the crane dropped.

"NOOO!" screamed Zhu, gripping the railing.

One of the figures fell a short distance before dangling under the crane like a Christmas decoration. The other gathered speed, and like a spider it dropped on a thin line before it disappeared behind a block of apartments.

Yang took a sniper rifle off a guard, positioned it on the railing, and pointed it at the dangling figure. "Is that him?"

Zhu took Yang's place behind the rifle and lowered his face to the optic. Through the magnified scope he could make out the features of the person hanging upside down with the rope tied to his legs. "Yes, that's him. It's him!"

Yang issued orders into his radio. "Take the prisoner to the western entrance to the market and wait for my order. Have every other unit form an outer perimeter. No one is to enter or leave the area without my approval." He looked out over the cityscape to the blob dangling from the crane. "And get the helicopter here immediately."

Chapter Thirty

SOUQ ARABI, KHARTOUM

THE WHITE PETROCON van screeched to a halt outside the western entrance to the souq. Two Chinese men dressed in coveralls jumped out and slid the side door open. They dragged the hooded prisoner from the van and stood him at the entry to the market. He was barefoot, dressed in the same torn, bloodied shirt and pants that he'd been captured in.

Despite the black hood, the sounds and smells of the market washed over Bishop. He could make out traces of spices among the smell of unwashed humans, dried meat, and smoke. The sounds of bartering in a multitude of languages and dialects mixed with the sound of the city's traffic. He knew they had brought him to a public place. His pulse quickened. They were going to release him!

He heard the snap of wire cutters and in an instant his hands were free. He squinted as the hood was torn from his head. Rough hands pushed him forward and he struggled to adjust to the harsh brightness of the sun. The noise around him was even more intense than before. His survival instinct kicked in and he pushed forward to put as much ground between him and his captors as possible. Dashing through the crowd, he joined the throngs of shoppers hunting for a bargain. His eyes darted left and right, looking for a trap, searching for someone following him.

"I can't see him, comrade," Aleks transmitted on his radio. The Russian was near the entrance and had caught a glimpse of Bishop as the PETROCON workers had pushed him into the crowd.

Aleks gently shouldered his way through the shoppers, trying not to draw undue attention. He was dressed in a traditional robe wearing a little cap and sporting a heavy beard. He looked like an Arab; the satchel that bounced at his hip was a common accessory.

"Keep looking. We'll find him," Mirza replied. He was on the other side of the entrance and, like Aleks, dressed in robes.

"We've got about two minutes before they recover the boy and the *Scheiss* really hits the fan," transmitted Kurtz. The German was a mile away; having rappelled from the crane.

Oblivious to the presence of his fellow PRIMAL operatives, Bishop was doing everything he could to blend into the crowd. He darted down a side alley packed with clothing. Robes, hijabs, and knockoff Western brands were stacked waist high on cardboard and hung from the rafters. He grabbed a T-shirt, discarding his old bloody shirt as he ran into an even tighter walkway filled with Chinese-made cooking utensils. He stumbled as he pulled his new T-shirt on, bracing himself against a stack of flimsy plastic chairs. The tower of Chinese goods teetered before falling sideways with a crash. An Arab dressed in a vibrant yellow robe accosted him with a machine gun flow of obscenities he didn't understand.

"I'm sorry, I'm sorry," he mumbled, bursting out the other end of the laneway into a pavilion filled with foodstuffs. He paused, gathering himself as he scanned the crowd.

"Shit!" He spotted a middle-aged African watching him closely. Was it one of Yang's men? The African started walking toward him and Bishop picked out the thin, clear cable running from under his shirt collar into his ear. Bishop turned and moved as fast as he could away down another lane.

"I've got him," Mirza announced. "He's in the main spice hall, western end. I think he's got a tail."

"*Da*, I'm moving there now," replied Aleks.

As the big Russian barged his way through the crowd a helicopter thundered overhead.

Kurtz's voice came over the radio. "We're running out of time. In a few minutes they'll be on us like Oprah on a donut. Every entry point I've passed is crawling with security." Kurtz was making a beeline for the safe house and extraction point.

"We're moving as fast as we can," replied Aleks.

"*Schnell*, big man, *Schnell!*"

Aleks barged his way into the spices pavilion. In the heat and humidity the open bowls of chili, saffron, cumin, and other popular ingredients were pungent. Sweat had already drenched his robes. It was running down his face in rivulets and the smell compounded his discomfort. He had been dragged out of an operation in Eastern Europe for this. Bish was definitely going to owe him a cold beer or six, he thought. He got a glimpse of his friend on the other side of the stalls. Bishop was not looking good. His face was badly bruised and he looked paler than usual. With his scruffy beard he could be mistaken for a homeless bum.

"I've got him, Mirza."

"Yes, I see you."

Aleks scanned the crowd. He could not see Mirza anywhere.

"We've got multiple hostiles in close vicinity," continued Mirza.

Aleks looked around. He counted at least two men dressed in plainclothes that were paying particularly close attention to Bishop.

"OK, I've got a plan," said Mirza. "Aleks, you grab Bish. I'll create a distraction and take care of the hostiles. On my count: one, two, three."

BUILDING SITE, KHARTOUM

The PETROCON helicopter hovered above the construction site. Below it, on the crane, two Sudanese police officers were hauling a terrified young man up from where he was hanging. It took both of them to winch the portly individual up onto the walkway that ran the length of the crane's boom. Once they had him secured, they waved the pilot down. The helicopter bumped its skids up against the boom and all three men scrambled into the cabin.

Zhu was waiting with Yang when the chopper touched down on the tennis court in front of the Corinthian Hotel. The police officers clad in their overalls and harnesses led the terrified youth from the aircraft. He was visibly shaken by the experience.

Zhu greeted him with a hug and a broad smile. Then as he looked over the boy, the smile dropped and his grandfatherly features turned to fury.

"YANG, WHO IS THIS?" he screamed.

Yang was confused. "It's your son, Ping!"

"Do you think I'm stupid? This is not my son! They have made a fool of us. Find my son, Yang! FIND HIM NOW!"

Yang grabbed the chin of the young Chinese man and studied his face. The resemblance was uncanny: the same squinting eyes, the pig-like features. Even the build and the clothing was spot on. The veins bulged in Yang's neck as he clenched his jaw. He lifted his radio and screamed into it, "All units converge on the market. Capture the American!"

Yang grabbed an assault rifle from a nearby guard and strode across to the helicopter. Wrenching back the side door, he sat on the floor of the aircraft, his feet braced against the skids.

The copilot handed him a headset and the blades beat faster as the aircraft generated lift. It rose off the tennis court, clearing the fence before it turned toward the market.

Yang had the crew tune the radio to his command frequency so he could coordinate the ground forces. He pressed the transmit button on the headset's cable. "The American is to be captured at all costs. Anyone providing assistance to him is to be killed on sight."

On the ground his guards relayed the commands to the Sudanese security forces. Heavily armed police established roadblocks and security checkpoints. Plainclothes police swarmed into the market. The hunt was on.

SOUQ ARABI, KHARTOUM

Mirza threw the distraction grenade as far as he could. It arced out of the entrance to the foodstuffs hall, landed on a hawker's awning, and detonated, spitting sparks as it erupted in a volley of simulated gunfire. Simultaneously he dropped a smoke grenade and kicked it under a bench laden with dried fruit.

The sounds of gunfire panicked the entire market. The Sudanese people were accustomed to the horrors of war and needed no prompting to flee. The food hall burst into turmoil as people pushed each other out of the way to escape.

Aleks reached out and grabbed Bishop's arm, dragging him into a narrow corridor stacked with bags of rice. Bishop swung his fist and Aleks caught it with his other arm. "Boss, it's me. It's Aleks."

Bishop looked into the big man's face and a grin spread across his own. "Thank God! It's so fucking good to see you." He wrapped his arms around the Russian. "Aleks, how the hell did you get me released?"

"Prisoner swap," said Aleks. "No time for details." He dug into his satchel and handed Bishop a robe. "Put this on."

As they sorted Bishop's outfit, two dark-skinned men shoved their way toward them, pistols drawn. Smoke had filled the stalls and the gunmen fought through the rush of panicked shoppers. They were not the only ones hunting. Mirza let the crowd push him toward the two men and his suppressed pistol spat twice, two neat holes appearing in his robe. Both gunmen collapsed in front of the alley. Mirza stood over them and fired a shot into each man's head.

"We need to move." He gave Bishop a nod as he stepped over the corpses.

"Weapon?" asked Bishop.

Aleks handed him a handgun and three spare magazines. He stuffed them into his pants under his robe.

All three PRIMAL operatives were now dressed in traditional Arabic garb.

"Kurtz, are you in position?" Mirza broadcast over his radio.

"*Jawohl*, I'm positioned due west of your current location."

"What's the reception—" Mirza paused as the PETROCON helicopter roared overhead. "What's the reception party going to be like?"

"About twenty heavily armed police, half a dozen PETROCON *Dummkopfen*, and that damn helicopter. It's good though. I have arranged a little surprise for them." The German laughed manically.

The three men kept moving with the crowds as they surged toward the exit. Aleks hung back with Bishop as Mirza pushed forward to scan for hostiles.

"They're checking everyone as they leave," transmitted Mirza. Ahead of him Sudanese policemen armed with AK-47s were checking the faces of everyone. They were even forcing women to one side where a female officer was inspecting under their burkas.

"Our disguises are not that good," said Aleks.

Mirza was only a few steps from the police now. Aleks and Bishop were half a dozen people behind. Bodies pressed up against them, forcing them into the checkpoint.

"Kurtz, I think it's time for that distraction," said Mirza.

"*Ja*, standby."

Mirza was nearly at the front of the line. "Kurtz, now would be good."

"*Ja, ja*, I am on it."

The man in front of Mirza was being eyeballed by a policeman. Mirza bowed his head and stepped forward, his right hand gripping the pistol under his robe.

The explosion caught Mirza by surprise. Across the street a car detonated in a massive ball of flame. The guard dropped to the ground and Mirza stepped past him, turning down the street. He glanced over his shoulder; Aleks and Bishop were hot on his heels.

Further up the street another vehicle exploded, with a huge fireball rolling up into the air. People were screaming and shouting. The bedlam from the market had now spilled onto the streets.

"Jesus, Kurtz, we wanted a distraction, not a massacre."

"Keep your panties on, Mirza. All bang, no frag. Just for show, *ja*!"

Mirza double-checked his iPRIMAL. The evacuation point was only a few blocks away.

"Kurtz, are you at the RV?" he asked.

"Affirmative. RV is secure."

"Roger, we're five minutes out."

"I'll pass it on to Mitch," Kurtz said.

They chose a less direct route to the rendezvous, using alleyways and back streets to avoid running into any Sudanese security forces. A helicopter could still be heard overhead but the streets they chose were empty; the explosions had sent people scurrying for their homes.

The evacuation point was a drab-looking building, three stories tall with a large flat roof. It towered over the surrounding single-story compounds. Solidly constructed, it looked like it had once housed a workshop of some description. One of Chua's agents in Khartoum had picked it, leasing it for a full month.

Mirza rapped his knuckles against the heavy steel door. It creaked open and Kurtz greeted them with a broad smile painted across his face. "You liked my fireworks, *ja*?"

"You're nuttier than a squirrel turd, Kurtz!" said Bishop. "But yeah, I liked your fireworks."

"So you OK, boss?" asked the German as they walked up a staircase to the top floor.

"A few scratches and a couple of bruises, mate. I'll live." He limped up the stairs, his bare feet leaving specks of blood on the concrete.

The top floor was a single room. Someone had ripped out all the furnishings, the broken windows suggesting everything had been thrown onto the street. There was a box sitting in the middle of the floor. Inside it was fresh fruit, a pair of slip-on shoes, and bottles of water. Next to the box were two AK-47s and a pile of magazines.

"Chua, no doubt. Thinks of everything." Bishop slipped the shoes onto his battered feet. "Perfect fit!"

"Aleks, Kurtz, long guns at the windows," Mirza ordered.

The two men grabbed AKs, loaded them, and positioned themselves at the openings, watching the street below.

"Aden, there is something I need to tell you," Mirza said softly.

"Yang told me Jess is dead. It's true, isn't it?"

"It was my fault, I... we..."

"That's bullshit, Mirza, and you know it," Bishop said angrily. "Yang's men killed her and we'll make them pay. It is that simple."

Mirza nodded, noticing his friend had tears in his eyes.

"*Achtung! Panzer!*" screamed Kurtz from his window.

"What?" Bishop yelled back.

"Tank!" confirmed Aleks. "And that damn helicopter."

Bishop sprinted to the window. Sure enough, at the end of the street sat a Type 88 main battle tank.

"Zhu's really pulling out all the stops, isn't he?" Bishop said. "Anyone would think we've got something he wants."

"We kind of do, boss!" said Aleks. "We've got his son."

Bishop looked confused. "Then who did you swap for me?"

"Someone kid Chua found on Chinese Facebook," explained Mirza. "Kurtz, how long till we evac?"

The German checked his watch. "Four minutes."

"INCOMING!" screamed Aleks, diving from the window.

The building shook as a 105mm round slammed into the bottom floor. The explosion sent dust rolling up the staircase and left their ears ringing.

The loud bark of an AK-47 added to the calamity as Kurtz fired his weapon at full automatic down the street. "*Mutter*fuckers!"

"Upstairs! Go, go, go! We've got ten seconds!" Mirza ordered, knowing a follow-up shot from the tank would not be far behind. "Autoloader," he explained as he grabbed Bishop by the arm and dragged him up the staircase onto the roof. They dove to the ground and Aleks slid in next to them.

Kurtz was still firing his weapon out the window below.

There was another boom as the tank fired. The round slammed into the weak concrete, blowing a hole in the side of the building. Kurtz sprinted across the floor for the stairs as it collapsed behind him. He barely made it, hitting the staircase as the entire floor collapsed.

"We need to get out of here!" he screamed.

"*Da*, thanks Einstein," said Aleks.

Another round slammed into the building, shaking its foundations.

"One minute," announced Kurtz.

"COME OUT WITH YOUR HANDS UP OR WE WILL FIRE AGAIN!" the megaphone on the helicopter hovering above the tank blared.

"It's that cocksucker Yang," said Bishop. "How the hell did he find us?"

"Must have tracked us with the chopper," Kurtz said.

"Give me the AK," Bishop said, reaching out for the German's weapon.

"No," snapped Mirza. "There will be time for revenge but now we need them to think we're going to surrender. We need to buy time."

"Fuck that!" Kurtz said as he knelt over the lip that ringed the roof and fired another burst from his AK.

Bullets snapped over their heads as the Sudanese police returned fire.

"Another excellent idea," said Aleks as they all pushed their bodies flat against the dusty concrete.

"THIS IS YOUR LAST WARNING. COME OUT NOW WITH YOUR HANDS UP OR WE WILL FIRE!"

Slowly the four PRIMAL operatives got to their feet.

YANG WATCHED them from the helicopter, satisfied he had them trapped. He hit the transmit button on his radio and ordered one of the police squads to secure the building and arrest the fugitives.

Zhu would be placated; they would now have three

more prisoners to negotiate the release of Ping. That meant he could let The Butcher wring as much information out of Aden as they wanted.

He looked down into the alley and watched the Sudanese police advance toward the building. After their last run-in with Aden and his colleagues, they were taking no chances.

"Put us down behind the tank," he ordered the pilot. Yang wanted to be on the ground ready to greet Aden, and he smiled at the thought. In his pocket his phone buzzed. He unfolded it, pulled off his headset, and held it up to his ear.

"Hello!" he yelled into the phone over the helicopter's noise.

He cupped his hand over the phone, pressing it up against his head.

"Yang!"

"Who's this?"

"It's me, Aden."

Yang laughed. "You have rung to surrender?"

"Not really. More to say FUCK YOU!"

"THANKS," Bishop tossed the phone back to Mirza. "Kurtz, time check."

"Now!" the German announced.

The tilt-rotor appeared from behind the building as Kurtz spoke. Its blades thrashed the surrounding streets with downwash sending a cloud of dust billowing out from the extraction point. It hung in the air like a predatory bird, its weapon pod unsheathed like a set of talons.

The roar of the minigun filled the air as the automatic

targeting system poured rounds into the Type 88 tank. The stream of armor-piercing rounds lashed it, smashing sights and tearing antennas.

Mirza, Bishop, Aleks, and Kurtz clapped their hands to their ears as thousands of casings cascaded down on top of them, a shower of hot brass.

Inside the tank the crew cowered as the deafening blast of rounds slammed into the armor. The crew commander jerked at the trigger, sending a final round downrange.

It screamed down the alley past the SWAT team and slammed into the bottom floor, tearing the guts from the building.

"MITCH, WE NEED EXFIL NOW!" Mirza screamed into his radio.

"Wilco, chaps."

Mitch fired one last burst, this time at the PETROCON helicopter that was landing behind the tank. The helo jolted and dropped, crashing into the street.

Mitch brought Dragonfly down on the flat roof, hovering with wheels inches off the surface. The building gave a groan and a shudder.

"She's gonna go!" yelled Bishop as he leaped through the door and into the aircraft. Kurtz was hot on his heels, throwing himself inside. Aleks followed, barreling into the cabin.

With a shudder, the entire building slipped sideways, the roof dropping from horizontal to a 45-degree angle. Mirza slid, scrabbling for a foothold.

"COME ON!" Bishop screamed from the doorway.

Mirza yelled as he sprinted as hard as he could, driving up the rooftop as it started to collapse. He reached the edge and leaped into the air, hitting the lip of the aircraft's door with a thud. As he slid backward, Bishop grabbed his arm and hauled him into the cabin.

"Punch it, Chewie!" Bishop yelled.

Mitch gave his best impression of a Wookie as he pushed the aircraft's throttles forward. Dragonfly's engines roared as the props transitioned forward, rocketing the little aircraft toward the horizon.

THE PETROCON HELICOPTER lay crumpled in the middle of the street, rotors bent and ruined. Yang had been thrown free and lay stunned as he watched the rescue in disbelief.

Twice now Aden had escaped him. The man was a walking, talking, wrecking ball, and Yang's aching body would not let him forget it. The Chinese operative rose stiffly to his feet, the pain reminding him of the other humiliating defeats. A blown-up cargo ship, shot-down attack helicopter, and now he had been shot down again; Yang wasn't sure if he was more furious or shocked at the turn of events.

For a few seconds he contemplated calling the Sudanese Air Force and scrambling jets to interdict the tilt-rotor. He shook his head. What would that achieve? Aden and his men may die, but he would be no closer to revealing the identity of their shadowy organization.

His phone started ringing. It was Zhu. Yang took a deep breath and answered the call. At least he had one last chance to seek vengeance and redeem himself.

Chapter Thirty-One

ABU DHABI INTERNATIONAL AIRPORT, UNITED ARAB EMIRATES

THE LASCAR LOGISTICS terminal at Abu Dhabi was extensive. Rows of heavy cargo aircraft waited to load and unload. A fleet of ground support vehicles assisted in the process, moving cargo back and forth from a freight terminal. The maintenance hangars were huge, large enough to fit the hulking four-engine Ilyushins. To the outside observer it all looked legitimate, another air-freight operator conducting day-to-day operations.

Mitch landed the PRIMAL tilt-rotor just after sundown. They came in fast with navigation lights turned off, landing vertically in the middle of the apron reserved for Lascar aircraft. Mitch taxied Dragonfly to the last hangar. The giant metal doors slid apart and they nosed in next to a business jet.

Dragonfly's side door slid open and Bishop stepped tenderly onto the polished concrete floor. The rest of the team followed, heading across to the briefing room. Behind them the hangar doors slammed shut. The Priority Movements Airlift facility was secure.

Bishop slumped into a sofa as Aleks made a beeline for the refrigerator. It was well stocked with beer. "Cold one, comrade?" he asked.

"Hell yeah, mate, all I want is a beer, a shower, and to hit the rack!"

Kurtz, Mirza, and Mitch all filed into the room and the Russian handed them cold beers as they passed the fridge.

"So now we work out how to kill that Chinese bastard, *ja*!" said Kurtz.

"Not me." Mirza shook his head. "I need to get back to Africa and help Jonjo take care of Garang."

"I'm with Kurtz," said Aleks. "The girl was killed by the Chinese. The Chinaman needs to die first!"

"It seems like you've all got vengeance on your mind," Mitch commented as he dropped onto the couch next to Bishop. "What about you, Bish? You're the one that took all the hits. Who gets it first?"

Bishop took a gulp of his beer and stared at the wall. "They'll all get what's coming to them, mate. I want payback for Jess more than anyone here, but the mission comes first and that means forcing Zhu to withdraw all military aid to Sudan. I'm guessing that's why we've got his son, yeah?"

"That's Chua's plan," said Mirza. "We've got orders scheduled for 1100 hours in the morning to discuss the next phase."

"So where's the kid now?" asked Bishop.

"No idea," said Mirza. "All I know is Saneh's babysitting him."

Bishop raised an eyebrow.

Mitch slapped him on the knee. "I don't think you've got much competition from him, champ. Right now he's probably sitting in the corner of a room terrified out of his mind as that woman of yours field-strips a pistol whilst hanging from the roof blindfolded."

They all laughed except Bishop, who drank the last of his beer, then stood. "Team, we've got six hours till the orders group with the Bunker. I for one could do with some sleep. Let's reconvene here at 1030 tomorrow, OK?" Bishop dropped the empty beer bottle in the trash as he left the room.

"How's he doing, Mirza?" asked Mitch shortly after.

"Bit bruised but he's OK." Mirza had given Aden a full physical on the trip back from Khartoum. "You know what he's like. He'll bottle up the emotion until he can focus it on the bad guys."

"I want to see him tear the arms off that Chinese bastard!" growled Kurtz.

"*Da*, like those people-smuggling pieces of shit in Budapest," agreed Aleks.

Before joining the Sudanese recovery operation, the German and the Russian had been tracking down a people-smuggling ring based out of Hungary. Now that Bishop was safe they were keen to kill Yang and get back to work. Both were heavily invested, emotionally, in the European operation.

Mirza rose next. "The Bunker will confirm what's happening tomorrow. I suggest you all get some sleep as well." He threw his own bottle in the bin and left the room.

Kurtz and Aleks followed, discussing some of the finer details of what they'd like to do to Yang. Finally it was only Mitch left. He let out a sigh, kicked his legs up on the sofa, and set his alarm for an hour's time. Five hours should be enough to run the preflight checks on Dragonfly.

THE BUNKER, LASCAR ISLAND

"Seriously, Vance, how long do I have to keep babysitting the kid?" asked Saneh.

"Twenty-four hours. Chua wants to let Zhu simmer a bit before he makes his demands." Vance was in his office talking to PRIMAL's only female operative via the island's wireless network. Saneh was only a few miles away on an isolated part of the island.

"Twenty-four more hours? I won't lie, Vance. There's a good chance I'll kill the spoilt little shit before then. He whines like a schoolgirl."

"He's on a tropical island with a beautiful woman, what's his problem?"

"I might've taken him for a run."

Vance laughed. "Tubby little guy struggled, did he?"

"A little. He vomited twice before we even made it to the first ridgeline."

"Just make sure you keep him alive."

"Fine. Vance, how's Bishop doing?"

"He's OK. Needs a bit of down time. The boys should be back tomorrow. Look, I've got to go. We've got an O-group in a few hours. I'll let you know what falls out of it."

"Thanks. Saneh out."

Vance walked from his office into the operations room. There were only a few people at their desks. The screen that outlined the status of all the units currently in the field was empty. All PRIMAL personnel were safe and sound. For the

Director of Operations that meant a good night's sleep for once.

"Good outcome all round," said Chua from the other side of the room. "We finish negotiating with Zhu, wrap up the traitor Garang, and we're done."

"Yeah, I can't help but feel we got real lucky on this one, bud. It could easily have been Bishop going home in a body bag." Vance turned to the watchkeeper. "That reminds me, what's happening with the girl's body?"

The watchkeeper looked up from his terminal. "Sir, one of the SFF fighters, Jonjo, returned her to the hospital in Juba. From there she was moved to the US embassy."

"OK. Her father is some kind of bigwig surgeon, right? I want to make sure he gets more than a short note from the State Department. He deserves to know his daughter died for a just cause."

Chua nodded. "The SFF have put a serious dent in both the Sudanese deniable capability and the Chinese will to continue the fight. From what I understand, Doctor Hutton played a critical role in that."

"Mirza spoke very highly of her. She saved a lot of lives."

"Her loss won't be in vain, Vance. We're in a good position now. We've cost PETROCON and China a lot of resources and should be able to force Zhu into withdrawing his support for the Janjaweed. Maybe even a Chinese vote in the UN Security Council for an increased peacekeeping force."

"You seriously think that's an option? You think Zhu has that much clout?"

"He regularly meets members of the People's National Council. He's got serious connections and wealth, and wants his son alive."

"Sir," the watchkeeper interrupted them, "you've got a call. It's Tariq."

Chua gave Vance a sideways look. PRIMAL's wealthy benefactor rarely called them. Chua took the call. The conversation was short; the owner of Lascar Logistics and former head of Abu Dhabi Police Special Branch was a busy man. Chua handed the phone back to the watchkeeper.

"We've got a big problem."

"What?" asked Vance.

"Yang has been spotted in Abu Dhabi."

"What the fuck?"

"The security system at the airport detected him but he escaped arrest," Chua explained.

"How the hell did he track the team?"

"There's only one way that could have happened."

"Bishop!"

"He's the only one they've had contact with. They can't have tracked Dragonfly. Mitch runs bug sweeps over it regularly, it's got no markings, and he ran a crazy Ivan flight path. It has to be Bishop."

"Wake the boys up. They've got work to do."

Chapter Thirty-Two

PRIORITY MOVEMENTS AIRLIFT HANGAR, ABU DHABI INTERNATIONAL AIRPORT

"ARE you sure you know what you're doing, Kurtz?" Bishop asked.

"Just hold still, *ja*!"

As soon as the Bunker had informed them that Yang had tracked them to Abu Dhabi Mitch had run a scanner over Bishop and his clothing. The PRIMAL technician had found a very low-frequency transponder emitting from the gunshot wound in Bishop's arm. Kurtz had immediately volunteered to remove the device, claiming he was an advanced medic during his GSG 9 days. With Aleks assisting, they proceeded to use the hangar's waiting room as a makeshift surgery.

"Aleks, give me the injection," asked Kurtz.

The big man passed him a prepackaged local anesthetic.

Kurtz plunged the injection into Bishop's arm.

"Fuck me! What are you, a goddamn horse doctor? It's my arm, not a cow's ass."

"*Du bist ein Mädchen.*"

Aleks laughed.

"What did he say?"

"He says you are a girl."

"Hmmph, fair enough. Now give me another scotch."

"*Nein,*" Kurtz said, shaking his hand. "Alcohol will mix with the local anesthetic and make you sleepy."

"No, we don't want that. I've got to find that bastard, Yang."

"Can you feel this?" Kurtz asked as he poked his finger into the stitched arm wound."

"Nope!"

"Perfect." Despite his lankiness, Kurtz could have been a surgeon. He cut the stitches and opened the wound with a deft hand. Then he reached into the hole with a pair of forceps and drew out the tracker, dropping it into the plastic container that Aleks was holding.

The device was the size of a large vitamin capsule. The Russian squirted it clean with a jet of saline solution and handed it to Mitch.

The technician gave a low whistle. "This is state-of-the-art, lads. You'd expect something like this out of the NSA or GCHQ, not the bloody ChiComs." He opened a small metal box and dropped it inside, shielding the signal. "I'll give it the once-over when we get back to the Bunker. Might be worth getting a few of our own."

Kurtz closed the wound on Bishop's arm with a row of neat tight stitches. A bandage completed the treatment. "There. Good as new."

Bishop grasped his friend's shoulder with his good arm. "You're a good man to have around, Kurtz."

The German beamed.

The door to the room opened and Mirza entered. "I checked the perimeter. No sign of Yang or any of his men."

Mitch nodded. "I don't think they were able to get an accurate fix on the signal. It may have led them to Abu Dhabi but that's it. My guess, one of the sensors at the Chinese Embassy got a sniff of it on the flight in, but inside the walls of this hangar the signal would have been cut off."

"They know we came in by aircraft, though. That narrows it down," stated Mirza. "And Yang knows we use the tilt-rotor."

"True," said Bishop. "Yang will probably be looking for Dragonfly."

Mirza was deep in thought as he took a bottle of water from the fridge. "I know I have only been with PRIMAL for a year, but this is the closest I've seen to our organization being compromised. If it weren't for the airport security, the Chinese would definitely have surprised us."

A new voice interrupted them. "You're lucky I'm keeping watch then," said Tariq Ahmed. Dressed in one of his signature suits the head of Lascar Logistics was standing in the doorway stroking his perfectly manicured beard. In his other hand he held an exquisite brown leather briefcase.

Bishop, jumped out of his chair to grasp Tariq's hand.

"Aden, I trust you're bug-free now?"

"Thanks to Kurtz I'm clean as a whistle. It's good to see you again, Tariq."

"Yes, it's good to see you're in one piece. But let's cut to business." Tariq pulled up a chair and sat, placing the briefcase on the table. "Your friend, Mr. Yang Tan, PLA Second Department, currently seconded to PETROCON, arrived in Abu Dhabi at 1030 hours yesterday. He flew in on a

Qatar Airways flight direct from Khartoum. Interestingly he entered my country under the name Tran Wang."

He reached into the briefcase and pulled out an A4 photograph showing Yang's face. Bishop picked it up off the table.

"No doubt about it, that's our boy," Bishop confirmed. "He must have jumped on a flight as soon as we bugged out."

"It would seem that way. Chua had him added to our watch list earlier in the week. He would have slipped through unnoticed except for the new facial recognition software."

"So what the hell happened at the airport? Why wasn't he detained?"

"He attacked and disarmed two of the airport guards. One of them has a broken arm. The other will never walk again."

"Yeah, he's one lethal little bastard. So did you track him?"

Tariq shook his head. "He was picked up by a car and escaped toward the Chinese quarter."

"So he's got a support base here."

"Abu Dhabi has a large population of Chinese workers. I have no doubt some of them are linked to Chinese Intelligence. If you want I can mobilize my people to find him. I still have a significant amount of influence over Special Branch operations."

"What will Special Branch do if they find him?" Bishop asked.

"He will simply disappear in the desert. It has happened before."

Bishop went cold. "No! PRIMAL will find him and I

will ensure he tells us everything about his Sudanese operations. Then I will finish him personally."

"It should be easy enough," Tariq said. "You already have the upper hand."

"How is that?" asked Kurtz. "We have no idea where he is in the city."

"Don't you? I mean you know exactly what he's looking for." The Arab turned for the door.

"One more thing, Tariq," said Bishop.

"Yes?"

"Can you get us a couple of police uniforms? Something official looking to go with our black SUVs."

Tariq smiled. "Of course. If you check the equipment container you'll find a variety of suitable uniforms. Now if you'll excuse me, gentlemen, I must return to my duties."

Chapter Thirty-Three

ABU DHABI INTERNATIONAL AIRPORT

YOU CAN FIND them at almost every airport across the globe. Highly dedicated individuals committed to the cult of plane spotting. Rain, hail, or shine they stand vigil, tracking aircraft across the globe, hunting for that elusive tail number or unique airframe.

The group staking out Abu Dhabi International Airport was no different. They were slightly awkward social misfits, passionate about their hobby, and willing to talk to anyone who showed an interest.

Yang did not approach immediately. At first he'd watched the airfield in his hire car, hoping to get lucky and spot the tilt-rotor. He had circled the airport perimeter a number of times with no luck. The radio scanner he was using failed to detect even the faintest trace of the tracking device in Bishop's arm. He was about to give up when he noticed the group of spotters camped on the fence at the end of the runway. Armed with binoculars and telephoto lenses they provided an almost twenty-four hour surveillance capability.

Yang set up his tripod and camera near the group, taking photos of random jets as they landed. Finally one of the spotters wandered over to talk to the newcomer.

"Busy, isn't it?" the man asked.

Yang gave him a sincere smile. "My first time here."

"Oh, it is a fine day for it. Wait a few more hours and it will get even more hectic!"

They chatted for a minute before Yang showed him a picture he had printed from a website. "Have you ever seen an aircraft like this?"

"Oh, the 609. Yes, I've seen it a few times, a gray one. It's not based here but flies in every now and then."

The geek gestured for Yang to lean in closer. "It flies at night, mostly. No tail markings," he tapped his nose, "if you know what I mean."

"I've never seen one in real life," said Yang. "Only on the web."

"You've come to the right place then." The enthusiast grinned. "She flew in last night. Should leave today or tomorrow. Never stays long."

"Where do they park her?" asked Yang.

"Not sure, but one of the boys will know, I'll ask." The young man addressed the other spotters in Arabic. A dialogue ensued before he turned back to the Chinese man. "There is a big gray hangar on the eastern side of the runway in the commercial aviation sector. There are no markings. Probably some sort of secret government outfit."

"I might go and have a look," said Yang. "Try and see if I can sneak a peek."

"Be careful. The police here are often paranoid. Speak of the devil, here they come for another ID check."

A black Mercedes SUV with heavily tinted windows turned off the highway and pulled in behind the cluster of cars parked along the dirt strip.

Yang's Toyota hire car was parked at the far end of the group. He contemplated making a run for it but decided to not draw attention to himself. His papers were in order and if it came to the worst, he could always make use of his diplomatic immunity.

"THAT'S HIM," said Bishop from the backseat of the Mercedes SUV. Aleks and Kurtz were sitting in the front, dressed in olive drab police tactical uniforms complete with pistol belts and handcuffs.

"The little guy with the camera, *ja*?" asked Kurtz as he adjusted the maroon beret on his head.

"No, the tall Arab guy with the binoculars," Aleks said. "Of course it's the Asian, you idiot."

"Fuck you!"

"You're like bloody school kids," said Bishop. "This guy is a dead-set ninja fuckmaster, so be extra careful, OK."

"Sure boss, very careful," said the Russian, cracking his knuckles.

"Why can't I just shoot him?" asked Kurtz. "I could just get out of the car, walk up to him, and pop one in his face. Job done, all good, back in time for jam and biscuits. He deserves it after what his men did to the girl."

Bishop shook his head. "Like I told you before, we need him for information. There is unfinished business in Sudan."

Aleks and Kurtz left the SUV and strode across to the group of spotters. Bishop checked his pistol but remained in the vehicle. He didn't want to risk being recognized by Yang and losing the element of surprise.

"We need everyone to leave right now," growled Aleks in heavily accented Arabic.

The spotters began packing their equipment, folding up their chairs, and moving to their cars. Yang made to do the same.

"Not you!" Aleks switched to English as he pointed at Yang. "We need to see your papers."

Yang eyeballed the two men suspiciously. He knew the Emirates hired a lot of Westerners for their military but he did not expect foreigners in the police force.

"Officer, I am a Chinese national from the embassy," Yang said as he produced his passport. "I'm just here to watch the jets."

"On your knees." Aleks drew his pistol and pointed it squarely in Yang's face. Kurtz did the same, ensuring he was at ninety degrees to his partner. "Put your hands on your head and get on your knees," Aleks repeated.

Yang threw his passport into the sand in front of the Russian and raised his hands. "I don't know what is going on here but I haven't done anything wrong." He dropped down to his knees.

Aleks holstered his pistol and pulled out a pair of handcuffs. "Hands together!"

Yang complied. "Check my passport."

"Shut the fuck up!" said Kurtz.

With Kurtz covering him, Aleks moved in. He grasped one of Yang's hands in an iron grip and made to snap the cuff onto his wrist.

Yang reacted in a flash. He broke the Russian's grip with a twist of his hand, reached up and grabbed Aleks's shirt. At the same time he spun, drove both his legs into Aleks, and rolled backward.

The Russian stumbled and collided with Kurtz, sending both of them sprawling into the sand.

Yang flicked himself to his feet and delivered a roundhouse kick that landed squarely on Aleks's jaw, knocking him out.

Kurtz rolled sideways and came up onto one knee with his pistol raised.

The Chinese operative was faster. His handgun barked twice, drilling the German in the chest dropping him to the sand.

Bishop saw it all from the Mercedes. He threw the car door open and leaped from the vehicle, drawing his pistol as Yang sprinted away from the crumpled bodies.

Firing one-handed, Bishop let loose a volley of .45 slugs. Dust erupted around Yang as he dashed to his Toyota and jumped into the driver's seat. The Camry Hybrid's front wheels spun in the dirt for a moment, then gained traction and accelerated along the highway.

Bishop jumped behind the wheel of the Mercedes SUV and it tore away from the gravel with a roar. The big-block V8 delivered 500 horsepower to all four wheels, catapulting the four tons of metal up to sixty miles an hour in five seconds.

The Toyota weaved erratically through the highway traffic and Bishop was starting to reconsider his decision. His injured arm ached as he wrenched the steering wheel from side to side, the speedometer touching a hundred miles an hour.

The powerful SUV rapidly ate up the distance between the two cars. The superior fuel efficiency of the Toyota meant nothing on the broad sweeping highways of the Emirates. Bishop muscled in behind it, forcing other traffic out of the way with flashing lights and the wailing siren built into the vehicle.

Yang swerved from side to side but didn't stand a chance. Bishop hit him from behind, shunting the Toyota forward. Its tires squealed in protest as Bishop accelerated. He angled the steering wheel, pushing the tail of the car sideways.

Yang lost control as he was plowed forward. It was like a ballet dancer trying to stop a sumo wrestler. He slid off the road, kicking up a cloud of dust. Tires buried themselves in the loose surface and the car flipped.

The Toyota slammed onto its roof, tumbled down an embankment, and came to a halt at the bottom of a ditch.

Bishop slammed on the brakes and came to a clean stop. He sprinted from the SUV and slid down the slope, his pistol held ready.

The Toyota was resting on its crumpled roof with the windshield shattered. Bishop circled with his weapon aimed at the driver's seat.

Yang was slumped against the ceiling where he'd dropped from his seat. Apart from the inflated airbags and shattered windows, his side of the car was intact.

The smell of spilled fuel hung heavy in the air and Bishop reached in to check his enemy's pulse. Yang was still alive.

He holstered his pistol and wrenched open the door. The limp body tumbled sideways into the sand.

"Seat belts save lives, dipshit," murmured Bishop as he reached down to drag the man clear of the wreck.

Yang's eyes snapped open and his fist blasted upward. Hit in the solar plexus, Bishop doubled over, gasping for breath.

Yang jumped to his feet, lashing out with a sharp kick that caught Bishop in the groin. He staggered backward in agony as Yang attacked again with rapid-fire blows. A punch slammed into Bishop's wounded arm, causing him to scream in pain.

"You've escaped me for the last time, Aden," Yang hissed as he gripped the damaged arm with his right hand, snatching the pistol with his left. One last kick swept Bishop off his feet and left him lying on his back gasping for air.

A moment passed before Bishop wiped the tears and snot from his face and looked up into the barrel of his own pistol. The black hole of the .45 caliber barrel blurred in and out of focus as Yang held it with a steady hand.

"I want you to know that once I've killed you, I'm going to find everyone you work with and kill them also." Yang's voice dripped with absolute hatred.

"Not if you want your boy Ping back, you won't," Bishop spluttered.

Yang laughed. "Do you really think I care about that fat pig? If he dies, then Zhu will become even more determined to destroy your friends."

"He'll never succeed, Yang. My friends will hunt you to the ends of the earth."

"What? Friends like those Europeans? They weren't so hard to kill." Yang thumbed back the hammer on the pistol.

Bishop watched the action with detached interest. It was a pointless activity; the hammer would cycle automatically. It was simply a gesture. A silent but final insult.

The bullet that hit Yang in the side of the chest snapped Bishop back to reality. The Chinese man spun, snatching at the trigger of his pistol as he fell. The bullet shot into the sand a mere inch from Bishop's head.

"Fucking Chinese piece of shit!" screamed Kurtz as he

charged down the embankment, his big HK handgun aimed at Yang's prostrate form.

Bishop struggled to his feet as the German skidded in next to him. The .45 caliber HK barked twice more as Kurtz pumped another two rounds into the dying Yang.

"Kurtz, stop!"

The pistol barked again sending a final slug into Yang's face, ending the moans.

"He was probably more use to us alive," croaked Bishop.

"He fucking shot me, Aden." Kurtz pointed at the two perfect holes in his shirt. Bishop could see straight through to the armor plates underneath.

"Crazy fucking German!" Aleks struggled down the slope, limping as a result of his confrontation with Yang. "He stole some sheik's car. Left me behind."

"*Ja* and got here in time to save Bishop, you fat, vodka-swilling gorilla."

Bishop knelt beside Yang's corpse. Half the face was blown off. He checked the body and pulled out a phone. Scrolling through the menus, he looked for the last-called number, hit dial, and held it up to his ear.

Whoever answered the call spoke in Mandarin.

"I'm guessing this is Zhu," said Bishop.

There was a pause. "Yes, who is this?"

"It's Aden."

"Where is Yang?"

"He's here but he's not really in a position to talk at the moment. Actually, make that ever."

"Where is my son?"

"Zhu, your son is safe and in good health. I can promise you that. He is currently enjoying fresh air, good food, and the company of a beautiful woman."

"If you return him to me I will make you rich. Very rich."

"Your money doesn't interest me, Zhu. But there is something you can do to ensure the safe return of your son."

"And what is that?"

"Cease all military aid to Sudan. Call off the Janjaweed operations in South Sudan and lobby your government to allow an increase in UN troops."

There was a delay before Zhu replied. "This business in Sudan has already cost the Chinese government too much. The return has been insignificant. It is my opinion that our resources are better spent elsewhere."

"Then we're on the same page. Let me have my people contact you and discuss the finer details of the return of your son."

"When?"

"That will depend on your actions, but I anticipate no longer than twenty-four hours."

"I would be most appreciative if that is the case, Mr. Aden."

"It has been a pleasure doing business with you. Just remember, we've taken him once, and we can do so again. Cross us and Ping will suffer the same fate as Yang." Bishop hung up the phone and turned his attention back to Kurtz and Aleks.

"You saved my butt, lads. I'm going to recommend a bonus and at least a month off when we get back to the island."

"*Nein*," Kurtz said. "I mean the bonus, yes, but we need to get back to our mission in Hungary. We have more business to take care of." He began climbing up the embankment back to their black SUV.

"That mission can't wait a few weeks?" Bishop asked as he followed.

"No, it can't," said Kurtz.

"He's got a girl in Budapest." Aleks laughed. "A beautiful stripper."

"She's not a stripper, *Dummkopf*. She's a dancer," snapped Kurtz.

"Nothing wrong with that, mate!" Bishop elbowed the German gently. "Just don't let your dick get you into trouble."

"It's not like that. She's different."

"Aleks, you in on this?" asked Bishop as they reached the SUV.

"*Da*. The mission is important. People smugglers, sex slavery; we're tracking down the biggest network in Eastern Europe. Very bad people with lots of connections. It's very important."

Bishop jumped in the back of the vehicle. Aleks drove while Kurtz rode shotgun. "You boys let me know if you need anything. I'm going to be on a beach conducting tan-ops with a cooler of beer."

"And a certain beautiful Iranian." Aleks grinned into the rearview mirror.

"Shut up and drive."

Chapter Thirty-Four

ENTEBBE, UGANDA

JONJO SAT at a table on the banks of Lake Victoria. He sipped an orange juice and watched a pair of cranes fly over the blue waters of Africa's largest body of fresh water. He marveled at the elegance of the two birds as they danced a slow waltz across the sky.

The seventeen-year-old warrior had waited patiently for ten minutes but was starting to worry. The instructions from Mirza had been specific; meet him at the Andrieta Beach Hotel at 1400 hours on Tuesday. He glanced at his watch again. It was 1405. He pulled at the collar of his crisp white shirt and wriggled his toes in the stiff brown lace-ups. This was the first time in nearly five years that he was not wearing his fatigues and did not have a weapon close at hand. He had never felt more uncomfortable.

"You look very smart, Jonjo."

He turned to face the voice. Mirza was standing on the

terrace of the resort, dressed in light slacks, a shirt, and a linen jacket. He was carrying a leather sports bag.

"Mirza, it is so good to see you." Jonjo jumped up, spilling his orange juice across the tablecloth. He grabbed his mentor's hand with his own, a broad smile painted across his face. "I was so glad to get your message and to know that Aden was OK."

"It is good to see you, my friend. I was worried I wasn't going to be able to pry you away from your war."

Both men sat down and Mirza waved a waiter over to deal with the juice.

"My war?" Jonjo said once the waiter had finished. "Your friends in the SAS have made it their war. It took them two days to split the SFF up and allocate all of my men to their different patrols."

"That's not a bad thing, Jonjo. Sometimes it's better to leave the fighting to the professionals."

"Yes, but what happens when they leave? That is the big worry. What if the Janjaweed come back? Then Doctor Hutton will have died for nothing." A sad look crossed the youth's face.

"I don't think that's going to be a problem. Your country has plenty of oil. Once it starts flowing, the West will make sure nothing jeopardizes it. The biggest problem your country will face is having young men and women with the education to be doctors, teachers, engineers, lawyers."

"Yes, we will need schools," said Jonjo. "And more people like Doctor Hutton to come and teach in them."

"What about you, Jonjo? What do you want to do now?"

"Me? I... I don't know. I cannot do anything other than fight, Mirza. It's all I know."

The waiter dropped off a bottle of water and Mirza

poured them both a glass. "You can learn, Jonjo. You can go to school and you can learn."

A smile spread across his face. "School? Me? Where?"

"America, Canada, Australia, wherever you like. The choice is yours."

"Really? But who will pay for this?"

"I can arrange a scholarship. But first I think we have some business to finish off, yes?"

Mirza reached into his jacket and dialed a number on his phone.

"Hello, Mr. Mirza? Is that you?" a deep African accent answered the phone.

"Yes, any update on the location?"

"No change," said Chua's agent. "He is alone as usual. The nurse left yesterday."

Jonjo watched with a look of curiosity.

"Very good. I will be there soon." Mirza terminated the call and turned to Jonjo. "There's someone I want to take you to see." He placed a few notes on the table, then picked up his bag, and they walked across the lawn and into the lobby of the hotel.

"Where are we going?" Jonjo asked as he followed.

"You'll find out in a moment. Tell me, Jonjo, what do you think you would like to study?" Mirza asked as they crossed the lobby and entered the parking lot.

"I want to be a doctor."

"I think you will be a fine doctor," Mirza said as they got in a white Land Cruiser and drove out from the hotel. They passed a lush green golf course and the prestigious Windsor Lake Victoria Hotel.

"It's very nice here," said Jonjo. "Maybe one day Juba will be like this."

A few more blocks and the neighborhood had changed,

the buildings becoming poorer. They pulled into a street filled with single-story fibro houses and parked the Land Cruiser by the side of the road.

Before they exited the vehicle Mirza pulled a suppressed Beretta Px4 from his bag and cocked it. He pulled out a second identical pistol, handing it to Jonjo.

"Who are we here to see?" asked the SFF warrior as he took the handgun.

"An old friend."

They approached one of the cheap houses, and without pausing Mirza kicked in the flimsy door, his pistol held ready. Systematically he cleared the rooms of the bungalow: first the kitchen, then the living room, and finally the bedroom. They found their target in bed.

Garang stared up at them with hollow eyes. "I knew you'd come," he croaked. "Nobody gets away from the CIA." The former SFF commander's right hand was missing; all that remained was a stump wrapped in bandages. The wound inflicted by Bishop's exploding phone had turned septic. His body was struggling to fight the infection.

Jonjo raised his pistol, pointing it directly at the face of the man he once idolized. Tears welled up in his eyes. "You cheated us, Garang. You betrayed us and now Doctor Hutton is dead."

Mirza stood watching.

The gun in Jonjo's hand shook. "Why did you do it? Why, Garang? Why?"

"I... I didn't think it would end like that," Garang said. "She wasn't supposed to be there. It was the only way. We could never have beaten them."

"But we did. We won." Jonjo wiped the tears from his face with his hand. He turned to Mirza. "I can't do it. I'm sorry." He lowered the pistol and left the room.

"Where's the money?" asked Mirza.

"Under the bed," replied Garang. "You can have it. But please don't kill me."

Mirza grabbed the aluminum attaché case from under the bed and aimed his Beretta.

It snapped once and the round drilled a hole through Garang's forehead. His eyes glazed over and blood leaked down his face.

"We always repay our debts," Mirza said. With that he left the house.

"What now?" asked Jonjo as they drove off in the four-wheel drive.

"You will go to school and become a doctor. There will be a scholarship that will pay for your education."

"Is there enough money for others to do the same?"

"Perhaps."

"Then I would like to go to school in Africa with other orphans of war."

"That is good. People like you are the only way your country will rebuild, Jonjo. People willing to forgive, forget, and help others."

"And what about you? Will I see you again?"

Mirza smiled. "Of course. I'll visit when I'm in this part of the world. There's still plenty of work to be done here."

Epilogue

LASCAR ISLAND, SOUTHWEST PACIFIC

"I'M STANDING HERE in the South Sudanese township of Malakal. What was once a small market town of five thousand has rapidly swollen to become a base for the recently bolstered UN mission in South Sudan."

The TV journalist was talking to the camera in front of a checkpoint manned by soldiers wearing blue UN helmets.

"In the last three days a regiment of crack French Foreign Legion troops, attack helicopters, and British Special Forces have all descended upon this border outpost."

Bishop was lying in bed and turned the volume up with the remote.

"Why this enormous increase in military power? All because late last week a motion put forward to the UN Security Council was, for the first time since the campaign in Libya, passed without veto by China and Russia. China insisted that Western forces reinforce what they called 'a woefully under-manned and under-resourced UN mission. Russia insisted that the atrocities against the South Sudanese must stop.'"

Bishop sighed and wondered how Jess would have felt if she could see this success.

"Within twenty-four hours of that vote, the peacekeeping forces started rolling into Malakal. French, American, British, and Australian Special Forces deployed at short notice. Within forty-eight hours the first patrols had pushed out to the border regions."

Bishop smiled. He would have loved to see that. The ragtag Janjaweed thugs up against some of the world's most elite soldiers. It would have been a one-way shooting range. The picture on the screen changed from the reporter to stock footage of Special Forces driving through the desert. Then it cut back to the journalist.

"Sources report they have forced back Janjaweed and other Northern Sudanese militias. With the huge increase in military presence, many warring tribes have chosen to lay down their weapons. For the first time in nearly fifty years, the region is reported to be secure, at least for now. Meanwhile, academics are asking how long will these forces have to stay? We cross now to Professor Ernest Dinkledum of the People for Peace Think Tank—"

"That's enough work, Aden." Saneh strode in and switched off the television. She had been for a run, swim, and returned for a shower before throwing on a robe and joining him.

Bishop was propped up in the bed wearing floral shorts. His torso was bruised in half a dozen places and the bullet wound in his arm was freshly bandaged.

"Just keeping track of the mission. Vance must be happy with the outcome."

"Not as happy as I was to get rid of Ping."

"Can't have been that bad. Chua told me the kid had lost five kilos, got a tan, and didn't want to leave."

Saneh dropped her robe to the floor. "Yes, it would seem that you're the only man that wants to run away from me all the time."

Bishop tossed the TV remote onto the nightstand next to his iPRIMAL as she slunk up the bed like a cat. His eyes consumed every inch of her supple body. He lingered on her breasts as she approached. Her hands ran up his thighs, tracing the bruises as they came up his torso. Their lips touched and he could feel his body responding to the energy arcing between them.

A loud message tone shocked them both. Bishop went to grab the iPRIMAL but Saneh got to it first and pushed it off the nightstand. "For at least the next hour you're mine. Then Vance can send you to whatever dump he wants." She kissed him hard. Another message tone sounded, this time from her bag. Her brow furrowed in frustration.

Bishop extracted himself from beneath her, leaned over, and read the message on his iPRIMAL. "Both of us have been recalled. My guess is the boys are in trouble in Budapest."

Saneh already had a singlet on and was pulling up a pair of cargo pants.

"But, what about..." Bishop hadn't left the bed.

"No hanky panky, Aden. We're on the job now."

"Oh, come on."

She pulled the cargo pants over her hips and zipped them up as she walked over to the bed. "How about you get ready and get us over to the briefing. Then if we've got time before we head out, then maybe..." She leaned forward and kissed him.

Bishop laughed, leaping out of bed to get dressed. "That's blackmail, Saneh, and you know how PRIMAL deals with blackmail."

"I think you mean 'deals in' blackmail. Now hurry. First one ready gets to drive."

Next in the PRIMAL Series

vinci-books.com/primal-fury

One woman's fight for freedom. One team's mission to deliver justice.

Turn the page for a free preview…

PRIMAL Fury: Prologue

OSAKA, JAPAN

The girl was delivered at 1949 hours, exactly one minute early. A curt knock at the apartment door signalled her arrival. The client, short and Japanese, was dressed in a pinstriped suit. He put his whiskey down on a side table, strolled to the door, glanced through the peephole, and opened it.

She was everything the website had promised: barely eighteen, beautiful, and Caucasian.

"Make yourself comfortable," he said, ushering her inside.

She smiled nervously and stepped into the room. Her classic Eastern European features were perfect: blonde hair, high cheekbones, and crystal-blue eyes.

"Sit." He pointed to the king-size bed as he took off his jacket and tie, draping them over the back of a sofa.

She sat on the bed, folded her hands, and looked around

the apartment. Clearly she was new to this. That excited him even more.

He removed his shirt as he watched her. "You speak English?" he asked, dropping his pants and removing the belt.

"A little." Her accent was thick. Her voice trembled.

"Good." He crossed the room and stood in front of her in his underwear, the belt in his hands. "Now show me everything."

She rose nervously and dropped the brown coat she was wearing onto the floor, revealing a lacy black bra, matching French-cut underwear, and sheer black stockings.

He ran his eyes over her firm body, like a buyer assessing a horse. She shuffled nervously when his gaze lingered on her breasts. The lace bra was a size too small and the flesh strained against the sheer fabric.

"Take it all off."

She reached behind her back and unclipped the bra. It dropped to the floor. She placed her fingers under the elastic of her underwear and paused.

A loud crack pierced the silence of the room as his open hand made contact with her face. He'd thrown his entire weight behind the blow and it sent her sprawling across the room. She screamed as he dragged her onto the bed by her hair and threw her face down. The scream stopped abruptly as he looped the belt around her neck and pulled it tight. With his other hand he tore her underwear off and proceeded to rape her from behind.

In another room of the apartment block, two men watched the encounter. A bank of screens showed the digital feed from the apartment and five other places like it. Racks of hard drives stored the video being captured by the hidden cameras. The men responsible for monitoring the equipment sat with their feet on the desk, drinking cans of soda and eating prawn crackers. They were watching a game of local baseball and occasionally glancing at the screens.

"Room five is getting a little rough," observed the younger of the men.

His companion leaned forward. "He's banging that blonde bitch hard."

On the screen the client was continuing to rape the girl, pulling on the belt with both hands as she clawed at it.

"Lucky son of a bitch," the younger man said as he looked back to the baseball game. "Do you think the Tigers will get up?"

"No chance."

They watched the game for five minutes before the older man glanced back to the screens. "Hey, the client's finished."

"She's not moving," his partner said. The man was dressing but the girl lay sprawled on the bed, motionless.

"You sure?"

"You'd better call Masateru."

He nodded, punched a speed dial on the phone, and studied the screen again. "Hello, *waka-gashira*, one of the girls looks like she is dead." He listened for a moment before replying. "Yes of course, we will see you in a few minutes." He placed the phone down and turned to his colleague. "He's coming up. You stay here and stop the video when we enter the room."

He opened a drawer in the desk and pulled out a chrome snub-nosed revolver. Stuffing the pistol into the back of his pants, he left the room. It was a short walk down the plush carpeted corridor to the elevators. He only needed to wait a few seconds before the elevator chimed and the doors slid open to reveal Masateru. He was a handsome man in his thirties, medium build, and dressed in an impeccable light-gray suit, crisp white shirt, and dark tie. He wore his jet-black hair slicked back in the style of 1930s gangsters.

The Yakuza henchman gave a sharp bow.

"Which room?" Masateru asked.

"Number five."

He led them down the corridor, pausing outside the room before rapping his knuckles against the door. There was no response. He reached into his jacket, retrieved a swipe card, slapped it against the receiver, and pushed the door open.

The client was fully clothed and standing in the center of the room. Masateru fixed him with a withering stare then switched his attention to the girl on the bed. She lay on her back, naked, her head turned toward them. Her once pretty face was distorted in death, her tongue poking out through blue lips, eyes wide and bulging.

As he strolled into the room he reached into his jacket and withdrew a pack of slim cigarettes. He turned to the now pale client and offered him one. The man declined and Masateru lit his with the snap of a silver lighter. "It would seem that we have a situation." He sucked heavily on the cigarette.

"I didn't mean to kill her... She, it was—"

"Yes, you did." Masateru let the cigarette bounce in the corner of his mouth as he spoke. "And why shouldn't you? She is, was, a *gaijin* of no consequence, and you are Japanese. You have paid to violate her body and it is your right to take her life, should you be able to pay for it." He inhaled deeply and walked across to a side table to ash his cigarette in a vase. "The problem here is not your right to kill this bitch. The problem is you have destroyed something that does not belong to you."

"Of course, of course." The man nodded in agreement. "I would be happy to pay." He pulled a thick wallet out of his jacket. "How much extra is it?"

Masateru reached into his pocket for his phone and punched numbers into the keypad. He looked up and showed the man the screen. "You owe seven million yen."

The client's jaw dropped. "That's crazy. How can an uneducated foreign whore be worth that?"

"She was young, my friend. Think of all the years of fucking we won't get out of her now." He shrugged. "I tell you what, for that price I'll let you keep the body. You can have another go."

The older man's surprise turned to anger. "You little shit! Do you know who I am?" He puffed out his chest and flashed a police badge. "I could end your little operation here with one phone call. You could spend the rest of your time in prison as a plaything for the Africans. Do not think for one second that you can intimidate me, you Yakuza lapdog!"

Masateru wiped the man's spittle from the lapels of his jacket and calmly stubbed out his cigarette on the table. "There seems to be a misunderstanding. If you cannot pay then I am sure another arrangement can be made. We are not unreasonable people. I mean, it's not like we need to release the video of tonight's activities to the media... Do we?"

The police officer opened his mouth to reply but thought better of it.

Masateru nodded. "No, I think it would be in everyone's best interest that you reach an agreement with the *oyabun*." Masateru dialed a number on his phone, waited for it to ring, and passed it across. "I think you will find him very reasonable."

"Superintendent Supervisor Tanaka..." The voice on the other end of the phone was as smooth as velvet, the voice of an experienced statesman. "It's a pleasure to talk to you. I hope that you enjoyed your evening?"

"Very much, thank you, although there was one minor problem." Tanaka turned his back on Masateru and walked over to the windows that looked out over the city of Osaka.

"Yes, I am aware of the situation, Superintendent. Rest assured that we will handle it with discretion. Consider this a one-time gift from me to you. In the future if you want to kill *gaijin* you will have to pay for the privilege like everyone else. However, I would recommend that you attend one of our other facilities for this pleasure. You will find the price more appealing."

"Thank you, *oyabun*." The senior police officer bobbed his head. "What about the tapes, the video footage. Will it be destroyed?"

"I will excuse the death of a whore and I will wipe your slate clean."

Tanaka glanced at the girl lying lifeless on the bed. "What do you want from me?"

"Please, Superintendent. I do not want anything from you other than to call you a friend."

"That's all?"

"Yes, you will find that being a friend of the Mori-Kai Yakuza comes with great benefits, the least of which you have experienced tonight. We are honored to call you a friend."

"No, *oyabun*, the honor is mine."

The head of the Osaka Regional Police Bureau handed

the phone back to Masateru. "What happens now?" he asked.

"There is a car waiting for you downstairs. It will drop you back at your office. Or perhaps you would like some more entertainment?"

He glanced at the girl's body. "No, I think I've had enough for tonight."

"Very good." Masateru followed the policeman out of the room and into the corridor. He spoke to the henchman waiting outside the door. "Ring the cleaners and have the whore dumped at sea."

PRIMAL Fury: Chapter One

CROATIA TO HUNGARY

The minibus nosed its way onto the car ferry that was tethered against the concrete wharf. Two men swung the gates shut behind it and the boat chugged out onto the Drava River. It was late at night and most of the twelve girls on the bus were sleeping. Only Kalista peered out of a window, watching the men guide the craft across the slow-moving river that cut the border between Croatia and Hungary.

She was the elder of two sisters, her seventeen-year-old sibling Karla snuggled next to her in a thick jacket. Tall, beautiful, and blonde, both girls had won a local beauty contest to earn their place on the bus. Men from Hungary had come to the village and run the competition before awarding the girls the opportunity to leave their families and head for the bright lights of Budapest. There, they were told, they would learn the skills of modelling before gracing the catwalks of Paris and Milan.

It had been young Karla's idea to enter the contest. She was by far the bolder of the pair. Some would have even called her reckless; always the first to throw herself into any adventure, forever trying to escape the drudgery of village life. Physically, the sisters were almost identical: the same high cheekbones, pale-gray eyes, and full lips. They had long been the most popular girls in the village. Boys would whistle as they rode past on bikes, long tanned legs flashing as they pedalled furiously, Karla always racing to be first.

The bus shuddered as the ferry nudged up against the wharf on the Hungarian side of the river. Karla murmured and nuzzled her head against her sister's shoulder. The other girls on the bus did not stir; like the sisters, they were all aspiring models, plucked from obscurity by the Hungarians. The bus drove off the ferry and up the bank to a border security post. There, the driver and a modelling agency representative got off, the second man carrying a large envelope.

"What's going on?" Karla mumbled.

"Nothing, just the border crossing. We'll need to show our passports." Kalista rummaged around in her backpack but stopped when the two men got back on the bus. The driver jumped behind the wheel, the bus started off again, and they drove through the glaring lights of the border checkpoint into Hungary.

THE MANOR, SOMOGY COUNTY, HUNGARY

"Wake up, wake up!" A man's voice jolted the girls from their slumber.

PRIMAL Fury: Chapter One

Kalista's head snapped to the front of the bus, where a rough-looking man with a heavy beard was standing. He glared at them with the intensity of a wild animal.

"Get up and get off the bus!" he screamed in English.

All the passengers were stirring and one of the younger girls burst into tears. Kalista grabbed her sister's arm and backpack and jostled into the aisle. They stepped out into a floodlit courtyard. More bearded men stood at the edges of the open area. Karla rubbed the sleep from her eyes and they grew wide as she noticed the large guns the men carried. A dog could be heard barking in the background.

The other girls spilled off the bus gathering in a huddle on the cobblestones, under the watchful eye of the heavily bearded brute and the guards. He yelled at them again, "Get into line, whores."

The girls stared at him in shock.

"I said get in line, bitches. Are you fucking deaf?"

Kalista stood defiantly. A guard moved forward and grabbed her by the arm. She lashed out, driving her foot into the man's crotch. He grunted, doubling over, and she hit him in the back of the head with her backpack.

"Karla, run!" she screamed, grabbing her sister by the arm. They sprinted around the bus and down the driveway toward the estate's gates. The metal gates were shut, flanked by tall stone walls.

The girls were fast, used to physical exertion on their father's farm. They covered the distance in seconds. Spurred on by the sound of a barking dog, they leaped onto the gate and started climbing.

Kalista felt a searing pain in the back of her leg as she was torn from the wrought iron. She screamed in agony as the Alsatian attack dog savaged her leg, pulling her down.

She hit the ground with a thump and the dog bit her arm, its fangs tearing into her flesh and meeting bone.

Karla leaped from the gate and landed on the dog. It yelped in pain and backed away snarling. As it launched forward to attack again, strong hands pulled it up short. The handler wrestled the dog away, disappearing into the darkness.

"You fucking idiots. Look at her, she's worthless now." The bearded thug yanked Karla off her sister and bent over the wounded girl. The dog had mauled her arm and leg, leaving deep wounds that were bleeding. The girl moaned, concussed from falling from the gate. "As a pair they would have been worth a fortune. Now this one is worthless. May as well put the bitch down." He turned away in disgust, heading back up the driveway to the stone manor and the other girls.

One of the guards scooped the wounded girl off the ground and carried her toward the manor. Another grasped Karla by the arm, dragging her sobbing to an adjacent building. The wooden barn once housed horses but now it was a basic dormitory. He pushed her through the double doors into a large room filled with beds. The doors slammed shut behind her, and a bolt slid across. All the girls from the bus were in the room, huddled in twos and threes on the metal frame beds.

"Where are we?" one of them asked.

"What's going to happen to us?"

"Where's Kalista?"

The chorus of questions continued until the lights were turned off. The girls wept in their beds, terrified of what the next day would bring. Karla sobbed uncontrollably. It had been her idea to try the modeling contest and now her older sister was badly hurt.

PRIMAL Fury: Chapter One

At precisely seven o'clock the next morning, the doors opened and a woman entered. She was brunette, petite and pretty, with the body of a dancer. The woman gathered the girls onto two of the beds and spoke to them in English, a language most of them understood. Karla interpreted for the few who didn't.

"I know most of you are very scared. You don't understand what is happening." She paused for Karla to translate. "My name is Aurelia, and if you follow my instructions and do as you are told things here will not be so bad. These men will not harm you. You will be taken from here to another place where you will be given to other men. If you listen to me and learn, then these men will also treat you well. They will lavish you with gifts and you will live like princesses. If you try to escape, you will die. It is that simple. Now we will eat breakfast and then we will start with your lessons."

She led them out of the dormitory and across to the manor, where the girls would be fed and trained. They glanced at the high stone wall that surrounded the estate and at the heavily armed guards patrolling the grounds.

As they filed in through the door to the dining hall, Aurelia pulled Karla to one side. "Your sister will live," she whispered, "but she won't be coming with you. I will look after her but you need to focus on yourself now."

Karla nodded and followed the other girls to the line for food. Tears welled in her eyes as she picked up a bowl of watery stew and took her place on the long wooden table. They ate in silence.

Over the next week, Aurelia prepared the girls for their new lives. She taught them how to apply makeup and how to

PRIMAL Fury: Chapter One

dress, walk, and entertain powerful men. She provided them with a wealth of advice, all of the tricks she had learned in her days as a professional dancer, including pieces of information that would help make their life in sexual slavery a little more bearable.

"Are they ready?" the thickly bearded Gusztáv asked. He was responsible for ensuring the girls were prepared before they were shipped off to the crime syndicate's headquarters for auction. He regularly summoned Aurelia to his rooms to update him, and occasionally for her to service his more personal needs.

Aurelia was dressing in the corner of his bedroom. "Are they ever ready? What woman could ever be ready for this?"

Gusztáv lay sprawled on his bed, naked except for a pair of shorts. His muscular frame was covered in tattoos; dragons and other mythical creatures wound their way around his arms and over his shoulders onto his hairy chest. "Deep down inside, every woman is a whore. These girls were born ready; you just polish them up a little."

Aurelia watched him with barely concealed hatred as he hunted in the drawer of an antique bedside table for a cigar. The bruises on her neck would be visible for days. She took her only solace in knowing that as long as he found pleasure in abusing her, the girls would be less likely to feel his rage. She might not be able to protect them once they left the manor, but at least here they were safe.

"Their photos are done." She took a USB drive from her handbag and threw it onto the bed.

"Good, we can ship them off early. Maybe András will give me a bonus." He found a cigar and fumbled on his side table for a cutter.

"What about Kalista? What will happen to her?" She walked to the table on the other side of the bed and picked up the cigar cutter.

"Kalista? Who the fuck is Kalista?" He snatched the implement from her hands and snipped the end of his cigar.

She handed him a lighter. "The girl who was injured."

"Oh yes, dog-food girl." He lit the cigar and puffed a pungent cloud of smoke into the room. "If she lives, I will sell her. If she dies, then the dogs can finish what they started."

Aurelia's eyes fell on the handgun that occupied the same table as the cigar cutter and lighter. How easy it would be to take it and shoot this devil dead in his bed, she thought.

She sat on the bed. "Where do the girls go from here?"

He took the cigar from his mouth and gave her a stern look. "I've told you before, Aurelia, ask questions like that and you will find out personally. You might be a little long in the tooth, but some Arab with an anal fetish will still pay good money for you. Then what would happen to your sick mother, hey? You should be thankful that I'm so generous. Now get the hell out of my sight."

Aurelia nodded and made for the door. She opened it, then turned back to face him. "My mother... do I still have your permission to visit her this afternoon?"

He puffed another cloud of smoke into the air. "Only because you still fuck like you enjoy it. Now go!"

After she left the room, Gusztáv picked up the phone by the bed. "Aurelia is allowed to go to the village but have someone keep an eye on her. That bitch is asking too many questions."

He slammed the phone into its cradle and turned his

attention back to his cigar. He puffed another cloud and stared at the door, deep in thought. After a few moments, he picked up the phone. "Load up the whores. I want them on the road to the castle in an hour."

Grab your copy...
vinci-books.com/primal-fury

About the Author

Jack Silkstone grew up on a steady diet of Tom Clancy, James Bond, Jason Bourne, Commando comics, and the original first-person shooters, Wolfenstein and Doom. His background includes a career in military intelligence and special operations, working alongside some of the world's most elite units. His love of action-adventure stories, his military background, and his real-world experiences combined to inspire the no-holds-barred PRIMAL series.